A Taste of the Apocalypse

A Taste of the Apocalypse

Chronicles of Jeremy Nash
Book 1

Frank F. Fiore

WordCrafts Press

A Taste of the Apocalypse
Copyright © 2012
Frank F. Fiore

Paperback ISBN: 978-1-962218-73-3
Hardback ISBN: 978-1-962218-72-6

Cover concept and design by Mike Parker.

Published by WordCrafts Press
Cody, Wyoming 82414
www.wordcrafts.net

Author's Note

In the *Chronicles of Jeremy Nash*, the underlying story deals with a conspiracy theory, unsolved mystery, urban myth, New Age belief or paranormal practice, but I keep the other aspects of the story as factual as possible. Whether it is history, science, politics, religion, or cultural traditions and beliefs, I base the *Chronicles* on real facts—then stretch the truth a little.

In *A Taste of the Apocalypse*, the organizations, cultural traditions, spiritual beliefs, history, and most of archeological artifacts mentioned in the story do exist. The urban legend itself, the supposed burial place of Jesus Christ, is an integrated piece of the plot.

Here are the facts of the story.

Essenes & Gnostics: Around the beginning of the Common Era, the Jewish Historian Flavius Josephus made interesting references to the Torah Codes in his description of the Jewish sect known as the Essenes. They were a religious sect that practiced gnosis. The Gnostics believed in the doctrine of salvation through knowledge—not faith. Jesus of Nazareth is identified by some Gnostic sects as an embodiment of the Supreme Being who became incarnate to bring gnosis to the Earth.

The Bible Code: Flavius Josephus said that if one used a special substitution cipher—or Torah Code, one could exchange certain Hebrew letters with other opposite letters and find a message. Once done, the Essenes applied a set of mathematical algorithms apparently taught to them by the Prophets of Old. The Essenes were able to predict the outcome of many events with great accuracy. This cipher is known today as the Bible Code, and there is much debate over its accuracy.

The Shroud of Turin: The Shroud of Turin is the supposed burial cloth of Jesus Christ, and there is much debate over its authenticity. In the late 1970s and early 1980s the Shroud of Turin Research Project (STURP) performed a set of experiments and analyses on the Shroud of Turin. STURP issued its final report in 1981. They concluded that the Shroud image is that of a real human form of a scourged, crucified man. It is not the product of an artist. The blood stains are composed of hemoglobin and also give a positive test for serum albumin. The image is an ongoing mystery and until further chemical studies are made, perhaps by this group of scientists, or perhaps by some scientists in the future, the problem remains unsolved.

Blood Theory of the Shroud: The blood theory of the Shroud put forth by the German researcher Kurt Berna sought to prove that the man in the Shroud was not dead when laid to rest. His blood theory seeks to prove that the man, Jesus Christ, did not die on the cross.

The Church of the Holy Sepulche: The Church of the Holy Sepulche in Jerusalem is the supposed tomb of Jesus Christ where he was laid before the Resurrection.

The Jesuits: The Society of Jesus, or the Jesuits (known colloquially as "God's Marines" or "The Pope's Storm Troopers") is the Church's defender of the faith and is engaged in evangelization and apostolic ministry in 112 nations on six continents reflecting the Formula of the Institute of the Society. The Church of the Gesu in Rome is the mother church of the Society of Jesus and the location of the Jesuit Refugee Service.

The Intermarium: When the Communists gained power in Russia in 1917, the Catholic Church saw communism as a threat. Between 1917 and 1923 the Church, with the Vatican at the head, took the initiative to fight against what it saw as the communist danger. Since 1920, the Church organized groups of action called the Intermarium. This organization was defined openly as anticommunists, and their declared objectives were the mobilization of the Catholic Church in the fight against Communism. After WWII, the Allies actively promoted and used known fascists in the Intermarium for intelligence purposes.

The Ratlines: The Intermarium helped many notorious Nazi war criminals escape prosecution by using a network called the Ratlines. The Ratlines was an intricate network, set up by the Intermarium, from Europe to South America to smuggle people out of Europe. The Ratlines were built by the Vatican with the guidance of the Jesuits and used by Western intelligences to facilitate and organize the protection and flight of the escaped fascists. It is rumored that the Jesuit Refugee Service is the inheritor of that process.

The Roswell Incident: In 1947, many believe that a flying saucer with two alien bodies was discovered in the high desert of New Mexico at Roswell. To investigate UFO activity in the aftermath of the Roswell incident, a committee called the Majestic 12—or Majik—was set up under Truman to study the incident. Out of that committee came what are known as the MJ Twelve documents that proved there was a UFO crash at Roswell. Whether the committee existed or not is steeped in controversy. Hangar 18 was where the supposed UFO crash remnants and alien bodies were stored. In the book, Section 18 serves this purpose.

The Dead Sea Scrolls: Between 1947 and 1956, the Dead Sea Scrolls were found in eleven caves in and around Qumran on the northwest shore of the Dead Sea. The scrolls are kept in the Shrine of the Book in Jerusalem.

The Ecole Biblique: In 1955, G. Lankester Harding, head of the Jordanian Department of Antiquities, asked Roland de Vaux, a Dominican priest and renowned scholar associated with Ecole Biblique, to head an international team of seven Hebrew and Aramaic experts to study the scrolls. Much mystery surrounds the control of the scrolls by the committee and their study.

The Talpiot: The Talpiot, the lost tomb of Jesus, is the supposed tomb of the Family of Jesus. *The Lost Tomb of Jesus* is a documentary co-produced and first broadcast on the Discovery Channel and Vision TV in Canada on March 4, 2007 covering the discovery of the Talpiot Tomb. The documentary, and the book that followed, are currently the subject of controversy within the archaeological and theological fields, as well as among linguistic and biblical scholars.

Prologue

The old aeronautical engineer felt the hairs rise on the back of his neck. He wondered if it was a change of airflow in his room—or trepidation.

It was both.

He turned around in his moonlit 5th floor hospital room at the Walter Reed Army Medical Center to see a slouched silhouette in his open doorway. A cold shiver coursed down his spine as if it had been dipped in ice.

Henderson squinted, his eyesight failing with age. But before recognition dawned on him, he knew something was going to happen.

And it's not going to be good.

Particularly for him.

The silhouette slivered towards him. Henderson backed away with fearful recognition.

"Vajda!" he whispered nervously under his breath.

Now fully immersed in a pool of silver light, the tall alarming figure nodded imperceptibly. He continued gliding forward in an unusual, stooped manner, like a jungle cat hunting its prey.

And I'm the prey.

Standing near the wide window, Henderson was suddenly having difficulty breathing. He was acutely aware that he was trapped in a small hospital room with nowhere to run. To make matters worse, Vajda was between him and the nurse call button.

The threatening figure said nothing as he closed the gap between them. Now fully in the moonlight, Henderson saw a tall muscular man with a shock of white hair growing out of a head of dark brown, dressed in a Romanian-style silk brocade coat that reminded Henderson of a certain vampire count.

"What do you want from me?"

He had little hope he would survive the night. Hell, survive the next five minutes, but he gave it his best shot. "I didn't tell them anything," he cried out almost inaudibly.

With stunning speed, Vajda pounced on him, gripping his throat with two strong hands. Henderson's air supply was immediately cut-off, and with it, any hope of calling out for help.

Vajda calmly watched Henderson with two different colored eyes—one an extremely pale blue and the other an almost colorless brown. A deep, brutal scar ran from under his left ear to his chin.

Henderson thought he was the ugliest son-of-a-bitch he'd ever seen. But then Vajda's hideous face started to blur before him. Like an encroaching oil spill, darkness crept along the edges of Henderson's vision. In an amazing feat of strength, Vajda pulled the obese man straight up off the floor, holding him suspended in the air.

"Where is he?" Vajda demanded with a slight lisp from his cleft lip. "Where is Nash?"

Henderson couldn't speak—hell, he could barely see. Vajda held him up a moment longer, and then slowly lowered the old man to the floor, grudgingly releasing his grip.

Gasping, Henderson would have fallen to his knees if the stooped man hadn't held him up. He painfully sucked in air through what he believed was a very damaged throat.

"I-I don't know," he gasped, stumbling over the poorly formed words.

"So you do not know where to find Nash?"

"I don't! I swear to you. I think he's dead."

"Then you are of no further use to us."

With that, Vajda grabbed Henderson by the collar and dragged the old man to the window. In one fluid motion, the brutal assassin kicked the barred window open, splintering the window frame and releasing whatever locking device it had. Glass and metal rained down to the parking lot below as a soaring wind rushed up into the room blowing up through Henderson's hospital robe.

This isn't happening.

Henderson could hear the sound of traffic below, horns honking, cars rushing by.

"I'll see you in *hell*," spurted Henderson.

And with that, Vajda shoved the old man through the deadly opening. Henderson flipped once, hit his head hard on the outside ledge, mercifully blacked out, and dropped five floors to the pavement below.

Friday
12:14 PM MDT
New Mexico

The rising sun cast its orange and pink glow over the windshield of Jeremy Nash's Cirrus SR20. A smattering of low cirrus clouds caught some of the early morning light, and Nash was reminded again how much he loved to fly at this time of day.

He turned the controls slightly and banked to the left, bursting through the thinning clouds. From here, he could see the high desert of New Mexico.

He would be approaching Roswell Airport soon.

The incessant beat of his SR20 propeller always had a calming effect on him. He loved being up here, loved getting away from it all. Loved, in particular, being alone with his thoughts. He did his best thinking up here.

And today, Nash's thoughts were on his grandmother. Two days ago, his sister had called to tell him his grandmother had passed. Nash was in Albuquerque researching a lecture on crypto-history he was to deliver a few weeks from now in Berlin. As an expert debunker of conspiracy theories, myths, and legends, he was often asked to give such lectures. Hell, half his time seemed to be spent behind a podium, poking holes in everything from Elvis faking his death, Bigfoot, and UFOs to the various 9/11 conspiracies.

The city of Roswell appeared ahead, under the warm noonday sun. He spotted the airport and angled toward it. He received confirming clearance from the tower, and a few minutes later he was applying the brakes as the plane touched down on the tarmac.

Nash taxied off the runway, heading toward the executive terminal. He parked the plane, shut down the engine, collected his laptop, and entered the small terminal. Sitting there in the waiting area, looking as lovely as ever, was his younger sister Alyson. She spotted him, smiled brightly, and stood.

It had been several years since they had last seen each other. Too long, and Nash had only himself to blame. He was a workaholic, but at least he was the first to admit it.

Though they were five years apart, Nash had heard all his life that he and his sister could have been twins. They were both around medium height, with auburn complexions, hazel eyes, and straight dark brown hair. Anyone could see the influence their Native American ancestry—Mescalero Apache—had on their appearance.

"Well, hi there, Sis," he said easily.

She rushed over, throwing her arms around him. Nash grunted doing his best not to fall over.

"I hate you," she said, still hugging him.

"Why?"

"You never return my phone calls. You are such a jerk."

"If I'm such a jerk, then why are you still hugging me?"

"Because I love you, you jerk." She planted a kiss on his cheek and released him. Nash laughed.

She turned to glance at a tall, athletic-looking man sporting a crew cut and standing stiffly a few feet away. Nash thought the man resembled a drill sergeant—only not as pleasant. Alyson was charged with enthusiasm. "Jeremy, this is my fiancé, Tom Gray. Tom, this is Jeremy."

"Nice to meet you," said Tom, reaching out with a wide, paddle-like hand. Nash set down his laptop case and took the offered hand. The man's grip was vice-like.

"Tom works for the FBI," said Alyson beaming proudly.

"No kidding," said Nash, working his hand while wondering what exactly Tom was trying to compensate for. "An agent?"

"Yeah. Field agent," he said. "Out of Albuquerque."

"Tom often works *undercover*," said Alyson. Both she and Tom laughed as Nash rolled his eyes.

The introductions finished, Tom led the way to Alyson's Bronco.

Nash was grateful for having grown up in the UFO capital of the world. Yes, he was born and raised in Roswell—an ironic twist of fate that was not lost on his colleagues.

Or just about anyone else, for that matter.

Growing up here, Nash had discovered something curious about himself. Furthermore, he was absolutely certain that had he *not* grown up in UFO City this personal quirk would never have manifested itself.

Considering that it had turned his life around and made him a lot of money, he was grateful for it.

Just about everyone in Roswell was determined to believe in the UFO stories, especially the infamous crash of 1947. As a young boy, Nash was determined to prove the opposite—that a UFO crash had *not* occurred, that UFOs did *not* exist, and that his entire city was insane!

That's how the great debunker and skeptic was born—from his drive to prove everyone else wrong.

As they drove, Tom looked over at Nash. "So, Alyson tells me your grandfather, Zed, was quite a character. Air Force Major, intelligence officer, archaeologist."

"And a paleo-linguist," said Nash.

"A paleo-what?"

"His expertise was ancient languages. He even worked on an original Dead Sea Scrolls research team."

"Very cool."

"Yeah.... Until he went crazy," mused Nash.

Tom looked at Alyson and winked. "So I'm told. A bit crazy."

"Certifiable. He was committed shortly after our parents were killed in an accident. That's when Alyson and I moved in with our grandparents."

"Committed? Alyson didn't tell me that part." Tom squinted as he drove. "I'm, uh, sorry to hear that."

They passed the International UFO Museum and Research Center, where the infamous—and bogus—alien autopsy had been performed on TV several years back. Orchestrated by Fox News, it was a brilliant publicity scheme, if nothing else. Nash had been one of the team of skeptics who had blown the whistle on it.

A few minutes later they pulled onto the property of the St. Mary's Catholic Church and drove the short distance to the cemetery beyond.

Friday
2:25 PM MDT
Roswell, New Mexico

The funeral was mercifully short since it took place in the intense heat of the mid-afternoon sun. During the service, Alyson openly wept. Nash found himself reverently lost in sweet nostalgia, remembering the good times he had shared with the kind old lady who had raised them. He could even forgive her insistence, and his resulting agnosticism, that he and his sister be raised in the Catholic Church. He never thought of himself as the sentimental type, but he shed a tear or two as well. Hoping his grandmother had gone on to a better place, he wondered where that might be.

He felt an unusual wave of guilt for having neglected his grandmother these past several years. He certainly could have done a better job of stopping by or calling her.

Hearing the end of the ceremony, he caught his sister watching him. He tried to smile, but his heart wasn't in it. He felt oppressively sad and regretted the arguments with this dear lady that had led him to forsaking the faith so important to her. Alyson, bless her heart, reached out and took his hand. They stood closely together as the casket was lowered into the earth.

13

Friday
3:10 PM MDT
Roswell, New Mexico

They were walking back to the Bronco when a small man dressed in a dark suit approached them from the parking lot. Nash briefly wondered how the man—who looked vaguely familiar—could wear such a dark suit on a scorching day like this.

"Alyson. Jeremy," said the man. "I'm Frank Evans, your grandmother's lawyer." They shook hands all around. Evans gave them his condolences and then got right to the point. "I have something for the two of you." He reached into his coat pocket, producing a sealed white envelope. "This letter was given to me by your grandfather to hold for you until your grandmother's death. I've taken the liberty of making arrangements with the pastor to use his office—if you two want some privacy."

He gave the letter to Alyson, offered his condolences again, and departed.

"Well," said Alyson, holding up the letter, "I guess we should see what Grandfather has to say to us."

The three of them hurried to the rectory.

14

Friday
3:20 PM MDT
Roswell, New Mexico

The pastor's office was small, dark, and—thankfully—air conditioned. Leaving Tom to amuse himself with some dull looking pamphlets outside, Nash breathed a sigh of relief as Alyson went straight to the desk and found a letter opener sitting in an empty coffee tin full of pens and pencils. She swiped the envelope, plucking the letter out. Scanning the page, Alyson frowned. "What's this?"

Puzzled, she handed the letter to her brother to read. Or, rather, he tried to. The page was filled with neatly printed rows of what appeared to be some sort of pictographic writing system. A very ancient system. He said as much to his sister.

"No wonder they locked him up," Nash said.

"So how do we get this translated?" Alyson asked.

Nash, folding the letter carefully, returned it to the envelope. "Actually, I think I know just the person."

"Who?"

"A colleague of mine at UCLA. I've worked with him on many occasions. He also worked with Grandfather years ago."

"And when will you have an answer?" she asked. "I kind of want to know what he has to say to us that's so important."

Nash wanted to know, too. He considered faxing the letter to his friend, but something stopped him. After all, there had to be a reason why his grandfather had written the letter in ancient, freaking Sanskrit, or whatever the hell it was. Perhaps their batty old kin might have left behind something very personal—even valuable.

He looked down at his sister, giving her a hug. "I'll fly over to Los Angeles today and see about getting it translated immediately."

She clapped and threw her arms around him.

Nash had a phone call to make. He hoped his friend was in.

Friday
3:37 PM PDT
En Route to Los Angeles

As Nash's small plane rose swiftly into the afternoon sky, he turned right and wondered how many citizens of Roswell were down there speculating that he was an interplanetary scout ship hunting its next bovine victim.

Sorry guys, he thought, *but it's just me, Jeremy Nash, your friendly neighborhood debunker.*

With the help of a tail wind, he made good time to Albuquerque. Before leaving Roswell, he called ahead to his old friend, Raymond Thomas, Professor of Near Eastern Languages and Cultures at UCLA. Although Thomas wasn't in, Nash left a message with a graduate assistant informing the professor he was coming.

He barely caught the next flight to LA.

As the big jet lifted off, Nash settled in. He was about to take a short nap when the overhead monitor turned on. Since the trip was too short for a full movie, the airline had elected to show various news shorts.

Nash jacked in his headset, casually listening and dozing in and out of consciousness. But once CNN began airing an interview with Jeremiah Hicks, his eyes popped open, gluing themselves to the screen.

The interviewer was a tenacious young news journalist. Nash immediately liked her style.

"Welcome, Reverend Hicks, to *Chapter and Verse.*"

"Thank you. I'm happy to be here."

"Reverend Hicks, you've come a long way from being a small country revivalist preacher. Now you're the head of the International Christian Zionist Movement, have your own religious radio program, a TV media empire, and have published many bestselling books on the Apocalypse."

Hicks, to his credit, at least tried to look humble. "Well, I don't think of myself as heading an empire, but I do expect my latest book, *Preparing Your Soul for the Apocalypse*, to do well within some religious circles."

"Well, Reverend, let's get right to it. Your organization's goal is to actually bring about the Second Coming. Is this correct?"

"Our goal is to prod it along, yes." Hicks apparently anticipated Blake's next question and added, "Peacefully prod it along, that is. The International Christian Zionist Movement is a non-political, non-violent movement whose sole purpose is to help bring Jews back to the Holy Land, fulfilling prophesy and ushering in the Second Coming of our Lord, Jesus Christ."

"Reverend, some say your organization is affiliated with the Jesus Saves the Earth UFO Foundation in Colorado, the so-called Warriors of Christ? Is this true?"

"Absolutely not—"

"And some also claim your organization is affiliated with the Armageddon Lobby—"

"I emphatically deny—"

"The same Armageddon Lobby that planned to carry out violent and extreme acts in the streets of Jerusalem at the end of ninety-nine to herald the return of Jesus to earth. The same Armageddon Lobby that then planned to commit mass suicide, a la Heaven's Gate."

Hicks' round face had reddened slightly. But to his continuing credit he had waited patiently for the young reporter to finish. When he was given permission to speak, he said calmly, "The ICZM has no connection with either cult."

"Is it true that both these *cults*, as you call them, believe Jesus will return in a flying saucer upon his Second Coming?"

Hicks opened his mouth to speak, but the reporter forged on.

"And didn't these so-called UFO Jesus cults specifically want to create a catastrophic event by provoking a deadly shootout with the police in Jerusalem?"

"I don't see how this is relevant—"

"Is it or is it not true that Israeli intelligence—the Mossad—connected both cults to you and the ICZM?"

"I'm unaware—"

"Isn't it true that Israeli authorities deported members of your organization under suspicion of planning acts of violence to coincide with the year two thousand?"

Hicks opened his mouth to speak, but the reporter relentlessly pushed on.

"According to these same reports, your members were plotting attacks on the Grand Mosque in Jerusalem. Is this true or isn't this true, Reverend?"

Now Hicks was visibly shaking. He looked like he wanted to stand. A vein pulsed on his left temple. Nonplussed, the young reporter blinked and waited calmly, letting the silence speak.

When Reverend Hicks spoke, he did so in a slightly strained voice. "It's not true. We abhor violence. Our members believe that we are the Chosen Ones and have a holy task to complete at the Second Coming. The ICZM will bring back Jesus peacefully. Plans are in motion, as we speak, to erect the Third Temple on the mount."

"Oh really?" the reporter asked, genuinely surprised. "And how will you pull that off without starting World War Three?"

The flush of blood in Hicks' face finally dispersed, leaving behind several blotchy patches. He sat back, seemingly relaxed again. "Through technology," he said. "Holographic technology."

"Excuse me?"

"My organization is planning to hover a holographic Temple above the Mount, thus re-constructing the Third Temple as

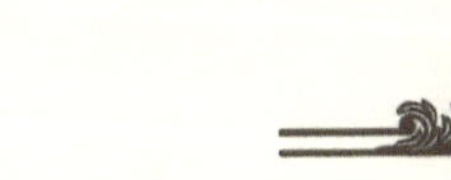

prophesy foretold without removing a single brick from the current mosque located on the Mount."

"And how will you go about hovering this, um, hologram?" the interviewer queried.

"The world will know next week," Hicks said, winking. "Next week."

The video clip cycled through other interviews, but Nash had seen enough. He removed his headset and sat back, thinking.

Though he'd never spoken to Hicks, Nash was quite aware of the Christian Zionists and his organization. In fact, Hicks and his organization figured largely in one of the chapters of Nash's new book. Still, the connection to the UFO cult was news to him, and Nash made a mental note to contact the pretty CNN reporter. There was still time to add an addendum to his book before it went to press.

Friday
5:05 PM PDT
Los Angeles, California

An hour and a half later, after touching down at LAX and hailing a cab, Nash found himself seated across from his long time friend, Dr. Raymond Thomas.

They were in his cramped office tucked away in the far corner of the Social Sciences building. The small window behind the desk was heavy with dust and seemed to lead to a narrow alley.

Nash swallowed, his mouth particularly dry. He was feeling a bit claustrophobic. The office was piled high with artifacts, many in the form of ancient clay tablets. It looked like a small wing of the Getty Museum. The two friends made small talk as Nash surveyed the clutter.

"Actually, you're lucky to have caught me," said the Professor. He indicated a small suitcase by the closed office door. He sat back in his chair and pulled a black lacquer pipe from his jacket pocket.

Nash was amused to see the pipe because directly above the professor's head was a **No Smoking** sign posted on the wall. "I leave for the Middle East soon."

"Hey, so am I," said Nash.

"Seriously?"

"No. I just wanted to be inclusive."

"Asshole," said Thomas. He sat back and grinned, puffing on his pipe.

"Actually," he said, "a colleague informed me of ancient scrolls found in Cairo that could prove links to languages spoken by the Proto-Indo-Europeans. Based on the initial reports these scrolls can add immensely to the study of the Proto-Indo-European language spoken by an ancient people who must have been the original ancestors of the European, Iranian, and Indo-Aryan peoples."

Thomas became more animated, and there was a gleam in his eyes. "As you can understand, this discovery, if true, might be quite significant to us ancient language aficionados."

"I'm sure you can barely contain your excitement," said Nash. "I know I can't."

"Why am I friends with you again?"

"Because I'm lovable," said Nash.

Dr. Thomas snorted. The professor, who was nearly thirty years Nash's senior, could have easily passed as an older brother. And whatever ravages smoking tobacco had on his body were not yet evident. The man's skin was tawny and tight, his hair flecked with gray, his arms rippled with lean muscle.

As usual, Nash was jealous of his friend's good health. And, as usual, Nash made a mental note to eat better and get more reps in at the gym.

More than anything, Thomas was a highly respected paleolinguist. Nash knew the man was born with the gift of deciphering the story of a life based on the incomprehensible chicken scratches found on the side of an ancient alabaster sarcophagus.

Hey, we all have our gifts, thought Nash.

"I don't want to keep you from your exhilarating work." Nash rolled his eyes and removed the folded letter from inside his jacket pocket.

"Did you just roll your eyes at me, Nash?" said Thomas.

"Never," said Nash. "At least not intentionally. Anyway, here's what I came for. Granted, it's not a dusty old tablet, but I think it still might get your old juices flowing."

Thomas raised one eyebrow and took the letter.

As his friend read the letter, Nash thought the man looked entirely too serious sitting there with his pipe hanging from his lower lip, bluish smoke curling up.

And then the pipe just fell from his friend's mouth. Thomas grabbed it, jumping up and dusting off ash and burning embers from his red argyle shirt.

Scratch the too serious part.

"Where did you get this?" Thomas asked, swiping at the embers on his pants, then sitting down.

"I found it in my fortune cookie," said Nash. "Took me forever to unfold."

"I don't have a lot of time, Nash."

"Where do you think I got it?" said Nash. "Hell, you knew my grandfather better than I."

"Only through our letters," said Thomas. "Your grandfather was a very strange man."

"A very *crazy* man," said Nash. "So what does it say?"

Thomas stood again, but this time moved over to his overflowing bookcase. Mumbling to himself around his pipe, Thomas thumbed through the titles of several books on what appeared to be ancient languages—big surprise there. He stopped at one, pulled it from the shelf, and flipped through it. Book in hand, he returned to his desk.

Nash laughed. "That wouldn't happen to be a book on deciphering the ramblings of a crazy old man, would it?"

"No," said Thomas. "Your letter, in fact, is written in Akkadian, the ancient language of the Middle East, commonly used from the third millennium BC to the early first millennium and surviving until about one hundred AD."

"Will this be on the test, Professor?"

Ignoring Nash's adolescent humor, Thomas continued.

"Akkadian was considered a special language, if you will, the language of diplomacy and culture. Like today's High German or Castilian Spanish." He looked at Nash and said, "You say this was written by your grandfather?"

"So I'm told."

"I could believe it. Very few modern scholars have such a deep

knowledge of this most ancient of languages, itself a very intricate tongue with many subtleties. Your grandfather was a semantic genius."

"He was also mentally ill and a hell of a bridge player," Nash added. "So can you translate it or not?"

Thomas grinned wryly. "Give me a few minutes. My Akkadian is a bit rusty."

Nash spent the time watching his friend pour over the letter as if it contained the secrets of the universe. Hell, maybe it did. Thomas often consulted his ancient Akkadian to English dictionary, or whatever it was. Watching this intense research was making Nash sleepy. From doing his own research in Albuquerque earlier this morning, to his various flying trips, including the stop for the funeral, and now UCLA, with the office air conditioner rattling softly, Nash could very easily just drift off to...

"Got it!" said Thomas excitedly.

Nash jerked and nearly fell out of his chair. For a very brief moment he couldn't remember where he was.

Ah, yes, a dusty old office...

"Good for you," said Nash, rubbing his eyes.

"No, good for *us*," said Thomas excitedly. "First of all, you were right. Your grandfather didn't have all his oars in the water."

"Tell me something I *don't* know. So what did the old coot say?"

"Perhaps it's best that I just translate it for you." Thomas said, clearing his throat dramatically. "My dearest Alyson and Jeremy."

Nash stopped him. "Just give me the *Readers Digest* version, please."

Thomas seemed disappointed. "Really, it's no problem at all. I've got most of the words—"

"Raymond," said Nash. "You're leaving soon, I'm tired as hell."

"You should exercise more," said Thomas. "It gives you more energy—"

"Just give me the condensed version, please. I'm in a hurry. I need to prepare for my lecture on crypto-history in Berlin in two weeks. So let's get on with this nonsense."

Thomas shrugged. "Fine. He says *Hi* to you and gives you and your sister his love. Blah, blah, blah. And with little or no segue, he goes right into something about a hidden diary."

"A diary?"

"Yep. He wants you to retrieve it."

Nash groaned and sat back. He knew he should never have gotten out of bed today. Or, more importantly, he knew he should never have volunteered to get the damn letter translated. But he knew his curiosity would have eaten him alive.

"Would you like for me to continue?" asked Thomas. "It's about to get quite good."

Nash sat a little straighter. "Alright. Go on."

"At this point in the letter, your grandfather seems to be addressing you in particular. He's giving you a man's name and a location of the diary. Do you know Stanton Roth? He's the guy who's supposed to have the diary."

"No. Do you?"

"Yes. He's an antiquities dealer. One with a shady past. Anyway, the letter says he's in Europe somewhere if you want to look him up."

"I'll pass," replied Nash. He got up to leave.

"But wait, there's more," said Thomas, enjoying this entirely too much. "According to your grandfather, the diary points to the location to the body of—oh, are you ready for this?"

"I'm quivering in anticipation."

"According to your grandfather, this diary points to the location of the body of one Jesus Christ."

"You're kidding?" said Nash.

"No," said Thomas, grinning. "And the look on your face is priceless."

"Grandfather was nuts."

"Maybe, maybe not. Either way, I am certainly enjoying this moment."

"Oh, shut up."

Nash drummed his fingernails on the wooden armrests.

The location of the body of Christ?

"Surely grandfather means where the body of Christ *was* buried," said Nash. "You know, *before* the Resurrection."

Thomas grinned. "No. *Is* buried. As in *now*. The language is quite clear on that."

Nash knew that the life of Christ had always been a hobby of his grandfather's. Perhaps more than a hobby.

An obsession.

"What else does the letter say?" Nash asked.

"Something about you personally recovering the diary and letting the truth be told. That your gift—and the very reason you were put on earth—has always been to reveal the truth to the world." Thomas paused. "Oh, brother. I think someone's grandfather thinks a little highly of his grandson."

Nash ignored the rib. "Is that it?"

"Yes. Wait...hmm. The signature isn't written in Akkadian. The letter is signed *Me'chatimo*. Hebrew for *His Signature*."

"As in *God's Signature*?" said Nash.

Thomas sat back and grinned. "More or less."

"Signed by God, huh?" Nash said in disgust. "So now he thought he was God?"

Thomas just shrugged his shoulders. "Yeah. Maybe the old man was nuts."

Friday
5:45 PM PDT
Los Angeles, California

Outside the Social Science building and into the cool night air, Nash called his sister in Roswell. Thomas had already departed, and was on his way to the Mid-East for his dusty old scroll worship.

Alyson answered immediately.

"I had the letter translated, Sis. I'm on my way back to Roswell tonight. Meet me at the airport at about nine."

"What did the letter say?" she asked.

"Too strange to discuss over the phone. You know, typical Grandfather shit."

"Typical shit?"

"Okay, maybe this isn't so typical. Look, I'll explain when I get there."

"But can't you just give me a little hint—" she pleaded.

"Sis, I have a plane to catch."

"Okay. Fine."

Nash heard the frustration in his sister's voice. She hung the phone up loudly—but before he snapped off himself, Nash heard a second click.

He made nothing of it.

Friday
5:56 PM PDT
Roswell, New Mexico

Alyson had just stepped away from her phone when she heard a noise in the kitchen behind her. Her first thought was that Tom had stopped by earlier than planned.

Her second thought was to wonder why Tom had suddenly put on a different-smelling cologne.

Then a rough hand covered her face with a chloroform-soaked rag. She struggled against the rag, but was soon overcome.

Friday
9:05 PM MDT
Roswell, New Mexico

*T**wice in one day. I've had enough of these alien freak shows,* mused Nash as he surveyed the Roswell Airport.

Unlike his earlier arrival, there was no smiling Alyson waiting to see him. Surprised, Nash called her home phone and Tom answered immediately.

"Tom, is Alyson—"

"Jeremy, I have bad news."

Nash could hear voices in the background. His sister's house sounded like it was teeming with people.

"What's going on? Where's Alyson?"

"She's gone, Jeremy."

"What do you mean gone?"

"We think she's been kidnapped. Wait there, I'll come get you."

Friday
9:20 PM MDT
Roswell, New Mexico

As they drove through town, Nash noted that the freaks seemed to be out in greater numbers that night. Annoyed and irritated Nash ignored the loons and listened to Tom give a rundown of the night. Alyson hadn't answered her phone. She and Tom were planning on a quiet dinner together. Tom tried calling her cell several times without success. He didn't think anything of it and assumed she was showering. When he arrived he saw something that chilled him to his core. The lock to her back door had been jimmied open.

"Jimmied?" queried Nash.

"Pried open, damaging the door frame." Tom hung a left and drove into a quiet residential street.

Or, rather, not so quiet now.

Cop cars and various nondescript vehicles were jammed into one end of the street. Neighbors were out in their front yards, pointing and talking amongst themselves.

"I expected the worse," said Tom, slowing down for a group of people crossing in front of them. "I mean, I thought I was going to find her dead on the kitchen floor. Instead, I found a note. Forensics has it now. They're going over it carefully."

"What did the note say?" demanded Nash. "Please!" he blurted out in desperation.

Tom pulled in behind one of the squad cars. A police officer recognized the FBI agent and waved him through. Tom parked haphazardly in front of Alyson house, among a dozen other vehicles.

He turned to Nash. "The note makes it pretty clear your sister was kidnapped."

Nash was finding breathing difficult. In fact, he thought there was a very good chance he might pass out unless he got some fresh air ASAP.

"Why?" he asked. "Why was she kidnapped?"

"According to the note, her kidnappers want a diary in exchange for her life. And they seem to think you either have it or know where it is. Does this have anything to do with your grandfather's letter?"

Nash pulled the translated letter from his jacket pocket and handed it to Tom. Nash watched his expression as he read it. "Is this for real?"

"Someone thinks so. They've kidnapped my sister for what's in it."

Tom frowned. "Well, there's more. The ransom letter indicates that they want to speak with you on an Internet Chat Channel on Sunday morning."

"Won't that make it impossible to trace them?"

"Yes," agreed Tom. "At least initially. Apparently, they want to speak with you and only you." Tom frowned again. It was obvious he clearly didn't like this idea. "Anyway, they gave us a contact name for the chat room. Enos Tucker. Does that name mean anything to you?"

"No."

"We're tracing it now," said Tom. "And one other thing."

Nash cracked open his door. He needed air. He needed to breathe. He was not sure he could handle *one other thing*. And still more police were coming, whipping into the street. Nash watched as plain clothed detectives poured in and out of his sister's house.

Where the hell is she? And then a horrible thought struck him. *Will they hurt her? Damn!*

"We want you to find the diary, especially if it means saving Alyson's life."

"Who's we?" groaned Nash, fear for his sister overwhelming him.

"The Bureau. Oh, and not to fear, I'll be working with you."

Nash relaxed a bit. "Then I guess we're off to Europe to find Stanton Roth. Can you get your office to track him down? That's what the FBI does, right?"

"Piece of cake," Tom replied.

Friday
10:55 PM GMT
Brenner Pass, Austria

At the western end of the Brenner Pass, with a full moon rising and a sharp wind blowing off the high ridge, a tall man dressed in railroad work overalls emerged from the darkness. He crossed over the guardrail and stood in the middle of the tracks, shivering and looking in both directions.

He was alone, as he expected to be. Still, along the world's most famous train route—the Orient Express—one never knew when and where guards would be randomly stationed, especially in light of terrorist activities.

Regardless, he was alone this night. Cold, but alone.

Satisfied, he headed over to the signal box and knelt beside it. At the moment, the red light was off, and the green light was brightly lit, thus informing any approaching train that the track was clear ahead.

Well, we can't have that.

He opened the Velcro straps of his knapsack and pulled out a cloth bag lined with a special non-light emitting material. He also removed electrical equipment and a fully charged portable battery. As the wind picked up and a wispy fog curled over the tracks, he carefully placed the cloth bag over the lit green signal lamp, effectively extinguishing its glow. Next he wired the portable battery to the bag.

Work for me, baby.

He flicked a switch and watched with relief as a red bulb attached to the bag burned a bright crimson.

His work done, the man scurried back over the guardrail, down the hill, and into a waiting Range Rover—and blessed warmth.

Friday
11:13 PM GMT
Brenner Pass, Austria

Enjoying the opulence of his private berth on the Orient Express, Enos Tucker could only see the reflection of his ruddy haired, pasty face in the window of his coach car as the Austrian Alps passed by in the night.

Except for his Peter Lorre eyes that made him look somewhat bizarre to the casual observer, his short squat body and close-cropped hair lent credence to the priestly robes he was wearing. On his lap was a brochure of the *Louvre's* exhibition of the *Arma Christi*. The exhibit had concluded the day before and was now on its way to Vienna for exposition.

And so was Enos Tucker.

As the train gently rocked, Tucker carefully stroked a small talisman that hung from a gold braided chain worn around his neck. The talisman marked him as a member of the Warriors of Christ.

Pride swelled in him, and he took a deep, reverent breath.

The minutes ticked by as he waited for the appointed time. Tucker prayed that the others had been successful in the Lord's work. He kissed the talisman again, perhaps for the hundredth time that night.

As the train passed through what Tucker knew to be the Brenner Pass, he casually rose from his assigned seat. He made his way through the other coaches, many of which were lined with plush booths and softly glowing lamps. As he crossed through the elegant dining coach that would have put many fine restaurants in his hometown of Los Angeles to shame, Tucker smiled devoutly at the various patrons. All of them were dressed to the nines, displaying their best formal dining attire and obviously enjoying the epicurean delights of the Orient Express.

He exited the dining coach, leaving its mouth-watering aromas behind, and stepped onto the noisy platform leading to the cargo car, the last car before the engine. A young guard stood before the doorway of this cargo car, pistol prominent in his hip holster.

"Sorry, Father, but you can't go in there."

Tucker smiled pleasantly, but the young guard, who wore a nicely pressed security uniform and official cap, remained impassive. Tucker figured the kid could not have been more than twenty years old.

"Forgive me, my son," said Tucker in English, although he adopted a passable French accent. "I was just wondering if you could extend me a favor."

"What favor, Father?"

"Are you a Christian, my son?"

The guard frowned. Tufts of blond hair poked out from under his cap. "Yes," he said.

"Good, and bless you. I'm from the—"

"Please, Father, you must leave this area. It is restricted." The guard shifted, lowering his hand near the polished handle of his pistol. He spoke English in a heavy Austrian accent.

"Humor me, my son. I won't be long. As I was saying, I'm from the Abbey of St. Michael in France." Tucker had no idea if there was such an abbey in France, but he was certain the kid didn't either. "We print and distribute a small magazine that we sell to the general public to raise money for the Catholic Relief Mission in Peru."

He was laying it on thick.

"Perhaps you have heard of our work?"

"Father, please—"

Tucker plunged forward. "I'm on assignment here to write an article about the *Arma Christi* and thought a few pictures of the actual transportation of the relics from Paris to Vienna would make a nice introduction to my piece. Don't you agree?"

The guard's hand now rested on the handle of his weapon. "The *Arma Christi*, Father?"

Tucker maintained a very pleasant demeanor. "Are you not familiar with the *Arma Christi*?"

"No, but I must ask—"

"It's a wonderful story, my son. Many of the relics in the *Arma Christi* are not well known. It's a tragedy that so few even know of their powerful existence, which is why the Vatican has put them on tour."

The young guard thankfully relaxed his grip on his pistol. The train rocked imperceptibly. Beneath Tucker's feet, he could feel the vibration of the wheels moving over the frozen tracks.

"What are these relics, Father?" the guard asked.

"Ah, my son. They are the Instruments of the Passion."

"Instruments of the Passion?"

Tucker nodded. "Or, as some call them, the Weapons of Christ." He let the words hang in the air. "They have a long tradition in iconography, dating back to, oh, around the 9th century." Tucker removed the gold braided chain from around his neck. He took a step forward and held the chain out to the guard. "This is a miniature of one of the relics. We of the brotherhood wear them to contemplate the price Jesus our Lord paid for our sins."

The young guard squinted through the half light of the platform. "It looks like an old nail."

"Indeed! It's a miniature of the nails driven into Our Lord's hands and feet at the Crucifixion."

The guard's jaw dropped a little. He leaned forward. "What's it attached to? A sword and shield?"

"That's the symbol for my abbey." Tucker lied. "So, my son, may I take a few quick pictures of the *Arma Christi*?"

"I really shouldn't—"

"Please, my son."

"OK. But please don't tell anyone I let you in here. I could get in trouble."

"Of course, my son. Bless you."

The guard pulled a set of keys from his jacket pocket and opened the cargo door. The two men walked towards the middle, Tucker a step or two behind, and passed several wooden cargo containers.

"Now, you do understand, Father, all you'll see is a few crates. The exhibit of course is boxed up."

"Of course—ah, there they are!" Tucker pointed to several crates marked *Arma Christi, Vienna*. He walked to the crates and pulled out a small camera from his robe. "Would you please stand next to the crates, my son? For the picture."

The young guard agreed and strolled over to the crates, but before he could reach them, he felt the train begin to slow down.

"That's odd," he said. "There's no scheduled stop here." He walked to the small barred window affixed to the sliding cargo door. "I can't see—" were the only words he could utter before a hard blow at the back of his head knock him to the floor. He turned over and looked up at Tucker who had a pistol pointed at his face.

"Give me your gun," Tucker demanded.

The young guard, confused and dazed from the blow to his head, tried to focus his thoughts.

"I said give me your weapon!" Tucker hissed.

The young guard complied.

"Now your keys. Quick!"

The guard hesitated.

"The keys. Now," spat Tucker menacingly.

The guard reached into his jacket and handed the keys up to Tucker as the train continued to slow.

"Stay where you are," Tucker commanded. The guard watched as Tucker unlocked and opened the sliding cargo door. A blast of mountain air rushed into the car. Tucker leaned out of the car, threw the guard's pistol out into the night, and looked ahead at the tracks. He strained his eyes to see, but it was too dark. As Tucker pulled his head in from the door, a pair of hands grabbed him by his robe and turned him violently around. Tucker looked up at the young guard who had his hand on Tucker's gun.

They both struggled for possession of the weapon as Tucker tried to remove the grip the kid had on his pistol. The young guard had at least a foot on Tucker in height and was stronger, too. But Tucker pushed him backwards across the floor of the car into the wall, knocking the breath out of him.

Tucker had regained the superior position. He beat the young man over the head and shoulders with his pistol as the guard threw his hands up in front of him trying vainly to ward off Tucker's blows.

Seeing him visibly weakened, Tucker saw his chance. He pulled his prey from the floor and dragged him to the open cargo door. The young guard grabbed desperately at whatever he could as Tucker pushed him relentlessly towards the opening.

The doomed guard was perched precariously on his knees. The sound of the clacking railroad tracks would cover any scream. The dark night rushed by the opening, and Tucker forcibly freed the clutching fingers gripping his robe. With one quick shove, he pushed the desperate guard through the door and into the night.

Tucker straightened his priestly robes. But he noticed something was amiss. His gold braided chain was gone. There was no time to look for it now. The train had come to a halt.

Friday
11:40 PM GMT
Brenner Pass, Austria

Two burley men dressed in black jeans, dark brown shirts, and ski masks quietly approached the stalled engine. They saw the engineer and conductor talking in the cab with their backs towards them. It looked like they made some sort of a decision as the conductor opened the cab door and started to leave.

This gave the sinister duo the opportunity they needed. It was quick and easy for them to enter the engine cab and overpower the two drivers.

One tied up the driver and conductor and tossed them out of the cab onto the cold rocky ground while the other sat in the driver's seat. All they needed to do now was to wait for Tucker.

He was already running towards them with his robes flowing behind him.

"Everything's set," Tucker exclaimed. "Disconnect those cars and let's get out of here."

One of the men went to the end of the cargo car, releasing it from the rest of the train. He gave the signal when done, and the other man put the train into forward gear.

Mission accomplished.

As Nash waited for Tom at Gate 6, Albuquerque International Airport, his cell rang. In his haste to snap it open, he nearly pried the phone in two. He was immediately disheartened to see that his sister wasn't calling. In fact, he didn't recognize the number. Then again, maybe these were her kidnappers—

Nash pressed the answer button, his finger shaking. "Hello?" he asked.

"Jeremy Nash?" queried a male voice.

"Yes." Nash's heart pounded furiously. Adrenalin surged through him.

"Jeremy, this is Bryan Henderson..."

Nash suffered his second set-back in so many minutes. He recognized the voice immediately. Bryan Henderson was an old friend from college. A real party animal. He had quite a head for math but a taste for psychedelics as well. His irresponsible partying eventually caused a rift between them.

They spoke for a few minutes, and Nash learned that his friend had bad news of his own and needed to talk. So bad, in fact, that Nash didn't bother recounting his own horrible news—*Oh, by the way, Bryan, my sister appears to have been kidnapped...*

As he spoke, Tom appeared through a crowd. Moving with such determination Nash was reminded of one of the terminator robots from those cheesy Schwarzenegger movies.

And for perhaps the tenth time that day, Nash thought—*God, what does she see in this guy?*

Nash offered his condolences to his friend, made a promise to try to attend the funeral, and snapped shut the phone.

"What was that about?" asked Tom.

Nash was about to tell the guy to mind his own damn business until he remembered that Tom Gray, super FBI agent, might just one day be his brother-in-law. And besides, the man was helping him find his sister.

"A friend of mine," explained Nash. "His grandfather just committed suicide."

"I'm sorry to hear that," said Tom. Nash saw a big 747 taxiing onto the ramp. Standing together at the gate, Nash waited for Tom's inevitable question... "So how did he, um, kill himself?"

"He was staying at Walter Reed—apparently the nut wing of the hospital—and leaped out his room's window."

"Jesus. What a way to go. Any signs of foul play?"

"Foul play? What do you mean?"

"You know, *foul play*," shrugged Tom sheepishly. "Sorry, it's the investigator in me. Hey, I have some good news. We found Stanton Roth, the guy mentioned in your grandfather's letter."

That *was* good news. "Where is he?"

As he spoke, Tom's icy exterior melted slightly, perhaps the truest sign yet that Global Warming was real. "He's in London. And hopefully the diary is with him, right? Anyway, Interpol has kept a tight watch on him."

"Really! Any reason why?"

"None that we care about," said Tom. "We just want the diary, right old chap?"

Old Chap? thought Nash. *And no. I couldn't give a horse's ass about the diary. I just want my sister back.*

And even as the words crossed his thoughts, Nash knew they weren't true. Yes, he wanted his sister back, alive and well, and he wanted her kidnappers behind bars or fed to the lions, but he had to admit, he was damn curious about what was in that diary, too. What could be important enough to have his sister kidnapped?

Saturday
2:05 PM GMT
Vienna, Austria

Sitting outside the police inspector's office, Agent Sabra Zamir, tall and ridiculously beautiful, read the Interpol alert regarding the *Arma Christi* robbery again and felt the excitement rise in her. Good God, this could be the break she was looking for!

But she knew she had to tread lightly when dealing with the Austrian police on three counts. First, the crime was way out of her jurisdiction, second, she was a woman, and third, she was a Jew.

As the Americans say, three strikes and you're out.

"The inspector will see you now," said a dour-faced police official. "Follow me, please."

Follow she did. Within minutes she was shown a seat before Inspector Nicholas Brunn, a large man with hands the size of small Volkswagens. As she sat, the balding Inspector furrowed his brow disapprovingly. Sabra wanted to shove his disapproving brow up his disapproving ass.

But that wouldn't be ladylike.

He glanced down at a sheet of paper in front of him. "You work for the Institute for Intelligence and Special Operations?" he said in German, which was fine with Sabra. After all, she was fluent in seven languages. He continued. "Isn't that just a fancy name, Miss Zamir, for the Mossad?"

"Israel doesn't officially recognize the existence of the Mossad," she said in perfect German. This was a line she always repeated.

"You are a spy, are you not?" he persisted.

43

"I am an intelligence officer," she said smoothly. "I gather intelligence and report my findings to my supervisors."

"You mean to the Mossad."

"I mean to my supervisors, Mr. Brunn. I always say what I mean."

"I'm sure you do," he retorted and sat back, the frown lines deepening. He tapped a pencil against his front teeth, a habit that immediately bothered Sabra more than she cared to admit. "So why is Israeli Intelligence interested in an Austrian train robbery?" he asked finally.

Sabra smiled brightly, knowing full well the effect her smile had on the male of the species. "Perhaps we can barter for information, Chief Inspector. I would be delighted to tell you more about our interest in this case in exchange for, perhaps, some information on your end."

"And what kind of information would this be, Miss Zamir?"

"We are interested in evidence gathered by your esteemed team of investigators."

She crossed her legs slowly, allowing her skirt to ride up a little higher on her thigh. She was pleased to see the movement was not lost on the Chief Inspector. He looked for a beat or two longer than his wife—yes, Sabra had noticed the ring on his finger—would have probably tolerated. He sat back and tapped his teeth some more with the eraser end of the pencil.

Sabra cringed.

"I know how the Mossad works, Miss Zamir. I spill my guts about our end of things, and you simply give me a bullshit cover story, something that seems plausible enough but certainly doesn't reveal the Mossad's true intent."

"You have my word, Inspector."

"Your word on what?"

"That I will be forthright about our investigation."

He laughed heartily and set the pencil down. "Now I've heard everything. Forthright and Mossad do not go hand in hand." He looked at her some more, then seemed to come to some conclusion.

"Okay, fine. I will tell you what we know if only to get a chuckle out of your cover story. I could use a good laugh. This has been one hell of a shitty day."

"I am sorry to hear that, Inspector."

He rolled his eyes a little. She knew he was buying little of what she said, even her sympathies. As long as the man kept talking, she could care less.

"We have very little to go on," he said, sitting back. "A professional job, we know that much. They spoofed the traffic control light and halted the train, which was then boarded by masked thugs who decoupled the storage car from the rest of the train. Then the engine was driven a few miles down the track where thieves apparently transferred the *Arma Christi* onto something else, perhaps trucks. By the time the railroad officials had arrived, the thieves were long gone."

"And only the *Arma Christi* was stolen?" asked Sabra. "Nothing else from the cargo car?"

"Nothing else."

"Wasn't there a shipment of securities and cash locked in the car's safe?"

Brunn opened a manila folder on his desk and looked at the train's manifest. "Yes. Several million Euro went untouched."

"Don't you think that's odd, Inspector?"

"I can't speak for the motivation of these thieves, Miss Zamir. For instance, I think it's equally odd that a representative from your *esteemed* office is sitting across from me, and showing me too much of her thigh. Makes me think the Mossad is playing on my sensibilities as a male."

She knew enough to say nothing in this situation, particularly as the Chief Inspector continued to leer at her legs.

He sighed. "If you knew anything about these Christian relics—and I suspect you do—then you would know that the *Arma Christi* is very valuable indeed. More valuable than the trouble it would have been to open the train's safe."

"Regarding the crime scene, what evidence have you found, Inspector?"

"Except for some tire tracks and footprints, the only thing we found was a necklace in the hand of the dead security guard lying in a gulley a few miles or so from the train. Poor man had a broken neck. We figured he was thrown from the car."

"The necklace. May I see it?"

Brunn opened a desk drawer and extracted a small manila envelope. Undoing the latch, he emptied the contents onto his desktop. A glittering gold necklace with an unusual pendant slithered out. From another drawer he produced a pair of latex gloves and handed them to her. She slipped them on and, with a nod of approval from the Chief Inspector, she carefully picked up the gold braided chain.

She immediately recognized the symbol for the Warriors of Christ—the small sword attached diagonally across a shield with the inscribed letters IHS. The small spike hanging from the sword and shield was a miniature of one of the *Arma Christi* itself.

This was more than she could have hoped for. She fingered the chain.

"Does that thing have any significance to you?" asked Brunn.

"None that I could see," she lied.

"So you do not recognize it?"

"As belonging to a certain group or a particular person? No, I'm afraid not. Do you have any suspicions, Inspector?"

"None yet, although we suspect it's a religious group. Fanatics perhaps."

"Perhaps," said Sabra in a hopefully vague tone.

"So what is your interest in this robbery, Miss Zamir?"

He was right about the bullshit spiel. She laid it on thick explaining a similar robbery in Israel. He didn't buy it, of course and smiled knowingly as she got up to leave.

"Perhaps you could stay for dinner," he said. "And tell me the real reason why you are here."

"Chief Inspector, you are a married man."

"In theory. So what do you say? Can we discuss the crime over cocktails?"

Pausing at the door, she smiled. "I'll call you," she whispered. And promptly left.

Saturday
3:10 PM GMT
Vienna, Austria

Outside the police building, Sabra placed her Bluetooth ear-piece into her ear and spoke her security code. A series of beeps and buzzes emitted from her Bluetooth and within seconds she was speaking to the Mossad station chief in Vienna on a secure encrypted line.

"This is Sabra. I want a team to meet me in London. Immediately." She disconnected and looked up at the graying skies. She knew that if the Warriors of Christ wanted to fence these ancient artifacts there was only one person in Europe who could do it.

Stanton Roth.

Saturday
7:56 PM GMT
London, England

Londdon was crowded, teeming with cars whipping through winding, narrow streets as if their drivers were hell bent on killing themselves and those around them.

Their cab driver was no different, and Nash was certain he would never make it to their destination alive. More than once his life passed before his eyes, a life that suddenly seemed entirely too short and without much purpose.

I have purpose, he thought, gripping the handrail above him again as the driver made a psychotically dangerous right turn. *I give people the truth. I set them free from their limiting beliefs.*

But a nagging thought persisted, a thought Nash didn't want to entirely accept. But there it was—*What if they don't want the truth? What if they prefer living in their comfortable ignorant bliss?*

Maybe. Maybe not. He didn't know. All he knew was he had devoted his life to dispelling untruths and flat-out lies. And he would be damned if he believed his life was without purpose. Granted his globe-hopping hadn't afforded him much time to have a personal life, but that would come someday. He was sure of it.

Or, at least, he hoped it would. Nash had never had much luck with relationships. More often than not he wasn't able to give women what they seemed to really want—*him.*

The driver whipped around a stalled commuter and cursed the guy out for his unfortunate luck.

Next to Nash, Tom didn't look so good. The FBI agent appeared a little green and sick to his stomach.

"They always drive like this?" Tom groaned.

"Only on good days," laughed Nash. This was, after all, his umpteenth visit to London. He had long ago accepted the suicidal driving.

Finally, after two near-fatal wrecks, their cab miraculously arrived in front of a stately mansion nestled between two smaller homes.

"Nice place," said Nash. "Reminds me of home."

"In your dreams," Tom sighed. He leaned out his side window. "You sure this is the right address?"

The cab driver assured them it was. They fumbled with the currency, paid their fare and stepped out into the driving rain, each carrying a small handbag. Nash tossed his over a shoulder, pushing through the wrought iron gate.

"He's expecting us, right?" asked Nash.

"Spoke to him myself," assured Tom.

Nash knocked on the oversized door and soon felt the gaze of a tall lanky domestic servant who peered down upon them from the length of his nose. Despite the disapproving thoughts obviously running through his head, he quickly ushered the two visitors into a cavernous entrance hall. They followed the dour butler through a long hallway lined with several Monet's—probably originals. The click of their footsteps echoed on the mosaic tile floors.

"Reminds me of a museum," Tom whispered to Nash. "An old, stuffy museum."

A few turns later, the two men were shown into an anteroom and seated. "I'll see if Mr. Roth is ready for you," said the butler in monotone syllables. He disappeared through a pair of double doors at the far end of the room.

Nash settled into a plush wing-backed chair and found himself thinking about his sister. Over the years they had grown apart due to the demands of their careers and religious beliefs, or lack there of on Nash's part. Still, Nash kicked himself for being so distant. After all, he could have called his sister more, visited more, taken more of an interest in her life. But he hadn't.

I'm a selfish asshole, he thought.

Once again he wondered where she was, who had taken her, and why. And once again, he had no answers. However, one thing he did know was that someone was going to pay for this, especially if they hurt her.

The thought of her being harmed made him sick. It also made him realize just how much they needed this diary. What had their crazy old grandfather gotten them into?

Nash distracted himself by scanning the small room, which was filled to the brim with religious paraphernalia from a plethora of theistic traditions. Nash was particularly drawn to one of the biggest displays, a life-size replica of the Shroud of Turin that hung on the wall directly in front of him. It was seriously cool, not to mention creepy, and he wanted one for his office at home. Next to it was a large banner that had a symbol Nash didn't recognize. He rose from his chair, walking over to study it.

"Tom, what do you make of this symbol?" asked Nash.

Tom joined him as rain splattered on the big window next to them. Tom looked at Nash—puzzled. "It looks like the logo for the US Department of Transportation."

"I wonder what it's doing here?" Nash said.

"Does it matter? He probably vacations on Route 66."

Nash shrugged. He didn't know what mattered anymore. The events of one day——too many thoughts and emotions coursing through his mind——sister gone, strange diaries, cryptic messages left behind by his equally cryptic grandfather.

So what the devil is going on?

He didn't know.

At least not yet. But one thing was for sure. He was going to find out, and he was going to get his sister back.

At that moment, the double doors at the far end of the room opened, and *Mr. Cheery* appeared. "Mr. Roth will see you now."

Tom mimicked under his breath: *"Mr. Roth will see you now."*

Nash grinned, despite the situation. Maybe he could get to like his future brother-in-law after all.

The two men passed through the doors and into a handsome and spacious study. Sitting in front of a wide desk was an elderly man in a wheelchair—an aged aristocratic-looking man with only one arm, which was currently resting in his lap. He smiled at them and introduced himself as Stanton Roth.

"I've been looking forward to our meeting ever since your phone call," Roth said pleasantly. "And who is the gentleman with you?"

"Tom Gray."

"Oh, yes. The one who contacted me." He resettled himself in his wheelchair. "So, Mr. Nash, have a seat and tell me a little about yourself."

"In all due respect, sir, I'm feeling very anxious. My sister…"

"Come, come," Roth interrupted. "Have Americans totally lost the art of polite conversation?"

Tom nudged him. Nash cleared his throat. *Hell, he might as well appease the old guy.* After all, the man *did* have something Nash desperately wanted. "Well, I'm a researcher and writer."

"Wonderful! And what are you researching now, Mr. Nash?"

"A book on eschatology."

Roth nodded knowingly and seemed about to ask something when Tom looked over at Nash, who didn't have to look at his new friend to know that there was a completely blank look on Tom's face.

Tom asked the inevitable. "What's eschata-whatever?"

"It's the study of the end of the world," Nash said, looking over at Roth for a reaction. The old man in the wheelchair raised his eyebrows and nodded.

"The End Times," said Roth.

"The End Times?" said Tom incredulously. "As in Armageddon and all that hooey?"

"Right," said Nash, grinning. "And all that hooey."

"Then there's no future in it, Jeremy," said Tom, laughing and slapping a knee.

Nash rolled his eyes. Tom was proving to be a bit of an enigma to him. Stoic and reserved at times, boisterous and unrefined during others. Admittedly, Nash liked the boisterous and unrefined version of Tom.

Must be the rebel in me, he thought.

Nash threw back, "You know, if I had a dime for every time I heard that joke—"

"And what is the name of your book?" asked Roth, thankfully getting them back on subject.

"*A Taste of the Apocalypse*," answered Nash.

"Sounds like a doomsday cookbook," said Tom, laughing again. Nash now began to question the boisterous side of Tom.

"What's your book about?" asked Roth patiently. The old man, to his credit, seemed to have taken a liking to Nash. Or, at least a liking to his occupational pursuits. Either way, Nash had to admit, he loved talking about his writing. An ex-girlfriend once told him she was tired of having a love triangle between herself, Nash, and his ego.

He said, "I'm debunking the different doomsday myths that we've had in history—especially the religious prophecies that predict the end of the world."

Tom rolled his eyes and sat back. "Good thing you're not wasting your time or anything. I mean, I would hate to think you might be doing something useful with all that research, like, I dunno, helping find a cure to cancer?"

Okay, Nash definitely didn't like the crude Tom.

Where's stoic Tom when you need him?

"Go on, Mr. Nash," said Roth. "What are some of your findings? I'm fascinated."

"Well, would you believe that the first recorded instance of predicting the end of the world was back in 2800 BCE? An Assyrian clay tablet was unearthed bearing the words: *Our earth is degenerate in these latter days. There are signs that the world is speedily coming to an end. Bribery and corruption are common.* Nash added, "Little has changed since then, has it? Words on a clay tablet then. Preachers on TV today."

"So, I gather you're not a religious man?" asked Roth.

"No."

"You don't believe in God?"

"Why should I care about the existence of God against all the evidence that our interest is not reciprocated?" Nash said. "Please forgive me, Mr. Roth, but I've recently received some very distressing news—news that has something to do with the diary my grandfather left you."

"Oh, dear me. I was so sorry to hear about your distressing news. I must apologize for overstepping my bounds. I was just curious to see how much of your grandfather was in you."

Nash felt terrible for jumping on the old guy. And a one-armed guy in a wheelchair, no less. "How did you know my grandfather, Mr. Roth?"

"For starters, your grandfather put me in this wheelchair."

Startled, Nash realized his jaw was hanging open and closed it quickly. Roth continued to smile kindly at him. The older man's eyes even twinkled.

"Perhaps I should explain, since apparently this is news to you," said Roth. "Your grandfather and I fought together in World War Two. We flew with the Eighth Air Force. Zed was the captain, and I was the co-pilot. We were on a bombing mission over Berlin near the end of the war, and we took the brunt of it. Or rather, I took the brunt of it. Something had gone straight through the starboard engine and blew off my arm. Somehow your grandfather nursed our B-17 back to England but ran just short of the runway. We crashed in a nearby field." He paused and looked at Nash. "As they say, any landing you can walk away from is a good landing. Well, I never walked again."

Nash was silent, taking in this shocking information, until he realized he needed to say something and mumbled his apologies. Tom did the same.

"But your grandfather did get us back alive, and I will be forever grateful for that," said Roth. "I will admit I've had days where I wished he hadn't gotten us back alive and that we had crashed our plane into a fiery oblivion. Ah, but I have long since accepted my lot in life as a one-armed cripple." He gave Nash a weak grin. "I am determined to get along in life, and not be a burden on others. So early on I cast around for work that I could perform from a limited physical capacity, and hit upon the antiquities market. As you can see, I've done quite well for myself."

Nash took in the massive study and the custom made bookshelves lined with hundreds if not thousands of books and pieces of ancient art.

Roth continued, "And in my spare time I took up various intellectual activities. One of them is biblical archeology. However, where I pursued my archaeological ambitions for fun, your grandfather would go on to become a leading paleo-linguist, working on none other than the original Dead Sea Scrolls. I must say," and for the first time Nash detected a note of animosity, "your grandfather certainly had all the luck."

"So, why would my grandfather leave the diary with you?" Nash asked, wanting to get them back on topic.

"We remained good friends. After all, you don't survive a harrowing crash together, become interested in similar scholarly endeavors, and then lose touch with each other."

"But why give the diary to you? Help me understand..."

"Maybe because I was a close friend or..."

"Or what?" asked Nash.

"Maybe he was scared."

"Scared? Of what?"

"More like of whom."

"W hom?" Nash questioned sitting forward.

"I don't know. However, he knew I would keep it safe. And I did. I kept it locked in my most secure vault."

"What's in the diary?"

"As you Americans say, that's the million dollar question."

"Did he tell you anything when he gave you the diary?"

"No. Only that I was to hold it until you came for it."

"How long ago was this?"

"Years ago." His voice lowered. "A long time ago."

"Have you read the diary?" Nash asked.

"Oh, yes, many times. Unfortunately, I can't make heads or tails of it. But perhaps you being here, Mr. Nash, will get us to the answer."

"How?" asked Nash.

"Your colleague there said you found me through a letter from Zed. The answer could be in there."

"There's nothing in there but some nutty rant about the burial place of Christ," Nash replied.

"You think your grandfather was crazy?"

"Certifiable. And not just me. My grandmother said he was committed to an institution."

"I can see you don't know very much about your grandfather," Roth mused.

"I know enough that whatever he wrote in that diary prompted some nut case to kidnap my sister. And unless I give it to them they will kill her." Nash became agitated. "So, if you don't mind, will you please give me the diary?"

"Perhaps it's best I give you what you came for." Roth rolled himself over to his ornate wooden desk. Once there, he picked up a small, tattered, maroon booklet the size of a teenager's diary, only thinner, and rolled back to Nash. "I believe this is what you want."

Heart hammering, Nash reached for the diary and saw one word neatly printed on the cover: *Apocalypse.*

Tom peered over Nash's shoulder. "So your grandpa's diary is also about the end of the world."

"Not necessarily," said Nash. "The literal meaning of Apocalypse means *pulling away of the veil* or *revealing the truth.* That's where we get the concept of Revelations in the Bible." Nash thought back to his grandfather's letter. Hadn't the old coot mentioned something about revealing the truth?

Nash opened the diary and thumbed through it. The slim booklet was filled with page after page of religious ranting, secular and religious drawings, and strange sketches of exotic looking figures and bizarre devices, all printed in his grandfather's neat, regimented handwriting

Roth broke the silence, "May I see the letter your grandfather left you?"

"It's just filled with the same ranting."

"Humor me," replied Roth.

Nash pulled the original letter and Professor Thomas' translation from his pocket. Roth studied both for a moment.

"The signature doesn't match the letter," said Roth.

"Right," said Nash. "The letter is written in Akkadian but signed in Hebrew."

"And do you have any idea what this signature means?"

"Well, yes. It's the Hebrew word for God's signature. Or so I was told."

"Close," said Roth. "But not quite."

"What do you mean?" asked Nash.

"I'm lost," said Tom. "And I'm hungry."

Roth rang a bell from his wheelchair, and out came the sour butler. Roth requested some sandwiches and cheese. The butler bowed and left. Nash wanted a butler, too.

Roth continued, "What we have here is the Hebrew word for the *signature* of God—which is different than God's signature."

"Now I'm really confused," said Tom.

"What's the difference?" asked Nash.

"I assume as a researcher in eschatology you're aware of the Bible Code. Yes?"

"Of course," said Nash, "but I'm not sold on its validity. In fact, I can make a case that many great works have similar codes—"

"Mr. Nash. I'm surprised at you," Roth admonished. "The Bible Code is sometimes referred to as the *Signature of God.*"

"I still don't see what you're getting at," said Nash.

Roth smiled patiently. "This Hebrew signature is your grandfather's clue to unlocking the diary."

Roth paused and shook his head. "Zed, you crazy old fool."

"Crazy is right," said Nash. "But what are you getting at?"

"Your grandfather hid a message in his diary, Jeremy." He grinned broadly. "And I think I know just how to find it."

Saturday

10:13 PM GMT

London, England

Sabra and her two-man team sipped their coffees across the street from Roth's mansion. They sat together in a black Lincoln Navigator, hidden behind tinted windows. Rain drizzled against the windshield, making comforting noises. Sabra thought the Navigator could have been cozy, if not for the fact that she was currently sharing it with two trained assassins.

She shivered at the thought and warmed her hands over her double latte. Sitting next to her and in the seat behind her, Ari and Jeron, brothers, quietly watched the entrance to the mansion. Too quietly. They rarely spoke, and when they did their voices were utterly devoid of warmth. Sabra knew the brothers had been orphaned at a young age by means they would not talk about. And at an equally young age, they had been recruited into the Mossad assassin academy. They had been trained as killers from the very beginning. Ruthless killers.

They gave Sabra the creeps, even after all these years as their team leader.

She brought the cup up to her lips and sipped some more of her coffee. She focused her thoughts on Roth. She knew whoever had stolen the *Arma Christi* would eventually end up here, at Roth's manor. She was sure of it.

Roth was the fence of choice for stolen religious artifacts. He paid top dollar and was confidential as hell. He was well known to the Mossad.

And to Sabra.

The rain intensified, obscuring the streetlights, drumming against the metal roof.

The two brothers sat silently. They reminded her of pumas stalking their prey. Both were vaguely handsome. She might have been interested in either or both of them—had they not terrified her to her very core.

And she was a trained killer herself.

She and the two brothers had been working the Warriors of Christ case off and on since the millennium, back when Israel had been forced to deport twelve of the cultists suspected of planning violent acts to hasten the Second Coming. Intelligence from a combined effort with the FBI had later confirmed that the cult never disappeared, only went dormant—and now they were planning something big.

Maybe big enough to finally flush out their leader.

Sabra took a sip of her latte—and thought she noticed a shadowy figure in the corner of her eye, moving up the street. She turned to get a clearer view, but the figure was gone.

If it had ever been there.

And as the rain continued to pound, she and the two brothers watched the house—and waited.

Saturday
10:56 AM GMT
London, England

Roth pressed the intercom button on his desk, and almost instantly a geeky young man appeared in the doorway. Nash thought he also saw the bulge of a handgun inside the young man's jacket, but that could have been Nash's overactive imagination. Roth gave his worker the diary and asked the man to scan the contents ASAP. The worker nodded, and when he turned away and strode from the room, Nash saw the white flash of ivory.

Definitely a handgun.

Nash's patience was reaching a breaking point. Whatever the hell his grandfather had gotten him into, he didn't know or care. Nash sat forward and made a concerted effort to control his voice. "Mr. Roth, I mean no disrespect to you, and I certainly appreciate your offer of uncovering the clues within the diary, but I'm not interested in what it says—or even what's hidden inside it. I just want my sister back, and that diary is the key."

"I understand, Mr. Nash. But they will not harm your sister while you still have the diary."

"You don't know that—"

"Yes, I do know that. I know exactly what kind of people you are dealing with, Mr. Nash. They have no interest in hurting your sister. They just want the diary."

"And how do you know the kind of people we're dealing with?" asked Tom, voicing Nash's own question.

The old man in the wheel chair simply smiled and flicked his gaze over at Nash. "What's the name of the man you are to contact?"

"Tucker," said Nash. "Enos Tucker."

Roth smiled again, but this time it was completely devoid of warmth. The smile of a man who knows too much, has seen too much, and suffered too much. "Do you have any idea with whom you are dealing, Mr. Nash?"

"No," Nash admitted. And he hadn't had time to research the name, either.

"He's related to Michael Dennis Rohan, who was his stepfather. You *do* know who he is?" asked Roth.

Nash nodded. "Rohan was a Christian Zionist. In nineteen sixty-nine he proclaimed to have been chosen by God to erect a Temple to Jesus on the Mount."

"But the Al Aqsa Mosque is on the Mount," Tom replied.

Nash looked over at his new friend, impressed.

Roth, excited, jumped in his wheelchair. "Details, details. Rohan tried to burn the mosque down. And very nearly did. Caused a good deal of damage, not to mention quite a stir in the Middle-East. If he had succeeded, he would have single-handedly started World War Three."

Roth paused and looked firmly at Nash. "As you can see, my friend, you are dealing with some very dangerous people here. I'd think strongly of bringing some protection with you."

"I have protection," said Nash, suddenly grateful that the somewhat lumbering Tom was indeed with him. "Tom is an FBI agent, and he's officially on the case."

"Good," said Roth, sitting back. "Then I would suggest you allow us to get on the case, as well."

"Us?"

"Me and my staff. Mr. Nash, I have valuable resources at your disposal."

"And what do you get out of this?" asked Nash.

Roth smiled wolfishly. "The satisfaction of knowing that I have helped my old friend's grandchildren."

Nash somehow doubted that was the man's true intentions, but he was certainly grateful for the offer of help.

Roth continued. "My best suggestion to you is that we first see if there's anything in the diary we need to know before you deal with these people, especially if they feel it's important enough to warrant kidnapping your sister. If I were you, Mr. Nash, I would very much like to know exactly what I was getting myself into. Forewarned is forearmed."

Nash didn't like it. His gut told him to get the diary and give it to the bastards and do whatever it took to get his sister back. But something held him back from demanding the diary. An investigator's curiosity and instincts, perhaps. Or perhaps there was something else, too.

Beating these bastards at their own game.

Nash hated bullies, and these were the worst kind of bullies. But was he willing to put his sister's life at risk to beat them? That thought sickened him.

God, what had their grandfather gotten them involved with?

Roth looked squarely at Nash. "Tucker and whoever he's working with may be, in your mind, religious *loons*. But let me assure you, they are religious *fanatics*. And fanatics are always dangerous."

Roth's intercom buzzed on his desk. A voice echoed out, "The booklet is scanned in, sir."

"Very good," said Roth into the intercom. He turned to the two men seated in front of him. "Now, let's see what the Bible Code says is *really* in the diary." The older man wheeled around and positioned himself in front of his computer on the desk. He flicked a button, and a large projected image appeared on the wall behind him, clearly visible to both Nash and Tom.

"I don't want to sound dumb," said Tom, "but I think I'm about to. What the devil is the Bible Code?"

"I take it you don't watch much cable TV?" asked Nash. "The History Channel, per chance?"

"I don't watch TV at all," said Tom. "I spend my time catching bad guys. So what's this Bible Code?"

"A cheap parlor trick," said Nash, looking over at Roth.

"You're quite the skeptic, aren't you?" commented Roth.

"It's kinda what I do."

"Ah, yes. The great skeptic. I have read your articles. In fact, I even subscribe to your magazine. You are quite the world traveler."

"I do what it takes to get the story straight. And the Bible Code has been proven—"

Tom raised his big hand. "Look, you two can argue about this later. I just want to know what the hell you're arguing *about*."

Roth answered. "Back around the beginning of the Common Era, the Jewish Historian, Flavius Josephus, made interesting references to the Torah Codes in his description of the Jewish sect known as the Essenes."

"And who are they?" asked Tom. And to Nash's surprise, the big FBI guy seemed genuinely interested.

"They were a Jewish sect that lived in Qumran on the Dead Sea during the time of Jesus." Roth clicked something on his computer, and Nash could see that a program was loading. Roth continued, "They were a religious sect that practiced gnosis. They were Gnostics."

"I've heard the name," said Tom. "No idea from where, though."

"They were different from any other religious sect at the time. For them, it was necessary for an individual to free oneself from the material world. To do that, one needed gnosis—spiritual knowledge. This esoteric spiritual knowledge could only be attained through knowledge—not faith—and only through intense study. Some Gnostics believed that Jesus was the embodiment of the Supreme Being who became incarnate to bring gnosis to the Earth."

"Sounds like a bunch of Buddhists," Tom said jokingly. "You know, contemplating your navel and all that stuff."

Roth didn't smile, but Nash found himself liking the federal agent's cavalier attitude more and more.

"You're closer than you think," said Roth. "Those who believe in the esoteric arts think there are many paths to God. Gnostics believe the journey to God is on the path of knowledge, not blind faith." Roth paused a moment. "Perhaps you saw the banner in the other room? It has a Gnostic symbol on it."

Nash spoke up, interested. "You mean the one with the symbol of the U.S. Department of Transportation on it?"

"Well, that's one use for it. But originally it was an Oriental symbol adopted by the Gnostics as an emblem of cosmic creativity, the threefold nature of reality or fate, and the eternally spiraling cycles of time."

"Oh, sure," mocked Tom. "Everyone knows that."

Roth frowned, and Nash nearly laughed. Yeah, Tom was going to make a hell of a brother-in-law. Now they just needed to find his sister.

Roth continued, "Now, between nineteen forty-seven and nineteen fifty-six, the Dead Sea Scrolls—you've heard of the scrolls, right?" He looked at Tom—the agent nodded. "Good," said Roth. "The scrolls were found in eleven caves in and around Qumran on the northwest shore of the Dead Sea."

"Ah," said Tom.

"Good. Now, back to Josephus. He reported that when the Essenes assigned numerical values to the various Hebrew letters in the Bible, they could predict the future."

"Huh?" said Tom.

"Follow me here," said Roth. "Josephus went on to say that if one used a special substitution cipher, one could exchange certain Hebrew letters with other opposite letters and find a message. Once done, the Essenes applied a set of mathematical algorithms apparently taught to them by the Prophets of Old. The end result was astonishing. The Essenes were able to predict the outcome of many events with great accuracy. Rarely, if ever, did their predictions prove wrong."

"That's pure bunk," interrupted Nash. "The Bible Code can

be used on any text, anywhere, at any time and provide the same predictive results. You only need to look as far as the *Moby Dick* debunk."

"What was that?" interceded Tom.

Nash leaned forward. He was in his element now. "Critics of the Code used Melville's *Moby Dick* to prove that predictions made by the so-called *Signature of God*—or the Bible Code—could be found in any book, and they proved it by showing that *Moby Dick* predicted the assassinations of Indira Gandhi, Leon Trotsky, Rev. Martin Luther King, and Robert F. Kennedy." Nash glanced over at the stoic Roth. "It's bunk."

"I'm still lost," said Tom.

But Roth ignored him. He looked at Nash. "I'm not going to debate you on the validity of the Code as far as its predictive ability is concerned. What I'd like to do is apply the Code to Zed's diary. I think that's what he wanted us to do."

"I don't see what good that will do," said Nash. "Quite honestly, I feel we are wasting time."

"Time for what?" said Roth. "You yourself said that kidnappers are expecting you to contact them in the morning. The way I see it, you have some time to kill."

Despite the stress of these past few days, Nash found himself smiling. The little man in the wheelchair was hard not to like. Nash sat back in the plush leather sofa, which had a tendency to make rude noises. "Fine. You win. Do your best. I could use a good laugh."

Roth grinned. "The great skeptic is softening. Very good, Mr. Nash. Let's unlock the secrets to your grandfather's diary."

Saturday
11:20 AM GMT
London, England

Roth turned his attention to the large screen on the wall above their heads. On the projected screen, Nash saw that the program was rapidly scanning the diary pages.

"This will take a few minutes," said Roth. "But the program, when finished, will display any hidden messages."

"What's that program you're using?" asked Nash.

"It's a version of the Bible Code cipher."

"So," continued Nash. "That's *your* background? Codes and ciphers?"

"Oh, no," Roth exclaimed. "I purchased this one. My background is the study of esoteric religion and philosophies—as you might have guessed."

Outside the massive window behind Roth's ostentatious desk, rain increased its rate, gusting at a slight angle. As if on cue, the fireplace in the study kicked into life on its own, flaring brightly at first, and then leveling off to a very cozy level. The acrid scent of smoke reached Nash's nose.

"Nice trick," observed Nash, indicating the fire.

"When you're a cripple, Mr. Nash, the price of convenience is never too high."

Touché.

"I liked that shroud thing you had hanging in the waiting room," said Tom. Nash nearly laughed.

"Shroud of Turin, yes. It's a replica, of course, and it's a personal project of mine. I have a partner, a young archaeologist, working

70

on a shroud theory. He's in Jerusalem now at the Church of the Holy Sepulcher. Ah, here we go."

The cipher program was finished. Roth clicked his mouse, and several pages appeared on the screen above.

JESUSEDNYHSYSBEUENETSABSTSG
V**C**XUJWUEBDKJWSDUIERMCMC**E**CMC
JC**O**CNSHSYSUNSGLRGNSUSKP**U**KRK
MND**F**ISIDJDDDOFIKDPDPWDP**R**WOW
TSGY**F**SHWHEOWWOEEKDPODOW**O**WDK
DJHWU**I**DOWHEOWADHODWOHDW**P**IDI
NDBDBD**N**DTEGEPOEPDPNNLKM**E**NVN

XXGTFYEDNYHSYS**J**UENETSABSTSG
B**Q**UJWUEBDKJWSD**E**IERMCMCM**S**CMC
CUMSNSHSYSUNSG**S**SUSKPOBB**E**KVM
A**M**D**COMING**DDDUK**U**PDPWDPCW**C**MMm
N**R**SGYASHWHEOWW**S**DPODOWBB**O**WDK
D**A**HWUHDOWHEOWADHODWOHDW**N**DIB
NNDDH**12Q11**POEPDPNNSxxDN**D**JA

XXGTFYEDNYHSYSMUENETSABSTSGF
HENDERSONDWAIE**A**YUORMC**MJ11**SXX
DDCUMDCFTRHcvc**J**SUSKPOBDDKVMX
NMDCINGDDDCCKB**I**KVKNNNDYETTEH
R**A**GYASHWHEOWWWd**K**DPODOW**1**BOWDKX
DH**S**UHD**MJ12**EOWAUODWOHF**2**NDICC
ANB**H**DHCDFRTPcCEPDPNNLKMSDRNVX

XXGTFYEDNYHSYSCUENITSABSTSG
B**Q**UJWUEBDKJWSDJIERNCMCMSC**1**C
XCUM**SECTION**SXESUCVVNPOBE**9**KV
AMDCOM**1**NGDDDVCIKDPIPWDP**4**WPM
NRSGYA**8**HWHEOWWTDPODOWB**7**OWDK
EOWA**INCIDENT**EODWOHDVVWNDIBL
YANBDBDHCDFRTPcBEPDPNNLMDNN

"What's all that gibberish between the highlighted numbers and letters?" queried Tom, sitting forward.

"The program only highlights the words the code sees," explained Roth. "It displays random letters for the other words and spaces."

Tom pointed to the first page of letters, real awe on his face. "It highlighted the words *coffin*, *Europe*, and *Jesus*." Tom looked at Nash, his mouth hanging open. "I assume it means Jesus is buried in Europe? But that makes no sense. If his tomb is anywhere, it's in Palestine. This is a waste of time."

Nash, his head supported with his fist, shrugged a single shoulder. He didn't really care what the display highlighted. He knew that such a complex program could easily find many word associations scrambled through texts.

Unless, of course, his grandfather purposely hid these key words. The idea intrigued Nash more than he was willing to admit.

Tom continued, talking excitedly, "Look, the next page says *Qumran*, *Jesus*, *Second*, *Coming*, and a number or something. *12Q11*. What's that?"

Roth wheeled his chair around and used a laser pointer, which he held surprisingly steady. He shone the light on the *12*. "This number here identifies a certain Dead Sea Scroll. The scrolls are identified by a number and letter combination, indicating the cave from which they were recovered. In this case, it identifies a scroll found in Cave Number Twelve in Qumran, Twelve Q. The second number is the catalog file number assigned to each fragment as it was archived. But there's a problem."

"What problem?" asked Tom.

"There is no Cave Twelve. This scroll doesn't exist."

To Nash, this was further proof that his grandfather's diary was just a huge waste of time. "You really think this missing scroll contains the date of the Second Coming?"

"According to the interpreted page here," replied Roth.

Nash rolled his eyes. "You do realize my grandfather was

committed when I was younger," said Nash. "This diary of his could be filled with the ramblings of a very disturbed mind."

"Your grandfather was a very special man," said Roth. "Very special. Was he eccentric? Oh, yes. Certifiable? At times. Genuinely insane? No. He was a genius."

Nash made skeptical noises in the back of his throat.

Roth smiled, acknowledging Nash's skepticism. "Yes, to the rest of the world—and even his own grandson—Zed would have appeared quite crazy, certainly. But the man I knew had an uncanny grasp of languages, symbolism, and ciphers. The man I knew would have been just as comfortable in ancient Palestine as he would have been in the modern world."

Roth removed his pipe from his desk, studied it, saw that it had gone out, and struck a match with his good hand against the side of a heavy matchbox. As he touched the burning flame to the pipe bowl in his mouth, he spoke around the stem. "After the war, because of his unique ciphering skills, your grandfather was assigned to Air Force Intelligence at the Aerospace Defense Command. One of the precursors of NORAD. He was a Major then. I hooked up with him several years later pretty much by accident. We both were on an international team to study the Dead Sea Scrolls."

Roth inhaled on the pipe. The bowl flared brightly. The fire in the fire place crackled. Nash wondered again how his sister was doing. Had they hurt her? Surely they wouldn't have hurt her. She was just a pawn in this game.

And what game was this?

Nash, admittedly, did not know. He wanted to tell himself he did not care, but he did care. By kidnapping his sister, they made him care.

Roth continued, "At the time we were hired to study the scrolls, your grandfather had just retired from the Air Force. He didn't seem to be the man I knew years before, though. He seemed oddly *driven*. The study of the scrolls was more than an academic exercise for him. It was his life. His sole purpose for existence."

Roth paused. "Anyway, after we concluded our work, he disappeared from my life. I didn't see him again until he showed up years later at my door with this diary. He asked me to hold it for him until his grandchildren came to claim it. And here we are."

"Yes," said Nash. "Here we are. Except one of his grandchildren has been kidnapped. I would say Grandpa didn't think this through very well. And now his diary is proving wrong. You yourself said there was no Scroll Twelve."

"True," said Roth. "But there is one thing I learned back when I was working with him."

"And what's that?" asked Nash.

"Never doubt your grandfather." Roth winked. "Now, let's see what's on the other pages."

Saturday
11:35 AM GMT
London, England

Tom had accepted his role of official reader for the group. He spoke up. "The next page says *Section Eighteen* and the year *nineteen forty-seven*." Tom frowned and looked at Nash. "What happened in nineteen forty-seven?"

"Lots of things," said Nash. "A whole year's worth. Hey, does anyone have a *Farmer's Almanac?*"

Roth ignored Nash's sarcasm. "Tom, read the next page."

Tom did, squinting up at the overhead projection. "Says *Majik* and *MJ twelve*. Hey, it's got your name in there Jeremy. Right there, it says *Nash*."

"Wonder of wonders," blurted Nash. "Since it was written by my grandfather, Tom."

The FBI agent shrugged and looked a bit sheepish.

Roth spoke up, "Do you know anything about *Majik* and *MJ twelve?*"

Nash did. Having been raised in the belly of the beast, he knew both terms well. "*Majik* is bogus. And there were no MJ twelve documents."

"I don't understand," said Tom, which was a bit surprising to Nash since the field agent lived in the area himself.

Nash explained, "Majestic Twelve, usually spelled numerically, is the purported code name of a secret committee of scientists, military leaders, and government officials, supposedly formed in nineteen forty-seven by an executive order issued by President Truman."

"Why?" asked Tom.

"To investigate UFO activity in the aftermath of the Roswell incident. Anyway, the UFO conspiracy nuts use these supposed MJ Twelve documents to prove that there was a UFO crash at Roswell because the *alleged* Majestic Twelve committee *supposedly* studied it." Nash flicked his wrist dismissively. "I wrote an article on it years ago for my *Skeptic's Magazine*, completely debunking this whole myth. The committee never existed, and there was no cover up at Roswell."

"Yes, I read your article, Mr. Nash. It was quite convincing."

"You don't sound convinced," said Nash. "And you can call me Jeremy."

"Very well, Jeremy. Have you stopped to consider that maybe the name Nash here," and Roth pointed his laser light at Nash's highlighted name, "is referring to your grandfather?"

"Sure, why not? It's his diary."

Roth was silent, his pipe forgotten. He stared up at the screen on the wall. The old house creaked badly. Either that, or it was seriously haunted.

When Roth spoke again, he did so with a bit of reverence in his voice. "Jeremy, I think this printout tells us that your grandfather might have been a member of Majik, and so was a fellow named Henderson, and the others mentioned on the remaining printouts."

Nash felt as if his spine had been dipped in ice water. He recalled his conversation with Bryan Henderson earlier that day. His friend's father had committed suicide. Jumped out of a window, in fact. Now why would a person who committed suicide be mentioned in his grandfather's diary?

Roth continued, "As for the words referring to a Section Eighteen incident in nineteen forty-seven, I have no clue."

"So why would my grandfather go to such convoluted lengths to tell my sister and I what he could simply have said in the letter."

"One word," answered Roth. "*Apocalypse.* The title of the diary. The revealing of the truth. Whatever he knows, he felt it so important, maybe even dangerous, that he had to shield it."

"Well, whatever it is, it's not worth the life of my sister." Nash stood. "So, thank you for an interesting evening, Mr. Roth. I'll take the diary now." He picked it off Roth's desk and pocketed it.

The old man frowned. "I'm surprised at you, Jeremy."

Nash shrugged into his jacket. "Yeah, why's that?"

"I thought a man of your curiosity would have an interest in pursuing what your grandfather thought was so important. Doesn't a mysterious scroll that predicts the Second Coming pique your interest at all?" An impish smile crossed Roth's face. "Would make good material for your next book."

"Not if it costs my sister's life."

The man in the wheelchair sighed resignedly, steepling his fingers in front of his face. "Very well, William will show you to your rooms. Perhaps we can discuss this further in the morning."

"Perhaps," said Nash. He turned to his friend. "Let's go Tom."

His sister's fiancé stood. "Sure, just let me check in at the office. They may have some more info on this Tucker."

"Fine. But no official interference," Nash replied. He turned to the man behind the desk. "Good night, Mr. Roth, and thank you for your hospitality."

As the two men left, they found William waiting for them in the hallway.

"I'll catch up with you," said Tom. He watched Nash and the butler disappear around a curving flight of marble stairs. And when they were gone, he pulled out his secure cell phone and logged onto the internet. With a few quick strokes he entered a virtual private network. A window appeared on his screen and asked for a user name and password. Once in, he started to type a message.

Sunday
5:11 AM GMT
Jerusalem, Israel

Douglas Peacock had believed the archaeological research he was doing for Stanton Roth in Jerusalem would be pretty straight forward.

As a freelance, highly-trained archaeologist, he had often taken on such projects for wealthy clients. Granted, he mostly worked with governments, but Peacock wasn't going to complain about where his next paycheck came from. After all, he lived from dig to dig, and it was a lifestyle that suited him tremendously. Long ago, Peacock, who was single with no kids (and planned to keep it that way), had vowed to never punch a clock again, and if that meant traveling halfway around the globe to conduct a secret expedition for an eccentric collector, well, Peacock was willing to bend the accepted archaeological rules a little.

Just don't ask him to steal artifacts. Peacock wasn't a grave robber. Leave that to Lara Croft.

He did, after all, have *some* morals.

With the morning sun hidden through the rock strata above him, Peacock frowned at his latest finding, admittedly confused. Dust was heavy in the air, and so was the smell of his own small body. Working below the surface, in such cramped conditions, was hard, sweaty work even for someone his size.

Something wasn't right.

He looked at the monitor set up next to him. He wiped away some dust that coated the screen.

It was the copper bands. They shouldn't be there. None of the historical records on the Church of the Holy Sepulchre that he knew of spoke about metal bands around a sealed chamber below the rock-cut tomb of Jesus—a tomb that was protected by an edicule, or a small enclosure, that had been destroyed and rebuilt many times throughout the centuries.

He continued studying the monitor in front of him, as dust sifted before his eyes, in and out of the lamplight. His breathing was difficult.

Yes, those were definitely metal bands strapped around a slab of rock, a slab that hid the contents within the adjoining tomb.

Metal bands? Strange. Very strange indeed.

He had to follow this up.

Roth had hired Peacock to discover what was hidden under the rebuilt edicule. After all, beneath this stone structure was supposedly the tomb of Jesus Christ, including a section of the actual stone used to block the tomb.

A simple enough job, right? After all, who wouldn't want to see what was beneath the edicule?

Peacock had asked—and then bribed with Roth's money—the Muslim family who controlled access to the site to lock him in the Church overnight. That way he could work undisturbed by the constant flow of religious pilgrims and tourists during the day.

Permission was necessary, and he had worked for a month getting it. This came from the various religious communities holding claims to the Church; sects that had been arguing over its control for centuries. Any attempts at disturbing the tomb would cause an ethnic and religious dispute. For the Church is not only the purported site of the burial place of Jesus, but also of his crucifixion. It was internationally famous for the rifts between various religious sects that had sometimes led to actual violence.

Peacock was given one chance—and one chance only—to do his investigation.

Understandably, he had worked feverishly through the night to wind the lighted endoscope—using an archaeological technique

called *photogrammetry*—through the cracks of the edicule. He hoped to get an up-close look at what was under its floor.

This had taken him most of the night, as he consulted various schematics that had been provided to him by Roth. Where Roth got these schematics, he did not know, but he suspected the old man had probably paid handsomely for them.

It was only after working through the night, with the sweat stinging his eyes and a mild sense of panic threatening to overwhelm him that—after all, he had only this one night to complete his project—he had completed the necessary steps to photograph the interior of the edicule, the chamber that guarded the way into Jesus's tomb.

With mounting excitement, fully aware that he might just be the first archaeologist in well over a hundred years to set sight on the room's interior, he had switched on his *photogrammetry's* monitor.

And discovered the odd copper bands surrounding the stone slab.

He checked his watch against the lamplight. He had to leave. The agreement was that he would vacate the Church before pilgrims entered to celebrate the Ceremony of the Holy Fire.

Peacock had no desire to sit in yet another foreign prison.

He began gathering his equipment, first removing the photogrammetry equipment, thinking hard as he did so.

There were certainly records from previous centuries of those who had peeked under the edicule on different occasions. He and Roth believed, based on these ancient records, that under the floor of the edicule was a quarry dating back to the First Temple period. That quarry area might hold signs of a preparation room where bodies were prepared before placing it the tomb. He and Roth both believed such a preparation room existed under the floor of the Church.

Completing his packing, he slid out from the cramped chamber he had been working under and breathed a sigh of relief. He inhaled the fresh air, and with his equipment in hand, he departed the church before any of the pilgrims arrived.

He had kept his end of the bargain.
And now he needed to see about the copper bands.

Sunday
6:48 AM GMT
Jerusalem, Israel

As the early morning sun rose over the ancient city, with the Dome of the Rock bathed in a hallowed golden glow, Peacock walked the few blocks to the office of the Israeli Antiquities Authority. The streets were mostly quiet at this hour, except for the sing-song voice calling Muslims to prayer.

As he approached the unpretentious antiquities office, he noticed a slouching figure behind the wheel of a car parked in the alleyway across from him. Peacock, who had been in enough hostile foreign lands to know not to make eye contact with such figures—in alleyways no less—nevertheless found himself staring at the figure. The man seemed deformed, somehow.

Peacock averted his eyes, but knew he had stared too long.

Worse, the man had been staring back at him.

Shuddering, the middle-aged archaeologist reached the antiquities office just as a security guard opened the doors for the day. He entered quickly and immediately forgot about the deformed man behind the wheel.

Peacock didn't need any help finding his way around the antiquities office. He'd been here before, both for this project and a few others he had consulted on.

Ten minutes later he had what he was looking for—the history of the edicule. He sat in front of the microfiche machine and read through it, wishing he had gotten something to eat first. After all, he *had* worked all through the night.

The records he sifted through showed that the Emperor

Constantine first encased the tomb of Christ in an edicule housed under the Rotunda of the Resurrection. The edicule was destroyed by Caliph al-Hakim in 1009, with repairs beginning in 1012. The Crusaders took on the rebuilding in 1099, but the work was not completed until 1167, a few years before Saladin took the city. The edicule suffered years of decay under Muslim rule, but was rebuilt again in quasi-Renaissance style in 1555. A fire in 1808 destroyed the edicule once more. It was rebuilt again in 1809.

A turbulent history at best.

The very last edicule, the one that stood today, was sheathed in a *steel cradle* to keep it from collapsing. The steel cradle was built by the Steel Corporation of Bengal—now defunct. That was the last record of when the edicule was touched. There was nothing about copper bands.

Peacock sat back in his seat and thought about that, until his growling stomach got the better of him.

But before he ate, he had an idea. Putting thoughts of food aside for the moment, he went downstairs to the research desk and asked the elderly Jewish woman, who looked vaguely like Golda Meir, for records on microfiche about the Steel Corporation of Bengal. She nodded and instructed him to come back in an hour. Good enough. That would give him time to eat.

The early morning streets were starting to fill as he left the antiquities office. The Ceremony of the Holy Fire had begun and throngs of worshipers were filling the streets. Many of the devout carried candles for the "Holy Fire Ritual," in which Orthodox priests descend to Christ's tomb in the Church of the Holy Sepulcher and emerge with a flame that they say appears spontaneously—miraculous proof, believers say, that Christ has not forgotten his followers.

Skeptics denounce the ritual as a 1,200-year-old sleight-of-hand whose secret is passed from one generation of high priests to the next. But for the thousands of gathered worshipers, it was proof of God's existence and Christ's resurrection.

As he made his way through the morning rush, he caught sight of something that chilled him to his core. The same man he had seen earlier, the strange-looking man in the car, had stepped out of the alley and joined the rush of pedestrians.

The archaeologist felt his heartbeat quicken. There was something very, very menacing about the tall figure, and it wasn't because of the minor facial deformity. Peacock sensed danger, and for a man who often ventured into hostile foreign lands, he had learned long ago to trust his instincts.

He quickened his pace and turned down the Via Dolorosa, the route of Jesus' crucifixion. Peacock glanced over his shoulder as he did so, and was dismayed to see the tall figure turn down the same road.

Packed with pushy vendors, the street was hard to maneuver through. As he hurriedly walked along the broken pavement, ignoring desperate vendors selling everything from Holy Water, t-shirts championing the Israeli army, and sandals to gaudy junk from India, Peacock hoped he could shake his pursuer in the crowd of tourists.

With this wish, he zigzagged his way down the route, looking back every few minutes to see if his pursuer was with him.

Damn! He was.

Even slightly slouched, the man was head and shoulders above the crowd and nearly impossible to miss.

Peacock avoided looking into the man's eyes and hastened his steps, darting down a small narrow side street and into a curio shop. He peeked out the door and up the street, ignoring the shopkeeper's insistence that he buy some supposed relic of the Passion that only he possessed. Peacock watched as the tall slouched man, dressed in a strange Romanian-style long jacket, shuffled past the shop window.

Heart pounding somewhere in his throat, Peacock waited a beat or two until he was sure the man was gone. Just when about to open the shop door, he felt a strong tug on his arm. Peacock nearly yelped. Had the tall man circled back, entered through a rear entrance? He turned, but it was just the insistent shop keeper.

"Sir, let me show you a piece of the original cross of Christ. I make you good bargain." The man spoke in a heavy accent, his words barely distinguishable.

Peacock tried to pull away from the man's vice-like grip. "No, thank you." He mused that there were so many alleged pieces of the true cross, Jesus must have been crucified on a whole forest.

"Then how about one of thorns from the crown of Jesus. See here is his blood still on it. I make you good bargain."

"I said *no*," said Peacock, and this time he had to physically yank his shirt sleeve out of the man's grip. He pushed through the swing door and left the angry man behind him. Peacock just hoped the shopkeeper didn't start shouting and thus attract his pursuer.

The man didn't, and the little archaeologist headed safely back to Via Dolorosa. After an anxious walk back to the antiquities office, Peacock stood in front of the research desk. "Did you find anything?"

The elderly woman handed him a thin pile of printouts. "This is all we could find on microfiche."

"Thank you." Peacock took the printouts over to a study carrel and read through them. As expected, there was mention of the contract with the Steel Corporation of Bengal—

Ah, but there was something else here. Peacock sat forward and peered closer at the print-out, his heart suddenly beating stronger in his chest.

He had a phone call to make.

Sunday
08:56 AM GMT
Jerusalem, Israel

Vajda entered his hotel room and slammed his fist into the dresser. He looked up at himself in the mirror and cursed the genetic disability that had plagued him all his life. Without it, he would have caught up to Peacock in the street.

And without it he might have had a normal life.

He shook his hand. *Damn!* He might have just broken a knuckle. And how the hell had that archaeologist eluded him?

I'm losing my touch, he thought.

He surveyed and cataloged in the mirror the symptoms of his Waardenburg Syndrome—two different colored yes, tufts of white sprouting from his black hair, cleft lip, deaf in his right ear, and the curvature of his spine that made him walk with a deep slouch impeding both his sight and forward motion.

I'm a monster, he thought, and not for the first time.

He cursed his deformed body—and cursed his Jewish mother and father who bestowed these defective genes upon him. Although a full blood Jew himself, Vadja hated his ancestry. And the more he hated it, the more he found reasons to hate it.

Until the hate consumed him.

Self-hate, a psychologist had once described it.

Whatever it was, it had led Vajda at an early age to discover various fascist beliefs. The more he read, the more he understood and believed that his heritage was a scourge on the earth.

The self-hate grew.

And then he came upon Intermarium.

86

His ringing cell phone jolted him out of his reverie. He snatched it from his pocket and looked at the caller ID. He had prepared his response.

He flipped the phone open. "I failed you, Father. But I will succeed today."

"No," came the reply. "You are to move on."

"But, Father I—"

"No, my son." The voice was insistent. "We have a new mission for you."

Vajda listened intently. "Yes, Father. I understand."

He snapped the cell shut.

Sunday
09:12 AM GMT
London, England

"Mr. Roth," said William's voice from the intercom. "You have a phone call from Douglas Peacock. He's on line one."

Roth put down his tea cup and picked up the receiver on his desk. "Hello, Douglas. What do you have for me?"

"A puzzle," Peacock replied.

"Tell me."

"Have you ever heard of a Section Eighteen?"

Roth blinked. *Section Eighteen. Interesting.* "Not until recently. But go on."

"As you know, last night and early this morning I was granted access to probe the interior of the edicule."

Peacock went on to describe the copper bands around the entry stone to what he and Roth thought would be a preparation room.

Roth frowned deeply at this. "Encased in metal bands?"

"And they looked recent; very little erosion. No more than seventy or eighty years old. I assume that's in nineteen forty-seven, the last record of when the edicule was touched."

"Who had access to the edicule in nineteen forty-seven?"

"Company called the Steel Corporation of Bengal," said Peacock, speaking uncharacteristically fast. "They re-enforced the edicule with a steel cradle."

"Were you able to contact them?"

"No. They're defunct. Which is unfortunate, because I would have liked to talk to them about something else I did find in the records. Something very strange."

Roth sat a little straighter. "And what was that?"

"This Section Eighteen got permission to do a day's work within the edicule."

Roth was silent, thinking, aware that his breathing had increased dramatically. "What did you find on them?" he asked.

"Not much was mentioned about them, although I did recognize a name. Someone we both know. Phillip Marcus."

Roth was silent. It was a name he wanted to forget. Marcus and he had been partners in the antiquities market years ago. Marcus had eventually made a pact with the Jesuit Church, selling them ill-gotten antiquities, and getting quite rich in the process. Their partnership had ended there.

"Will you be coming to Jerusalem?" asked Peacock.

"No. I can't." Roth, despite his better judgment, told his archaeologist about Nash, his kidnapped sister, and the diary that mentions Section Eighteen. He finished with, "Douglas, I want you to find Marcus, and I want you to find out what you can about Section Eighteen."

"Sure, boss. But where do I start?"

"He might still be doing work for the Church—the Jesuits— in Rome. Maybe someone there will know where he is. Try the Vatican's Information Service. They may give you a lead."

Roth hung up. He sat back in his wheelchair and wondered why Phillip Marcus was connected to something mentioned in a sixty year old diary.

Sunday
11:27 AM GMT
London, England

Nash was frustrated.

He'd been logged into the assigned internet chat channel all morning, with no sign of Enos Tucker.

"Any luck?" asked Tom as he walked into the mansion's study.

Nash looked up from his laptop and rubbed his eyes. "No. Just sitting here getting a monitor tan. Where the hell is he?"

Just as he finished speaking, a message popped up on his screen. It was from Tucker. The man got right to the point.

```
DO YOU HAVE THE DIARY?
```

Nash typed back:

```
YES.
```

```
AND THE CAVE TWELVE SCROLL?
```

Nash looked up, confused. The scroll mentioned in his grandfather's diary, the scroll found in Cave Twelve. Except, according to Roth, there was no Cave Twelve. "How the hell does he know about the scroll?"

Tom scratched his head. "Ask him."

Nash did so, and the reply came back instantly:

```
NO MATTER. DO YOU HAVE IT?
```

```
NO.
```

```
THEN GET IT. FOR YOUR SISTER'S
SAKE, MAKE IT SOONER RATHER THAN
LATER.
```

And then Tucker promptly exited the chat room. Nash closed his laptop, thinking hard.

"Well," said Tom. "That's that. Looks like we have to get the scroll."

"What's this about the scroll?" Roth asked, rolling into the study.

"Just chatted with Tucker," said Nash. He felt sick to his stomach. Something was wrong here. Nash had a sense that things were very much slipping out of his control. "He somehow knew about the Cave Twelve Scroll. Now he wants both it *and* the diary in exchange for my sister."

"That changes things," exclaimed Roth. He wheeled to a stop before Nash and looked at him compassionately. "So, what are you going to do?"

"Whatever it takes to free my sister." Nash looked at the little man in front of him. "How do you think Tucker knew about the scroll?"

"Couldn't say," said Roth, picking up the change in Nash's voice. "And I don't like your insinuating tone, my boy. You think I had something to do with it?"

Nash didn't answer, but instead asked. "How reliable is your staff?"

"They have all been with me many years, and have all proven their loyalty many times over. I trust them all with my life." Roth paused, seemed to control himself. "Jeremy, my staff is not the source of the information. I personally have no reason to tell anybody. You came to me, remember?"

"My apologies," said Nash relenting. "Then who's the leak?"

"Perhaps none," said Roth, his tone softening. "Have you considered that those who kidnapped your sister knew of the scroll before us? After all, they knew of the diary. And they knew it contained information they wanted. They may not have known the *details* in the diary, but they must have had a pretty good idea of its contents—or else why bother threatening your sister?"

The man made good points. In fact, they were all very logical points. Nash sat back, expelling a long stream of air. "I guess you're right. So now I'm supposed to look for a Dead Sea Scroll that doesn't exist which was found in a cave that doesn't exist."

"Doesn't look good," Tom chimed in.

"Maybe this will cheer you up," said Roth. "I just received news about something else mentioned in the diary."

"What news?" Nash asked.

"My partner, a freelance American archaeologist, was working at the Church of the Holy Sepulcher and ran across some information on Section Eighteen."

"Go on," said Nash.

Roth recounted his phone conversation with Peacock, mentioning everything of note, from the copper bands to his ex-partner's name being mentioned in the records dating back to 1947.

"And who, exactly, is this Marcus fellow?" asked Nash, who found himself pacing the spacious study. Nash needed to do something, anything. Changing the rules on him was infuriating. He had recovered the diary, as requested. As *demanded*. They owed him his sister, damn it. Nash felt like a caged animal.

An *enraged* caged animal.

"Marcus and I were in business together. We acquired and sold antiquities that the Nazis had stolen during the war. Together, he and I would find these and other valuable items and return them to their rightful owners."

"For a price, I assume," offered Tom.

Roth smiled. "Yes, of course. It was a very lucrative business, though some of the transactions were, shall we say, somewhat unconventional?"

"Meaning you had problems with the police?" said Nash.

"No. Not really. Marcus had contacts within the Catholic Church, and at times they would run interference for us. Kept us off the radar screen of the secular authorities."

"And why would the Church do something like that?" asked Nash.

"We did them some," he cleared his throat, "let us say, favors."

"What kind of favors?" Tom prodded.

Roth folded his good arm over his sunken chest. "I don't

believe either of you two gentlemen have ever heard of the Ratlines?"

Both Nash and Tom shook their heads.

"The Intermarium?" asked Roth.

They shook their heads again.

"No. What are they?" Nash snapped at the crippled man, but he almost didn't care.

If Roth noticed, he didn't seem to mind. "First, let me give you a little history lesson. One that you'll not find in popular textbooks. I suggest that you sit for this, Jeremy."

"No, thanks," Nash retorted cooly, and he continued pacing.

"Very well. When the Communists gained power in Russia in nineteen seventeen, the Catholic Church saw communism as a threat. Between nineteen seventeen and nineteen twenty-three, the Church, with the Vatican at the head, took the initiative to fight against what it saw as the communist danger. Since nineteen twenty the Church organized groups of action called the Intermarium. The groups composing this organization were defined openly as anticommunists and their declared objectives were the mobilization of the Catholic Church in the fight against communism."

Roth paused and lowered his voice for effect. "Now this is where it gets interesting. The Intermarium could count on the participation of notorious Nazi fascists."

"Nazis?" said Tom. "Even after World War Two?"

"Yes," said Roth. "Think about it, with the war now over, who was the new enemy?"

"Communists," said Nash.

"And who had the remnants of an intricate spy network behind the Iron Curtain?"

"Nazis," answered Nash. He felt a bit like he was in a lecture hall and could see why his grandfather had been good friends with Roth. There was something oddly infectious about the little man.

"So," said Tom, "you're saying the Allies actively promoted and used known fascists in this...what did you call it, the Intermarium?...for intelligence purposes?"

The FBI agent sounded skeptical. Nash didn't blame him. This was a lot to swallow.

"Indeed," replied Roth. "And in return for their services the Intermarium helped many notorious war criminals escape prosecution by using a network called the Ratlines."

He went on to explain that these Ratlines were built by the Vatican with the guidance of the Jesuits. They were used by Western intelligences to facilitate and organize the protection and flight of the escaped fascists.

"Jesus!" Tom cried.

Roth lowered his voice, and for the first time Nash saw real emotion on the old man's face. "My Jewish relatives had their gold teeth removed before they were sent to the gas chambers. The gold ended up in the coffers of the Vatican. It was used to enable these same Nazis to escape to South America. Incredible, eh?"

"So how did the Vatican get the Nazis out of Europe?" asked Nash now totally engrossed in the tale.

"The Office of the High Commission with the Refugees of the Vatican gave them false identities. Based on that, the International Red Cross unknowingly gave them identity papers. Piece of cake," said Roth," and the end result is this. The Intermarium became a tool of Western intelligence behind the Iron Curtain, coordinating fascist spying to aide the fight in the Cold War."

"So what does this have to do with your friend Marcus?" asked Nash.

"Marcus helped the Vatican organize the Ratlines for the Intermarium. That's how he received his, shall I say, *protection*."

"And you two lived happily ever after," Nash interjected sarcastically.

"No. Not exactly." Roth's voice became vindictive. "When certain activities of Marcus with the Intermarium started to surface, he needed to deflect attention from himself. He made it look like *I* was selling Nazi stolen antiquities to financially support the escape of noted Nazis to South America."

"You beat the charges?" asked Tom.

"Barely." Roth paused a moment. "But that's not important now. What's important is to find out what Marcus has to do with this Section Eighteen and why your kidnappers may be interest in it. It's in the diary, so it must have something to do with their objectives—whatever they may be. If we can get to Marcus before we give the scroll and diary to Tucker, we may be able to get a handle on all of this and use it for the safe return of your sister."

"And that means we have to get the scroll," said Tom.

"Correct," Roth replied. He looked at Nash for agreement.

Nash nodded.

"I hate to be the one to state the obvious," Tom said to Roth, "but didn't you say there *wasn't* a Cave Twelve? Doesn't that mean we would be looking for a scroll that doesn't exist?"

"Not necessarily," Roth replied. "There's been a lot of secrecy around the scrolls. Some say even a conspiracy."

"A conspiracy?" questioned Nash. "What do you mean?"

Roth chuckled. "I thought that might get your attention. In nineteen fifty-five, G. Lankester Harding, head of the Jordanian Department of Antiquities, asked Roland de Vaux, a Dominican priest and renowned scholar associated with Ecole Biblique, to head an international team of seven Hebrew and Aramaic experts to study the scrolls. These two men decided to impose strict rules of secrecy on the project and to limit access to the manuscripts only to team members."

"And you were on that team?" Nash exclaimed.

"No. Zed and I were on one of the many study groups that received from the international team what ever they deemed fit to release. All kinds of rumors flew. Many of us believed that the scrolls contained revolutionary or explosive revelations about Jesus and the New Testament. Many in the church were quite fearful of their potential contents."

"Why?" asked Nash.

"Remember what I said about the Essenes? They were Gnostics and believed that the path to God was through knowledge, the personal experience of God."

"That sounds a lot like esotericism," Nash replied. "The type of religions practiced in the East."

"Correct! And practiced here in the West, too. But you rarely hear of them. For example, the Kabbalah, Christian Mysticism, Sufism, Gnosis—even primitive mysticism. You've read the books by Castaneda?"

"That flake?" Nash blurted out.

"No. Not Castaneda himself, but Don Juan, the Yaqui shaman. He tried to open Castaneda's mind to the spiritual world of God. There is a common thread running through all these esoteric approaches to God."

"Fine. So, what does this have to do with the fear of Christian authorities?" asked Nash.

"Ever hear of the saying 'You can't see Jesus before Paul?'"

"Yes. It refers to Emperor Constantine's attempt at making the Bible palatable for converts. He was fed up with all the bickering between the different sects of Christianity at the time—who Jesus was and what he taught. So, he chose Paul's interpretations of Christ. All other beliefs and texts, what are called the Lost Gospels, were suppressed and left out of the Bible we have today."

"Good. You know your history," Roth replied. "Those holy writings were deemed heresy and left out of the New Testament we read today. Anyway, the recovered manuscripts—the scrolls— didn't speak unanimously. Some of the early Christians believed in one God, some in two, and others in thirty. Then Paul came along and sought to turn a heretical Jewish sect into the Christianity we know today."

"You guys know a lot of shit," Tom observed with a touch of mock awe.

Roth grinned and leaned back in his wheelchair. "Now. Why do you think Paul pushed for his version of Christianity?"

Nash shrugged. His knowledge of Christianity's roots had been plundered dry.

"Simple salesmanship. Paul knew how to sell a product, and the product that the Gnostics had would not sell. That dog wouldn't hunt, so to speak." Roth smiled.

"What exactly do you mean?" asked Tom. "What was he selling?"

"What passes for Christianity today," Roth replied. "Look. If you're going to start a new religion, one that can spread quickly around the known world, you need to tailor it in such a way that everyone—not a select few—can join. Like any good salesman, you don't raise objections like having to be circumcised, or not being able to eat certain foods, and other such cultural restrictions not palatable to your average gentile. You also have to build an organization."

"OK," Nash agreed. "But again—what did that have to do with the Essenes?"

Roth had a notable gleam in his eye. The man loved to lecture. Just like his grandfather.

And for the first time in a long time, Nash felt a tinge of regret that the old man had passed.

"The Essenes were Gnostics. The Gnostics were elitists. Being elitists, they felt that only a small fraction of humans were capable of salvation. They were a democratic organization—if you want to call it that—having no titles like bishop, deacon, etc. Women participated equally with men. You could imagine how this irked those who were building a church with the hierarchy and discipline to withstand Roman persecution."

Roth continued, "The Essenes believed that to reach paradise you had to work at it. You had to follow the path of knowledge—not just blind faith. You had to reach *self-realization*. You had to become one with God, not just believe in God." Roth paused and smiled. "I call it my Cleveland hypotheses."

"Your what?" asked Tom with amusement.

"I'll explain. Suppose you want to experience Cleveland. Well, you can *read* books about Cleveland, *view* pictures of Cleveland, *review* maps of Cleveland—and even *talk* to people who'd been to Cleveland. But you'll never *experience* Cleveland unless you actually *go there*. Substitute God for Cleveland and you'll understand the belief of the Essenes."

Nash thought about that. He saw his friend Tom trying to puzzle it out. Nash almost laughed.

Roth went on, "The Essenes believed that if you don't *practice* Gnosis—the path of self-realization, the path to God—you will not reach heaven. And even if you do practice Gnosis, there are no guarantees because the path to self-realization takes work—a lifetime of work. Try selling that to the masses and build a religious following. Good luck!"

Despite himself, Nash found himself nodding. This was making sense. "So when the scrolls were found and the writings of the Essenes were translated, the findings threw the religious authorities into a tizzy?"

"That's correct." Roth leaned towards the two men. "Which is why I believe there might just be a Cave Twelve Scroll, a scroll that is being kept from us. The scroll your grandfather somehow knew about."

"The scroll must say something the Church doesn't want told," reasoned Tom, catching on surprisingly fast.

"I think you've hit the nail on the head," said Roth.

"So how do we find it?"

"One step at a time," warned Roth. "First, let's see what my assistant uncovers in Rome. But for now, I'll call and get the plane ready."

"Plane?" asked Nash. "What plane?"

Alyson Nash awoke slowly.

She closed her eyes again and listened to a distant thumping. No, not distant. It was close.

It was her heart.

Where am I?

There was something wrong here. Very wrong. Something had happened to her, she was sure of it.

Or was she dreaming?

Damn, her head hurt like hell.

If she were dreaming, then why did her head hurt so much?

Alyson tried to focus her eyes. Images swam into view. A bed post. The ceiling. A stained ceiling. Water damage.

Images flashed across her confused thoughts.

Her in her kitchen. Her receiving a call from her brother. A sound in her house. An image of a man in the corner of her eye. A hand reaching around her mouth—

No, no, no.

She was dreaming, surely. That hadn't really happened, had it?

Alyson tried to sit up and nearly vomited. She took a few deep breaths and realized she had absolutely no idea where she was.

Something very bad is happening.

And it's happening to me.

Now.

She sat up again and saw that she was sprawled on a rumpled bed in a large humid room. No windows, little light.

Now she heard another sound, a sort of sing-song ringing. She had heard this sound before. She forced her brain to work.

Then she had it. It was the sound of Muslims being called to prayer.

She was alone in the room, the bed against the far wall. Actually, there were windows, but they appeared to be boarded. A single, dusty light bulb cast little illumination across the spacious room. Other than her bed, the only other furniture wasn't really furniture at all. It was an odd wooden display on the opposite side of the room.

She swung her feet off the bed, half expecting to be tied down.

Thank God, she wasn't.

Her feet were bare. Hadn't she been wearing shoes the last time she remembered? She had. She had been waiting for Tom. They were going to have dinner.

God, that seemed like an eternity ago—and yet, it was her last memory, too.

How long have I been out? What's happened to me?

She found her feet and slowly stood, as a wave of nausea swept over her. She held on to one of the wood posts of the four poster bed, fought to retain consciousness, and then proceeded forward, shuffling on feet that suddenly seemed much too heavy.

There was just enough light from the tepid bulb for her to make out the odd display at the far end of the room. Whatever it was, it was surrounded by roughly-hewn beams of wood, forming a sort of frame. Within the frame was an ancient-looking cross. Around the frame were—

"Admiring our handiwork, Miss Nash?" came a voice from behind her.

Alyson gasped and spun around. A short, squat man with cropped light hair stepped into the room through a narrow door. He shut it behind himself.

"Who are you?" she cried, noticing her speech was slightly slurred. "Where am I?"

"My name is Tucker, Miss Nash. And you are in a safe place."

"Why was I brought here?"

"Your brother is doing a little task for us, and you're our insurance policy that he does so."

Alyson stared at the little man. Had she heard him correctly? Maybe her brain hadn't kicked into gear yet. "What are you talking about. What task?"

The little man smiled patiently. "It is God's work."

"I don't understand."

"You'll be told in time." She sensed the finality in his voice. She also sensed something else—danger. Call it women's intuition, but she suspected she did not want to push this man too far. For now, he was pleasant enough, but all her instincts told her this guy could turn on a dime. Until she knew what the hell was going on, she decided to play it safe.

For now.

She then noticed the chain worn around Tucker's neck. It had a miniature nine point scourge hanging from a small sword diagonally attached across a shield with the letters IHS on it. She immediately recognized the symbolism. It stood for, *I Have Suffered*.

Hands clasped behind his back, Tucker stepped beside her and admired the display on the wall. "Are you a Christian, Miss Nash?" he asked, without looking at her.

She nodded, watching him.

He glanced at her, obviously catching the movement from his peripheral vision. "Good. Then you'll appreciate what's on the wall here. Come closer and look at this." He reached out his hand. "Come. Don't be afraid."

Alyson moved closer, but didn't take his hand. He frowned, disappointed, but there was no way in hell Alyson was taking this creepy asshole's hand. He stepped closer to the display, pointing.

"Look here. Do you recognize any of these holy relics?"

"I don't know. What are they?"

He smiled reverently. "They're called the Instruments of the Passion or the Armi Christi—the Weapons of Christ."

Alyson mentally cataloged the relics: A heavy ancient nail, a scourge, spear, a pair of dice, a bloody robe, a reed, a crown of thorns, a stone, torch, ladder, and bucket.

Tucker continued. "All of these holy relics were once connected to Our Lord's crucifixion, scourging, and taunting."

"What does this have to do with your God's work?"

"That's the Shield of Christ you're looking at, and when the proper time comes," a devious smile ran cross Tucker's face, "our Lord's sacrifice upon that cross will guarantee our success."

Alyson felt a shiver run up her spine. More than a shiver. She felt as if someone had dipped her spine in ice.

She was sure the man named Tucker was insane.

And she was trapped.

What the hell was going on?

"Good night Miss Alyson." Tucker bowed slightly and walked out of the room. She heard a heavy bolt slide into place behind him.

Sunday
5:35 PM GMT
London, England

Roth's limousine pulled into a private airport outside of London and into a brightly lit hangar. Roth was helped out by his assistant, and Nash and Tom stepped out to see before them a gleaming twin-engine private jet.

"Beautiful," said Nash, admiring the plane, tempted to run a hand over its polished surface.

"Nash flies, too," commented Tom.

"Really?" said Roth. "Now why doesn't that surprise me?"

"I do, but nothing fancy like this. I have a Cirrus SR20."

"Build it yourself?" asked Roth.

"No. Bought second-hand."

Roth rolled next to Nash and looked up at him. "How would you like to be my co-pilot?"

"*You* fly this?" Try as he might, Nash couldn't hide the surprise in his voice. He felt like a shit the moment the words left his mouth.

"You seem surprised, Jeremy."

"Look, I'm sorry—"

Roth waved his hand dismissively. "Don't worry about it. You wouldn't be the first person to underestimate me. The plane, as you might have guessed, has been engineered to my particular needs. All is forgiven. So, will you be my co-pilot?"

Nash grinned and replied, "Count me in," just as a small panel truck pulled into the hangar.

"Ah. Here we go," said Roth.

Two men exited the truck, opened the back door, and immediately began unloading boxes labeled "Lab Equipment."

"What's all that?" asked Tom.

"Most of it is a portable clean room. If we're going to examine the scroll we don't want to damage it. The rest is my lab gear." Roth motioned to the two men. "Let's get on board."

Within minutes, the jet taxied and took off from the runway. When they reached cruising altitude, Roth turned to Nash. "Want to take over?"

Nash nodded and handled the controls. He had to admit, he was always happiest a few thousand feet above all the bullshit that was planet Earth.

"Tell me something, Roth," Nash said a few minutes later when his spirits had lifted. Flying always put him at ease. "What's the deal with that copy of the Shroud in your home?"

"Exhibit A of my research."

Nash looked at him, pulling his gaze away from the beautiful morning skies. "What kind of research?"

"I believe that Jesus didn't die on the cross—and I'm going to prove it."

"That's quite a statement," Nash offered in surprise. "How do you intend to prove that?"

"By the blood stains and other evidence on the Shroud." Roth saw Nash's puzzlement. "I assume you've never heard of Kurt Berna?"

Nash shook his head.

"That's understandable. His book was written in German and is now out of print. However I acquired a little known translation of his book in English. When I read it, I knew he was onto something."

"And what was that? asked Nash.

"To start, Berna stated that all the reports about the death of Jesus, as recorded in the Gospels, were true—considering the *definition* of death at that time."

"I'm not sure I'm following you."

"Let me explain. Take blood on the hair. Most forensic investigators know that blood in the hair dries quickly and when combined with hair, forms a hard, impermeable crust."

Nash was glad he had decided to forgo breakfast this morning.

Roth continued. "Obviously, fabrics don't absorb dried blood, and the traces of the stuff visible on the Shroud can only have originated from the blood that had been *flowing* from open wounds. See where I am going with this?"

"I'm following. Go on."

"Now, in regard to the crown of thorns, Berna wrote that any blood after Christ's death would be dried up and congealed. This is the natural behavior of blood which leaves the body and is exposed to air."

Nash wondered where the old coot was going with this, but kept his mouth shut for now. Besides, he was enjoying flying this amazing craft too much to care about much of anything else.

Roth continued. "Now, when a crown of thorns is removed leaving small wounds on the skin at the back of the head—what happens? Nothing!" he stated excitedly, startling Nash. "Absolutely nothing! There is no blood pressure in a dead body, and, as everybody who understands anything about human blood circulation knows, without pressure blood does not flow from a wound. Once death has ensued, blood circulation in the human body follows the same law."

"So what does this have to do with your theory about Christ *not* dying on the cross?"

"We're getting there, Jeremy, I promise. And keep your eyes on those instruments. It looks like we're heading into cloudy weather ahead." The old man, who was clearly in his elements—lecturing and flying—pounded excitedly. "Now where was I?"

"Blood circulation," said Nash, taking note of the gray clouds on the horizon.

"Oh, yes! Now a living body's skin will appear a reddish color because blood penetrates to the capillaries. But in death, when the heart stops pumping, the veins draw the blood back. The result? The capillaries are the first vessels to be emptied because they are at the extreme end of the circulatory system. What happens soon after a body dies?"

Nash shook his head.

The skin turns white. This is what happens to a corpse some eight to ten hours after the heart has ceased to beat. Not only is there no blood flow to open wounds because of lack of pressure, but the blood retracts a little in the veins."

Nash was certain he had heard that last bit on a recent episode of *CSI*, but he didn't say anything.

"Ah, but what happens if there is *still* blood pressure?" asked Roth. "What happens if the heart is *still* beating?"

Nash glanced at the excitable little man. "I don't know, you tell me."

"In the case of the crown of thorns, the smaller wounds would fill with blood, and the blood would flow from the head, through the hair, and onto the Shroud. That is why it cannot have been a corpse that was in the Shroud because the body was not dead. Plain and simple."

Roth sat back, pleased with himself. Nash had to grin at the man's enthusiasm.

"If you believe this blood theory," said Nash, "then why do you have your man Peacock at the Church of the Holy Sepulcher?"

"Because I believe that Jesus survived the crucifixion, lived a long life, died, and is entombed at the Holy Sepulcher."

"That's a big stretch," observed Nash.

"*Someone* is entombed at that Church, Jeremy. And I think your grandfather has stumbled upon who it is. That's why we have to pursue what's written in his diary."

"I could give a damn what's in the tomb," said Nash, setting his jaw and staring out at the gray skies ahead. "I just want my sister back."

"How's our little guest downstairs?" Benjamin Hicks asked Enos Tucker. They were in a small, stuffy office. Outside, the setting sun was just dipping below the distant foothills.

"Scared," Tucker replied. "But that's good. It'll keep her quiet for now. We'll have no trouble with her."

"Good." Hicks opened his briefcase and pulled out some legal papers. "Abraham Katz from the Temple Mount Movement will be here any moment. His group, as we discussed, is the perfect cover for our plans."

Tucker grinned. Perfect indeed. The Temple Mount Movement had dedicated themselves to the goal of rebuilding the ancient Jewish Temple on the Temple Mount. The movement's current idea—its current *brilliant* idea—would serve to their advantage.

"What about the weapon?" asked Tucker.

"It will be ready for pickup tomorrow. I want you to handle the transfer. Understood?"

Tucker nodded. He would have it no other way.

There was a knock on the door, and Hicks said, "That's our shill. Let him in."

Tucker opened the door, and a tall elderly gentleman with an Arctic-white beard and long hair swirling down past his shoulders entered the room.

Both men greeted the older man, and Tucker showed him to a seat at one end of the desk. As Katz sat, he spoke gravely, "I can't tell you, Reverend Hicks, how much your help means to us. Without the financial support of the International Christian Zionist Movement we would not be able to bring about the coming of the Third Temple."

"Thank you. We're all part of God's holy work." Hicks ruffled through the papers on the table and produced a check. "As we agreed, here's your final installment. Now, when can you show me what you've accomplished with our funding?"

The older man glanced at the check, then folded it carefully and tucked it away in a shirt pocket. "You shall see tonight, my friend. I have arranged for a demonstration of the holographic technology. It's in the desert about twenty kilometers outside the city, far enough away from prying eyes." He glanced at his watch. "In fact, we can leave anytime you want."

Hicks slapped the flat of his hand down on the table. This is what he liked—results. "Perfect," he said. "Enos? Are you ready to see how we will erect the Third Temple on the Temple Mount?"

Tucker smiled and closed his eyes. An odd sense of peace passed through him. "I have been ready for this my whole life."

After a long flight, Roth's jet landed in Palestine and pulled into a small private hangar at the Atarot Airport, just outside Jerusalem. The sun had set, and the hangar was brightly lit with fluorescent lights. The jet came to a halt, and the three men exited the plane.

"Why did we land here and not in Tel Aviv?" asked Tom.

Roth maneuvered his wheelchair to the opening of the hangar. A hot desert wind found its way inside. Roth looked out into the night, frowning. "Quieter and just as safe. It's overseen by the Israeli Defense Force. Besides, if we need to make a quick exit from Palestine, I don't want to be delayed in an international airport."

"Good thinking," replied Tom.

Roth eased further out onto the tarmac.

Nash stepped behind. "What's wrong?" he asked, stretching his back.

"I ordered a van to pick us up," said Roth. "I guess it's late."

"Or they forgot," said Tom.

"Are you always this pessimistic?" asked Nash. "I won't have my sister marrying a downer."

Tom laughed. "Only when it's a hundred degrees at night. God, it's sweltering out here."

"And this coming from a guy who lives in the deserts of New Mexico."

"It ain't hot like this."

The airport was mostly empty. One or two motorized carts

zipped by in the distance, but that was it. There was no van in sight. Just an eerie silence under a warm blowing breeze.

"Tom," said Nash, "Can you go up to the office and see if anyone knows anything about our transportation?"

Tom nodded. Roth pointed out the main offices, and the FBI man dashed off into the night.

"I'm going to look around," said Nash. "Maybe they pulled into the wrong hangar."

"Good idea," Roth replied. "But don't wander off too far. If the van comes, I want to get on the road right away. This airport is run by the IDF, and I don't want to answer any embarrassing questions."

Nash nodded and walked off. He got about twenty steps outside the hangar when he saw a van parked around the corner.

That's it, he thought. His first instinct was to head right over to it, but it was his second instinct that gave him pause. Something felt wrong. The van seemed empty, lifeless.

A dry wind swept over the grounds, bringing with it an unusual smell of dust combined with the smell of copper.

No, not copper, thought Nash. *Blood.*

He hoped he was wrong. Against his better judgment, he carefully approached the silent van. The lights were off, and no one seemed to be in the driver's compartment. He breathed a little easier, except for—

The smell of copper was stronger.

He walked up to the vehicle and tried the passenger's side door. It opened with a resoundingly loud creak. He winced at the noise and looked inside.

Nothing. No one.

He walked around the back of the van and tried its rear doors. They opened, too. In fact, they seemed to burst open. Two bodies, leaning against the door, tumbled out and landed at Nash's feet. Both had the back of their heads blown off, and blood and brains splashed out all over Nash's shoes.

Nash stared down in utter shock, then felt his gorge rise violently. He turned his head and vomited, and when he was done retching, he realized he was in serious danger.

He backed away from the scene, scanning the area. He seemed to be alone, but that didn't mean there wasn't somebody nearby pointing a gun at him.

He tried to ignore the way the bodies shifted and turned as he moved away—and the trail of blood he was leaving behind.

He covered his mouth, fighting the need to vomit again. There was no time for that. He needed to get the hell out of there.

And now he was running, as fast as he could, back toward the hangar in a blind panic.

He was a professional journalist and skeptic, after all. He didn't come across many murdered bodies.

As he rounded the corner into the hangar, gasping and stumbling, he pulled up short. There, standing next to Roth and pointing a gun to the crippled man's head, was a tall slouching figure.

The man jerked his head around, bringing the gun with him.

Nash gasped, raised his hands out before him, and could not imagine a more horrific human being. The man looked misshapen and hideous, face twisted into something demonic. Knowing that two men had just had their brains blown out made the man in front of Nash all the more horrendous.

Nash's bowels turned to water as he saw the man's finger tighten around the trigger.

The man grinned, and Nash realized the last image he would have on this earth would be that of this grinning demon.

The sounds of running footsteps erupted behind him. The man with the gun frowned and looked over Nash's shoulder. Nash risked a glance himself.

Three people appeared from the darkness.

He looked back at the demon with the gun, and the man was gone. He caught sight of the hunched figure as he disappeared through a side door.

The three figures all appeared behind Nash—and all were brandishing handguns themselves, sleek flat handguns.

Good Christ! thought Nash. *What the hell is going on?*

"Where is he?" shouted a woman wearing a long black jacket.

Nash could only guess who she was talking about, and he could only pray that she was one of the good guys. Nash pointed. "He went that way, through the side door."

She motioned, and one of the men ran through the hangar, and out through the same door. He came back shortly. "Gone," he said in clipped English.

"Did you see who it was?" asked the woman.

The man nodded and stood by her side. He said a single word, "Vadja."

The name meant nothing to Nash, but the woman and the big guy next to her both nodded solemnly, as if it had explained everything.

"Pardon my French," exclaimed Nash. "But what the *fuck* is going on here? There were two dead men outside! And who the hell are you?" he said, pointing to the woman.

She ignored him and glanced at the man who had dashed after this Vadja character. She jerked her head once and the man ran out the wide hangar doors.

"My name is Sabra," the woman said. "And I'm with—"

"The Mossad," said Roth suddenly. He pointed to her pistol. "Walthers. All Mossad agents carry Walthers."

The woman called Sabra stared down at Roth in his wheelchair, seemed to make a decision, and then nodded her head once. "Very good, Mr. Roth. Yes, we are with the Mossad."

"Spies?" asked Nash. Tonight could not have gotten any stranger. Hell, this weekend couldn't have gotten any stranger. Nash had to admit, this was all getting a bit much for him to absorb.

The woman ignored him. "That man who was pointing a gun at you two is called Vadja. He's a paid assassin. A very good paid assassin. You can both consider yourselves very, lucky to still be alive."

"What the devil would he want with us?" asked Roth.

"That's exactly what we'd like to know," said Sabra.

"And why are you here?" demanded Roth. Nash had to admit, he admired the Englishman's spunk. He just hoped the Englishman's spunk didn't get them all killed.

"We're here because of you, Mr. Roth," said Sabra. She turned to one of her men. "Get the Rover. And you two," she said to Roth and Nash, "are coming with us."

"No can do," stated Roth forcefully, maneuvering his wheelchair before the stunningly beautiful woman. "We have other plans. So, unless Mossad doubles as the Israeli police, I don't believe you can legally detain us. We've done nothing wrong. In fact, I have every intention of reporting this incident to the Israeli Defense Force. After all, we have two dead men and a killer on the loose, and for all I know it could be terrorist related."

Sabra looked at her companions. They each nodded as if reading her mind. "Okay, Mr. Roth," she agreed, "we'll lay our cards on the table if you do the same."

Roth nodded in agreement. "First you."

Sabra holstered her weapon. Nash noticed the other two kept theirs ready. "We're tracking an organization called the Warriors of Christ. Do you know of them?"

Roth nodded. "Of course. A Christian fringe group that wants to single-handedly help bring about the Second Coming."

"Guys," said Nash, cutting in. "I hate to break this up, but we have two dead men outside here and I think—"

"Let us handle that," interrupted one of the agents, speaking in an accent so thick that he was nearly impossible to understand.

Indeed, as the agent spoke another vehicle, a station wagon, appeared out of the dark, driving swiftly over the tarmac. It pulled up outside the hangar, about where Nash had come across the van and bodies. Nash heard doors opening and closing, and then the sounds of men working. Next, he heard water being sprayed, and Nash looked from Sabra to the other two men. Nobody moved or spoke. Nash looked at Roth. The crippled man shrugged his shoulders. The car started again and sped off into the night, and Nash had the unsettling realization that the dead men had been disposed of.

Sweet Jesus.

There was a sound up to their left, and the two agents drew their weapons.

It was Tom casually walking down the stairs from the upstairs offices as if nothing had happened.

"Where the hell were you?" spat Nash.

Tom looked at the armed Mossad agents and his jaw dropped. He explained that he had heard nothing in the offices he searched since they were soundproof.

"Now," said Sabra with finality, "back to our discussion. Yes, we are aware that the Warriors of Christ are planning something big to bring about this event. It is they, we feel, who recently robbed the Orient Express of some ancient religious relics called the Weapons of Christ. Perhaps you've heard of them?"

"Yes," said Roth. "I'm quite aware of them."

Sabra went on. "We're certain they stole the relics to finance whatever plans they have afoot and knew that the best man to fence them in Europe would be you."

Roth nodded. "I'm honored that you think so."

"So we staked out your mansion and waited for them to arrive or for you to leave and meet them."

"How did you follow us here?" asked Roth.

"Flight plan. You filed one."

"It could have been a fake if what you said about me fencing goods is true."

"Sure," nodded Sabra. "Your reputation as being wily was not lost on us. So, we had a backup plan." She smiled. "Those men who loaded your equipment at the airport. They were Mossad. They dropped a little GPS tracking device in one of your cargo containers just in case. Now, it's your turn."

As Roth explained the story of the diary, scroll, and the kid-napping of Nash's sister, Nash wondered just how much of what Sabra had told them was true. Had they shown their hand too easily? Nash didn't know, but if they helped him find his sister, then he really didn't care.

When Roth had finished, the disturbingly striking female looked at Nash. "Enos Tucker is a member of the Warriors of Christ. We are after the same man."

"And he wants the scroll," replied Nash.

"So you are here in Israel to find the lost scroll?" asked Sabra. "Which you will then trade for your sister?"

"Yes," said Nash. "That's the plan."

"And aren't you curious about what the missing scroll contains?" asked the agent.

Nash set his jaw. "I just want my sister."

Sabra crossed her arms and stepped in front of him. Nash was surprised to see that she was nearly as tall as he. She held his gaze for a heartbeat or two as a small commuter plane touched down across the far field. "Let me help you find your sister, Mr. Nash. And in return, you help us take down Enos Tucker."

Her empathy was real, Nash was certain of it. Whether or not her offer was real, Nash didn't know. But the way he saw it was this—to save his sister, he needed all the help he could get. Even if it was with a clandestine government agency.

"I don't know how I can help you," he admitted.

Sabra smiled, and Nash was not very surprised that when she did, his heart beat a little faster. After all, she *was* a stunningly exciting woman. Her compassion, real or not, was most welcome.

"For starters, Mr. Nash," she said firmly with a soft touch, "help yourself by finding that damned scroll."

"And to do that," said Roth, rolling over to them, "we will need to make a little house call."

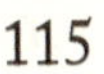

Along the south shore of the Dead Sea the night was thick and still. Hicks and Tucker watched as Katz gave order after order to a small team of engineers working on a set of four high-powered, water-cooled lasers that were laid out in a wide circle. The lasers surrounded a large flat rock protruding several feet from the desert floor. A six foot by six foot transparent plastic cube sat atop the rock.

Katz looked up into the cloudless night sky. "It's a perfect night for a light show." He looked at his watch as his crew assembled the last pieces of the equipment. "We should be ready in a few minutes," said Katz. "Now remember, this is just a demonstration. Just a scale model of what you will see above the Mount."

"That poses a question," asserted Hicks. "How did you ever get permission to do this demonstration?"

"Surprisingly," Katz replied, "both the IDF and the Islamic Trust had no qualms about it. I suppose they see our attempts at re-establishing the Temple on the Mount using a holographic projection as a harmless jester and proof that our belief in the Second Coming is ungrounded." He laughed. "They're writing us off as *meshugenehs*."

A moment later, Katz got the nod from his chief engineer.

"It's time, gentlemen," he said and walked to a control panel fifty yards from the outside of the circle of the laser projectors and powered up the guns. "Behold! The Third Temple of Solomon!"

Katz threw a switch, and the four lasers immediately started

116

humming. A deep vibrating seemed to emanate from the desert floor itself, and Tucker and Hicks looked at each other.

When the humming and vibrating reached a sort of crescendo, four powerful blue beams of light shot into the transparent cube. Despite himself, Tucker stepped back and noticed Hicks had done the same.

Their jaws dropped when an ephemeral, twenty-five foot flickering replica of the Temple of Solomon appeared before them as if by magic, hovering several feet above the flat rock.

"Sweet Jesus!" exclaimed Hicks.

For the longest time the men stared at the shimmering image of the small Temple. It was Katz who spoke first. "I have always thought myself to be God's architect. And now we can summon the Messiah without the need for bloodshed. The trigger will be a peaceful, technology-fueled spiritual revolution. A velvet apocalypse, if you will."

"Wonderful!" Tucker sighed in awe. "But, how will you produce a life-sized image of the Temple? You would have to place a plastic cube several hundred feet in diameter directly on top of the Mosque on the Mount, would you not?"

"No, we won't," Katz explained. "We will suspend the much larger cube from a blimp above the Mount and shoot the lasers into it both from above and below to give the Temple image a blessed detail not seen before." He looked both men in the eye, and quoted, '*The future Temple, which we are expecting, is built and perfected and will be revealed and descend from heaven.*'"

"Thank you for the demonstration, Mr. Katz," said Hicks sincerely. "Our money was well spent. I want you to be ready to deploy it at a moment's notice."

Katz nodded agreeably. "We can deploy within an hour."

As Katz walked away, Hicks turned to Tucker. "Now, Mr. Tucker, I believe you have an appointment in Haifa."

Sunday
11:55 PM GMT
Jerusalem, Israel

"Mossad?" the voice on the phone said in surprise. "How do you know?"

"I saw the Jew whore," Vadja said as he ran his fingers along the scar on his face. "I don't know where they came from or why they were there, but I still can complete my holy task, Father."

"No," the voice said emphatically. "We're too exposed now that Mossad is involved." There was a pause on the other end of the line. "But they can be useful later."

"Father, I—"

"Please, my son. Now listen carefully. Here's what I want you to do..."

Monday
12:00 AM GMT
Tel Aviv, Israel

"That's the one there, on the left," said Roth from the front passenger seat. He pointed to a stately home in the upscale neighborhood just outside of Tel Aviv University.

The Rover pulled over, and the Englishman turned back to Nash. "Help get my wheelchair out and come with me."

Nash helped Roth up to the front door. The older man rang the bell located just below the Jewish *mezuzah* attached to the door frame. A few moments later, a mature woman in her late fifties opened the door.

"My God!" she cried out immediately. "Stanton Roth! You old goat!"

The Englishman chuckled. "I see you haven't forgotten your old colleague, Mishka."

"What on earth are you doing in Tel Aviv?" She looked over at Nash, then on to the Rover parked in front of her home. "And who are your friends?"

Roth lowered his voice. "I think it's better if we discussed this inside."

She frowned, then nodded, and opened her door all the way.

A few minutes later, the motley crew of multi-nationals were sitting around an elegant dining room table while Mishka prepared some tea. As she poured them each a cup, Roth completed his introductions of Nash, Tom, Sabra, and her two teammates.

"I haven't seen you since our days at the Shrine," Mishka said to Roth as she sat next to him, holding her own cup of tea. Nash

119

noted that she kept a careful eye on Sabra and the others, although she seemed to warm naturally to Roth.

But before Roth could respond, Sabra jumped in. "The Shrine of the Book?" she asked. "Where the Dead Sea scrolls are kept?" She turned to Roth. "So, you two worked together on the scrolls?"

Mishka studied the Mossad agent for a moment or two before answering. "If you want to call it that," she said, then smiled and winked at Roth. "I never saw a man so good at chasing women around—and in a wheelchair, no less!"

Nash intoned, "A man of many talents."

To his credit, Roth blush mightily. He said, "Yes, well, we did get quite a lot of work done, too, if you'll recall. And that's the reason for our visit."

Roth filled Mishka in on their mission and the strange series of events that brought them together with Mossad. As he spoke, she calmly drank her tea while the others sat patiently, chiming in occasionally when necessary. When he was finished, Nash noticed that Roth was watching the woman closely. "Mishka," said the elder man. "We need to see the Cave Twelve Scroll."

The woman nearly dropped her cup. "How did you know about that?"

Roth told her about the coded page in the diary, finishing with, "It exists, correct?"

Mishka opened her mouth to speak, then closed it again. She looked down into her cup of tea.

Roth prodded gently. "Mishka. It's me, Stanton. Please. It's important. It's truly a matter of life and death."

The Israeli woman took a deep breath and looked around the room. During Roth's explanation he had tactfully omitted any reference to the dead drivers at the airport or of the Mossad's involvement. She seemed to come to some conclusion after considerable thought.

"Your friends," she said, "are they trustworthy?"

Roth looked around the room, his eyes settling on the Mossad agents. Nash almost laughed as all three agents did their best to appear trustworthy. "I think so," he said. "Yes."

"You *think* so?" she said, wringing her hands. She clearly didn't like the answer.

What happened next surprised Nash. Sabra, clearly the leader of this Mossad cell, stepped forward and showed Mishka her agent ID. They spoke heatedly in Hebrew, and after some back and forth, the older woman finally nodded. Sabra patted Mishka's hand and stood back with her colleagues.

The female agent noticed Nash's quizzical expression and simply said, "I told her I was with her own government, and her information was of the utmost importance to national security."

Roth, who obviously spoke Hebrew—or at least ancient Hebrew—nodded to both Nash and Tom. He rolled his wheelchair over and took Mishka's hand. "We need your help," he implored. "*I* need your help."

The older lady nodded, took in some air, and then spoke carefully, "Yes, there was indeed a Cave Twelve Scroll. The Committee, after much debate, decided not to release its contents or even acknowledge its existence."

"But why?" asked Nash, genuinely intrigued.

"I'm sure Stanton here has told you the story of the scrolls' connection to the Essenes prophesies," said Mishka.

Nash nodded, looking over at Sabra. She nodded as well. Mossad agents, he realized, were obviously very well briefed.

Mishka continued, "Well, this one was filled with all kinds of Apocalyptic, end-of-the-world predictions. The committee thought such unsubstantiated material was not what the world needed to know. With beliefs in Nostradamus, the looming Mayan calendar 2012 predictions of the end of the world, the Second Coming of Christ, and the Coming of the Mahdi—well, the Committee decided that it was best to keep that scroll secret for now. What we didn't need to do was throw more gasoline on the fire. And I agreed."

Roth had opened his mouth to speak, but Sabra surprised them all by stating, "My father worked on the Cave Twelve Scroll project."

"And who was your father?" questioned Mishka, raising her eyebrows.

"Isaac Zamir."

"You're Ike's daughter?" Mishka asked in surprise.

"Yes," said Sabra. "And despite what you might have been told, he was not killed in a senseless robbery. He was murdered. And it had something to do with the Cave Twelve Project. I just don't know what. Yet. But I'm going to find out."

The room grew silent, and after some prodding by Mishka, the Mossad agent told them all more about what she knew. Her father had been killed in front of her. They had been coming home from dinner together when a man appeared from an alley and dragged her father inside. Young Sabra—only ten years old at the time—had tried to fight the man off but the attacker was just too strong. The man had thrown her aside, and as she painfully picked herself up from a pile of trash, she had watched in horror as he proceeded to stab her father repeatedly. She found a nearby bottle—a broken bottle—and attacked the man, giving him the scars he wears today.

Sabra paused in her narration. Her eyes were alight with tears—and something else. Hate. She went on, "After I joined the Mossad, I used their resources to track down the man who assassinated my father. It was easy. I would never forget his face—especially a face that I had forever scarred. That man is Vadja. Mr. Roth and Nash were both introduced to him tonight at the airport."

Nash nodded. He recalled the look of startled recognition on Sabra's face at the airport. Looking at her now, he could clearly see the range of emotions on her face—with hate and anger being the top two. Nash could imagine Vadja's chances if the man ever found himself alone in a room with a now fully grown Sabra!

The table was quiet until she spoke again. "Vadja's services are often employed by a little known US Intelligence project here in Europe."

"American?" said Tom, raising his voice.

"Financed by Americans," said Sabra. "The man in charge ordered the hit on my father, and now the same killer has shown up at the airport tonight."

"It has something to do with the scroll," said Nash suddenly.

"Yes," said Sabra. "I believe that. Somehow your grandfather's diary, the scroll, and my father's murder are all connected."

Mishka stood up and leaned towards Roth. "Stanton. This is serious. If what Sabra thinks is true, you need to back out of this now."

Nash stood up suddenly. He needed the scroll to find his sister. Roth looked at him and gestured for him to sit. Nash did, reluctantly.

"I will be fine, dear friend. I have been in dicey situations before. It's what keeps me alive. Besides, we need that scroll to get Nash's sister back. It's the ultimate bargaining chip."

Mishka sighed. "And how, pray tell, do you plan to get the scroll?"

Roth smiled. "We steal it."

Mishka's draw dropped.

"With your help of course," Roth added.

"Oh, no!" she cried.

Roth rolled over to her and parked directly in front of her. She was still shaking her head as he reached for her hands. "All we need is your access pass to get into the secure areas of the Shrine. You don't have to be there. Just tell them your pass was stolen."

"And I suppose Mossad has no problem with committing a shady act?" Mishka said. "What am I saying? This is probably right up your alley, Sabra."

"Yes. What about that?" asked Roth.

Sabra smiled. "And I suppose your CIA or NSA are not above performing dark ops?"

"Point taken," Roth replied.

"What about you, Tom?" asked Nash. "You're the FBI. I assume something like this would be frowned upon by your superiors?"

"On the face of it, yes," Tom replied. "But if this helps lead us to the kidnappers, well...?"

"Good. It's agreed," said Roth. "We steal the scroll." He looked at his hostess and pleaded. "Mishka? For the young girl—and old times sake?"

She looked the group over, and her eyes settled on Nash. "And here I thought I was going to settle in for a pleasant evening with tea and my crosswords. Now look what I've gotten myself involved with."

"Please," begged Nash, holding her gaze. "I need the scroll to save my sister's life."

"Yes, I understand, dear," she answered softly. And then a small, mischievous smile touched the corners of her lips. "I will deny everything, of course."

"Thank you!" said Nash softly. "Thank you so much." He wanted to hug her but thought the show of emotion might have been a little much for the reserved woman.

She looked at Roth. "You *will* be careful with it?"

"Mishka, please," he replied.

Tom turned immediately to Roth. "And how do we go about stealing the scroll?"

"Oh, I think we'll leave that up to our friends from the Mossad," said Roth. "That's more their line of work—don't you think Sabra?"

The agent nodded. And Nash noted the complete lack of emotion in her blank gaze.

She's a killer, thought Nash. *An honest to God killer.*

"By the way, Sabra," asked Roth. "Did you ever find out who ordered your father's assassination?"

"Yes," said the Mossad agent quietly. "A man named Phillip Marcus."

Roth almost gagged on his tea.

Monday
2:01 AM GMT
Haifa, Israel

A good place for a murder, thought Enos Tucker, as he fingered the satchel he carried and looked again over his shoulder. He was waiting outside an abandoned warehouse on the docks of Haifa, nervously smoking a cigarette. In the near distance, out on the dark, flat water, a foghorn sounded hollowly.

Tucker shivered and flicked his cigarette away. It sizzled in a small, filthy puddle.

At the sound of footsteps behind him, he jumped and spun around. There, at the far end of the warehouse, emerging from the fog and darkness and into the flickering light of the single overhead security light, were the silhouettes of two quickly approaching figures.

Here we go, he thought.

The first silhouette coalesced into that of a tall, thin man carrying what appeared to be a medium-sized metal suitcase, the type in which sensitive equipment is shipped. The second figure, a short, squat man, carried what looked like a laptop computer.

"I'm happy you could make it, Mr. Tucker," said the tall Walter Bletch.

Tucker was surprised by the man's looks. *This was a notorious arms dealer?* Bletch looked anything but notorious. In fact, he looked downright effeminate. Blond hair and blue eyes, with softness about him. If not for his known activities on the black market with access to the most sophisticated and deadly weapons, the Walter standing before him could have passed himself off as being Walter Mitty.

125

"We were afraid the Warriors of Christ had changed their mind," said Bletch, with a hint of an accent. Danish, if Tucker recalled correctly. "Have you brought the payment?"

Tucker found himself eyeing the second man. This powerful-looking man had two of the biggest hands Tucker had ever seen. He had no doubt the man had used those hands to inflict harm on others. "Have you brought the goods?" Tucker asked. His voice, admittedly, sounded nervously high even to his ears. He swallowed hard.

Bletch snapped his fingers, and his short companion brought over the metal suitcase. The Dane opened it up.

Tucker leaned forward and peered in. His initial apprehension turned immediately into irritation. "This is what you brought me?" he snapped, looking up at the tall man. "This is nothing but a shoulder-held, soldier-launched light munition." He stepped back. "You brought me an anti-tank weapon. Why?"

Bletch raised his eyebrows and nodded. "You seem to know your munitions, Mr. Tucker. Yes, this is an individually launched weapon. Light and easily transported." He paused and peered almost lovingly into the box. "But an anti-tank weapon it most certainly is not."

"This isn't what I ordered. We're paying a lot of—"

Bletch raised a hand, cutting him off. Tucker took a deep breath and backed off, reminding himself that he was dealing with, among other things, world class criminals. Bletch motioned, and the short man promptly snapped open the laptop and held the glowing machine before him. The little man, Tucker noted, made a perfect pedestal.

Bletch stepped over to the open laptop. "Let me show you what, exactly, you are buying, my friend."

Tucker watched as Bletch called up a video file and ordered it to play.

"Now watch closely," Bletch advised. "This is state-of-the art. The Brits have deployed this in Afghanistan. Denied, of course. It uses a technology based on the thermobaric principle."

Tucker eyes scanned the video as it showed a large cinder-block building in the background. In the foreground, a British Marine had the very same weapon resting on his shoulder. The soldier pulled a trigger and rocked backwards as a small lick of flame appeared from the weapon. A moment later—hell, a half a moment later—the cinderblock building exploded in a hail of rock and rubble. The building looked like it was incinerated—no, both incinerated *and* blown to bits. And when the smoke cleared, Tucker's eyes just about bugged out of his head. He knew his mouth was hanging open. He didn't care. He sensed Bletch smiling next to him.

Sweet Jesus. The building was completely and utterly gone.

The Dane closed the laptop. "That was a steel enforced cement block house, by the way." He gave the laptop back to the short man. "And there's a side benefit—you could say—that the weapon provides, one that I hope does not make you squeamish."

Tucker still couldn't get the image of the disintegrated block house engulfed in flames out of his mind. He was impressed.

"Side benefit?"

A devious smile crossed Bletch's handsome face. "If there happened to be people in the structure, say people at prayer?" he winked, "those near the blast are obliterated but not before the shock and pressure waves cause minimal damage to brain tissue. You see, victims are not rendered unconscious by the blast, but instead suffer for several seconds, even minutes, in agony while they suffocate."

"*Good God.*"

Bletch looked straight at Tucker. "No, my friend. No God who is good would have allowed such an unholy weapon to be built. Even those just outside the blast area were likely to suffer internal injuries including severe concussions, burst eardrums, ruptured lungs, and other internal injuries. Oh, and possibly even blindness."

Tucker swallowed hard. Far off the foghorn sounded again.

He stuck his hands deeper into his jacket and shivered. "How does it do this?"

Bletch glanced over at the suitcase containing the weapon. To Tucker, the Dane appeared to be looking at a favorite pet. Bletch said, "It disperses a gas which is lit at a second stage, allowing the blast to fill all the spaces of a building. No one escapes." The tall arms dealer glanced at the satchel under Tucker's arm. "Now, can we get to business?"

Tucker nodded and handed him the satchel. "Ten million dollars in bearer bonds."

The Dane gave a half smile.

"You were perhaps expecting thirty pieces of silver?" Tucker asked sarcastically.

Bletch laughed. "No. These will do quite nicely." He turned as he started to leave the warehouse. "Now go and do God's work!"

He was laughing as he left.

Nash, Sabra, and Mishka were seated around the elder host's outlandishly spacious outdoor veranda. Nash couldn't help but note that the veranda was nearly as big as his apartment at home. Roth, Tom, and Sabra's teammates had left earlier to "set up a clean room," although Nash still wasn't entirely sure what that entailed.

"They've been gone quite a while," observed Nash with concern after Mishka served them more tea. He knew the others heard the frustration in his voice. His sister was missing and in some serious trouble, so why the hell are they taking so long?

"Setting up a clean room takes time," said Sabra calmly. "Roth has a place reserved in some office complex downtown. My boys will make sure it's debugged and ready to go."

Nash took a sip of his tea. He tried to calm himself down. Sipping tea while his younger sister was facing God only knew what horrors, was frustrating beyond words. So frustrating that he did the only thing he could to keep himself from going crazy. He resigned himself to the situation.

Endeavoring to divert his worries, he asked Sabra, "Are your teammates going to be in on the heist?"

"No. I can't risk it. If something goes wrong, I don't want them involved. This is my decision, and I'll take responsibility for it." She looked into her tea. "When my team gets back with Roth and your FBI pal, I'll send them off to HQ."

"I'm sorry to hear about your father," offered Nash, and he meant it. Having recently lost his own grandmother, and now with his sister, well, it was safe to say that his heart went out to anyone who had suffered similar losses—especially one who witnessed her own father's horrible murder.

"Thank you," said Sabra. She gave him a small smile, and Nash, despite himself, swallowed hard. He noted that his heart had, ever so slightly, quickened. She continued, "He was not just my father, but my mentor. Even so young, I helped him in his work on the scrolls, you know. In the process I learned a lot about his beliefs and how he used them to live a full and productive life."

"What beliefs?" asked Nash. He decided that he loved hearing the Mossad agent talk. In particular, he loved her Hebrew accent.

"As Jews, we weren't very orthodox, but my father taught me a lot about the Kabbalah, and that a life lived without meaning is no life at all."

"And did the Kabbalah give him—and you—meaning?" Nash asked, genuinely intrigued. He, of course, knew something of the popular Jewish mystical tradition known as the Kabbalah. And thanks to a handful of practicing Hollywood pop stars, much of the world knew a smattering of the arcane religion, as well.

"For him, yes. Myself?" Sabra, for the first time since Nash had met her, suddenly seemed unsure of herself. "I don't know. His study of the Kabbalah was his search for inner meaning. I never took the time to fully understand it."

"My opinion?" said Nash. "Don't bother. Religion has been the bane of mankind for thousands of years. The opiate of the people, and all that."

Mishka, listening quietly, finally spoke up, "There are many paths to God, Jeremy, and none of them are the domains of organized religion."

"The subject of God is open to debate, too," said Nash.

"Yes, you are truly a skeptic. That's good. Skeptics keep the world in check."

"Someone has to," commented Nash.

"And you are correct about religion being an opiate. The common condition of man is that he—and she—is asleep."

"Asleep?" asked Nash.

Mishka continued. "Yes. Those who want to reach God understand that reality is just a form of sleep. The goal for those of us who believe in a Creator is to awaken the true self and experience God. And that's what the study of the esoteric paths to God like the Kabbalah, Sufism, Gnostics, and others teach you."

Nash rolled his eyes. *The goal*, he wanted to say, but bit his tongue, *should be to awaken from the pathetic delirium that there was a higher power of any kind and to take ownership of one's own actions.*

"I don't understand?" asked Sabra. "What's the point?"

"Exactly—" Nash began, until Mishka cut him off.

"The point," replied Mishka calmly, "is that you have to learn to control any and all states of awareness you experience in order to experience the one true reality—God." The elder Israeli leaned forward with a gleam in her eye. "You have to learn how to reach self-realization by controlling your states of awareness."

"Nirvana," said Nash, "is best reached in the arms of a woman."

Sabra laughed, surprised, and nearly choked on her tea.

Mishka ignored his remark. "Like I said, the Kabbalah offers one way to God. One way to awaken, so to speak."

"But if we know we are asleep," asked Nash, "isn't that enough? I mean, why go through all this esoteric navel gazing if we understand we are asleep. Why not just wake up?"

Mishka smiled. "Because you're more machine than person."

Nash was confused. "Now you've lost me."

"According to esoteric teachings, we *are* machines," she said. "A machine in respect to the fact that human beings act in response to external influences. Most, if not all of our movements, actions, words, ideas, emotions, moods, and thoughts are the end result of external influences. What we are is really just an automaton with a certain set of stored memories of previous experiences. Everything that you think you *do*, really just *happens*."

"Are you saying we're robots? I don't buy that," Nash retorted boldly. "Life is not a Matrix movie. We have free will."

"Do we?" Mishka replied.

"Of course we do," said Nash. "Any of us—at any time—can do whatever we please. We are not programmed."

"Let me suggest this," replied Mishka with a now frustrating smile of knowledge that Nash was beginning to find infuriating. "We are machines, but very peculiar ones. A machine which, under the right circumstances and with the right knowledge, *knows that it's a machine.* And if you realize this, you may then find a way to cease behaving like a machine. The first step on this road to knowledge is to understand that you are not one integrated person. You are many."

"New Age mumbo-jumbo," muttered Nash.

"Call it what you will, but these are the basic tenants behind spiritual teachings like the Kabbalah. Mr. Nash, as an educated, open-minded researcher, I know you are at least willing to listen to my mumbo-jumbo."

Nash shrugged reluctantly. She had used the one card that he could never get around. Yes, he was—in theory—open-minded. But not so much that his brains fell out. It was going to take *a lot* to convince him of anything other than the cold hard facts of reality.

She nodded and continued, "Those who study the esoteric path believe that you have one unchanging *I.* But we also understand that this is an illusion. We are *not* unchanging. The human condition is in constant flux. Look back over a typical day. One moment you are one Jeremy Nash, happy and fun-loving. Another moment, you are another Jeremy Nash, annoyed at someone cutting you off in traffic. A third moment, you are yet another Jeremy Nash, and so on and so on. You are really different people at every moment of the day."

Oh, boy, thought Nash. *Now how the hell did we get started down this road?* But because they had time to kill, and the old lady was going out of her way to help them, Nash decided to hear her out. Besides, she seemed particularly knowledgeable of the esoteric angle of the spiritual teachings, an angle he was not often exposed to. Grudgingly, he found himself mildly intrigued.

Mishka was still talking. "Your illusion of a whole person is created first by the sensations of your physical body. You look in the mirror and...there you are! You look down at your body and feel whole, unique, apart from the rest of the world. Your name, Jeremy Nash, makes you believe that you are one total person and the many mechanical habits that you repeat throughout the day reinforce this illusion even more."

She continued, happily realizing she had their full attention. "Having the same physical sensations, the same name and the same number of mechanical habits instilled in you by your society and education makes you believe that you are *always* the same. But in reality, there is no *oneness* to you. You are made up of many different parts. Every thought you have, every feeling you feel, every sensation, every desire, every like and dislike is a different *I*. You believe that you are the same *I* having all these different sensations, feelings and thoughts because you *remember* yourself having them. What you think you are is really many different *I's* having many different experiences, with you remembering yourself having these experiences. These many different *I's* are not connected or coordinated in any way. Each depends on changes in your external environment and the changes in your response to them."

"I'm beginning to feel like that gal who had multiple personalities," Nash quipped.

Sabra rolled her eyes. Nash wasn't sure if the beautiful Mossad agent was rolling her eyes at his quip or at Mishka's exhaustive rhetorical monologue.

"You're close," Mishka replied. "Each of your *I's*—when you are remembering them that is—want to represent *who you are*. When you say I did this or I did that, or I feel this or I feel that, or I know this or I know that, these are only a thought, a passing mood, or a passing desire. In an hour's time you may forget *who you were,* and, with the same conviction, become someone else. In most cases you believe that you are the last *I* you can remember."

"Who am *us,* then?" Nash asked, getting swept up in the woman's enthusiasm despite himself.

"A machine," answered Mishka. "And as a machine, human beings have four different functions—thinking, feeling, instinct, and movement. *Instinct* is all the inner workings of your machine, and *movement* the outer. The *thinking* function includes all impressions and realizations of the world and all your representations and concepts of it. The thinking function also includes reasoning, comparison, affirmation, negation, and the formulation of words, speech and imagination. The *feeling* function, or those of emotions, includes joy, sorrow, fear, and astonishment."

"So," asked Sabra fully enjoying this woman's smooth flow of thought, "each one of these functions, with all their varied parts, acts as a different *I* for each of us?"

"Correct," Mishka replied. "Your task on the path to self-realization is to become *aware* of your many *I's,* understand them, and control them. To succeed, you need to learn to stop reacting to what happens to you and start *acting* on them."

"Or," added Sabra, "as Stewart Brand once wrote, "We are as gods, so we better get good at it.""

Mishka nodded. "Yes, I like that." At that moment, Mishka's front doorbell rang. She looked at her two young guests. "The boys are back."

As she exited the veranda, Nash leaned closer to Sabra. "So, any idea on how we're going get the scroll out of the shrine building? Getting in will be easy using Mishka's ID. Getting out with it under Roth's arm is quite another matter."

A smile crossed the Mossad agent's face. Nash liked her smile, even if it looked a bit sadistic at times. She said, "I put some thought into that while our gracious hostess was rambling on about the various *I's* and *we's* and *us's.* Jeremy, have you ever wanted to be a spy?"

"I don't understand—"

"Welcome to the Mossad, Mr. Nash."

Monday
5:20 PM GMT
Rome, Italy

Douglas Peacock was exhausted.

He had spent the entire day at the Vatican's Information Service building, pouring over anything and everything he could find regarding one Phillip Marcus. He found much—but no mention of Section 18 in connection with him or even the existence of Section 18 itself.

Damn.

He was sitting at a massive, ornate table with a single, dusty lamp at his side. He was alone in the cavernous building, which seemed to creak on command. Peacock rubbed his tired eyes and looked again at his notes. Phillip Marcus had, according to his research, acted as a consultant to the Vatican—the Jesuits in particular—on many occasions in the area of antiquities and antiquity preservation. Unfortunately, the Information Service had only a post office box for him in the States.

Peacock was stumped and at a dead end.

Damn again.

It was getting late, and he was hungry. He gathered his gear, returned the books and other research material, and left the creepy building to look for a restaurant. In Rome, one never had to look far for such things. Almost immediately, he found a charming cafe that sat on a piazza. He sat under a red umbrella and ordered a glass of wine and some brochette. Once done, he called Roth. No answer. The man was infuriatingly difficult to reach at times.

Peacock sipped his wine and watched as bright cars flashed

136

pell-mell around the circle next to him. He idly wondered how Italian drivers ever reached their 30th birthdays. What was it he'd heard about Italian drivers and stop lights? Green meant go and red was just a suggestion?

He chuckled and drank some more wine as one car in particular caught his attention. Then he sat forward a little. The damn thing was veritably skidding around the circle on two wheels.

Crazy jerk, Peacock thought. *He's going to run someone over.*

Now it was slowing down and pulling over to the curb nearby. As it did so, Peacock raised his eyebrows, genuinely intrigued to see who was behind the reckless driving. When the sedan was next to him, Peacock noticed the man in the driver's seat looked familiar. In a flash of recollection that nearly made his heart freeze in his chest, he recognized the figure.

It was the same person who stalked him through the streets of Jerusalem.

But what Peacock saw next was even worse.

The man had a pistol in his hand.

And it was pointed at him.

To his horror, as cars honked and whipped through the piazza beyond, the man opened fire. Peacock reacted instinctively, his military training kicking in. He dove under the table as more shots rang out. Dishware shattered on the table above. Vermilion liquid dribbled down the white tablecloth, his wine bottle destroyed. People seated nearby screamed.

Peacock, through a blur of running feet and chaos, managed to scramble his way between a half dozen outdoor tables, some now overturned, and shove his way through the restaurant's glass double doors.

Just as he did so, a bullet shattered one of the doors. Peacock ducked, tripped, and landed hard over a small, empty table. He found his feet and, staying low, dashed through the restaurant, and out the service entrance and into the alleyway.

Waiters and cooks were already running hard through the

alley, and Peacock thought that was a damn good idea. Just as he was about to do the same, a black sedan burst into the alleyway and blocked his escape.

Shit.

The window to the sedan rolled smoothly down. An elderly man's face appeared in the window, someone Peacock had never seen before.

"Get in if you want to live," yelled the man calmly.

Peacock looked down the blocked alley. More screams echoed from the front of the building.

"Get in before he comes back," said the old man, opening the door. "Final offer."

Regretting his decision almost immediately, Peacock dove into the sedan and pulled the door shut behind him. The vehicle sped off down the narrow alley as if a host of devils were after it.

"What the hell is going on?" asked Peacock.

The old man looked calmly at him sideways. "That remains to be seen, my friend."

"Who the hell *are* you?"

"My name's Nash," said the man. "But you can call me Zed."

"Look at that," said Tom, pointing to the white-tiled dome that loomed in front of them as they drove past the Israeli Knesset and towards the Israel Museum. "Looks like a giant Hershey's Kiss."

Despite himself, and despite the perilous situation he had found himself in, Nash laughed. He liked Tom. The FBI agent had a way of putting things in simple, inelegant terms.

Sort of like my sister, thought Nash. *No wonder they are in love.*

"That's the Shrine of the Book building," said Roth. "The dome you see covers the Shrine, most of which is located two-thirds below the ground. The roof was made to look like the lid of the first jar in which the Dead Sea Scrolls were found."

"I guess it's a good thing it wasn't found in a peanut butter jar," said Tom.

Nash groaned. Everyone else ignored the FBI agent.

As they got closer to the structure, Nash asked, "What's that black wall opposite the Shrine?"

"The contrast between the wall of black stone and the white-tiled Shrine represents the dualism of the scrolls," Roth replied. "The war of the children of light against the children of darkness."

Sabra's Land Rover pulled up to the entrance of the shrine, and Nash and Tom helped Roth out and into his wheelchair.

"You all know what to do," Roth said. "Give me about fifteen minutes to locate the scroll, then do what we planned to get me out with it."

Nash nodded with the others. He wondered if their stomachs

were as knotted with nerves as his own. He watched as the old man rolled his way toward the building.

Nash idly wondered if anyone had an antacid.

Stanton Roth was excited. God, he loved a good adventure, and this, he had to admit, was far more than he ever bargained for.

As he rolled his wheelchair toward the entrance, he could see the building was closed for visitations.

Boldness, Roth knew, was the best strategy here.

Above and to his right, a security camera turned toward him. Roth smiled and waved to them as he slipped Mishka's passkey from his pocket and swiped it through the security device. When it asked for his PIN, he typed in the one given to him by Mishka.

The doors clicked open, and he pushed through into the main corridor. Roth knew that the fragility of the scrolls made it impossible to display them on a continuous basis, so a system of scroll rotation was developed. After a scroll had been exhibited for three to six months, it was removed from its showcase and placed in a special storeroom where it was given a sort of rest from exposure.

This storeroom was his target. There, he knew, he would find the Cave 12 Scroll.

Roth passed beneath a display in the center of the room designed to look like the massive end of a scroll handle. Wrapped around it was a reproduction of the great Isaiah Scroll found in Qumran Cave One. Fragments of other scrolls were displayed around the wall of the museum.

He exited the room, found a side hall, and worked his way toward the storeroom. He knew the Cave 12 Scroll would not be in the regular inventory. Mishka, God bless her soul, had given him detailed instructions on how to find it. Once there, he used Mishka's passkey and entered the bitingly cold room.

He wasn't alone, as he knew he wouldn't be.

There were three researchers leaning over long tables, inspecting several scrolls. One researcher, who was taking notes in longhand, looked up, frowning. Roth simply smiled and did his best to pretend he belonged there.

Which he had, of course, many years ago.

A lifetime ago, he thought.

He casually rolled towards the far side of the storeroom where Mishka said the Cave 12 Scroll would be stored. There he found the hermetically sealed cabinet he was looking for and opened it. He carefully removed the contents.

On his lap was a 30x15-inch glass and metal reinforced case.

And in it was the scroll.

Despite himself, Roth's heart pounded a little harder, and his mouth felt a little dryer.

Jesus, I'm going to have a heart attack over a damn scroll?

But it wasn't just any old scroll, was it?

No. It was the Cave 12 Scroll.

As Mishka said, there wasn't much to look at. The thing inside the case was torn and faded and looked much worse off than the scrolls he had studied years ago. He tried to read the writing, but it was too fine and faded.

A voice inside his head instinctively warned—*Read it later. Get the hell out of here.*

And so he did. Or tried to. He rolled over and placed the scroll on a nearby worktable and waited for Sabra to work her magic.

"Are you two ready?" asked Sabra.

Nash and Tom nodded obediently.

"Then let's do this," she said. She led the way to the front door of the building with the two Americans following. Nash, admittedly, did not mind following behind her. Sweet Jesus she was a sexy woman.

At the door, she flashed her Mossad ID at the camera above

her head, and a voice, filled with static, came over a speaker to her right. "Your purpose?"

"We have to evacuate the building," she said, raising her voice an octave or two. "We have a bomb threat."

There was a moment of silence, followed by some more crackling, and then the voice said, "I'll be right down."

Sabra looked casually over at Nash. "Nervous?" she asked.

"A little," he admitted. "Do you think we'll get away with this?"

"We'll soon see," she said as the front door opened and a well-dressed security guard in a pressed uniform and sporting a neat goatee appeared in the doorway.

"We have to evacuate the building," said the Mossad agent firmly. "We have a credible threat, and my team here will help you clear the premises."

Nash tried to look as intimidating as possible but wasn't sure he reached the desired affect.

The security guard pulled on his goatee, and Nash could see he was mulling it over. "I need to contact my superiors—"

"No time for that," stated Sabra irritably. "Stand aside and let us through. People's lives could be at stake."

The security guard looked over his shoulder, then back to Sabra, and finally nodded reluctantly. "Okay. Do what you must do. But I'll have to inform my supervisor."

Sabra ignored the comment and pushed past the suddenly sweating security guard. Once inside, she turned to the man and said, "Quickly, gather your people while we go through the building and clear the area of personnel."

"But what about the bomb?" asked the guard.

"The bomb squad is on their way here now."

Jesus, I'm in some deep shit, thought Nash. This whole thing seemed to be spiraling out of control. But Sabra never once blinked an eye or faltered from her story. She seemed so believable that Nash had to remind himself she was lying through her teeth and that he really didn't work for the Mossad.

She is an artist. A con artist. Nash had heard somewhere that spies were gifted with bold face lying. This was living proof.

Sabra did not wait for a response. She led the way through the glass foyer and into a side hallway. Nash knew this hallway would lead to their target—a nondescript storeroom.

"I'll go with the guard," said Tom to Sabra, which caused Nash to stop short. That wasn't part of the plan.

Sabra didn't blink an eye. "Why?" she asked, snapping off the question as the three of them pounded down the hallway.

"Might not be a bad idea to make sure no one in security is left behind," he replied.

Sabra looked at him briefly, nodded once, and then said, "Go."

Tom peeled away and headed back to the entrance.

Within seconds, Nash and Sabra were in the storeroom, where the Mossad agent commanded those within to immediately clear the building. The researchers blinked, looking at each other. Sabra held up her credentials and barked the orders again, and the room immediately cleared.

Roth, of course, lingered behind.

When the others were gone and the cold room was clear, Sabra pounced on Roth, "Did you get it?"

He nodded holding up the scroll container. "Now let's get the hell out of here."

As they worked their way through the quiet halls, Nash heard footsteps running toward them from around a corner.

Ah, shit. Here it comes.

He waited for what he was sure would be the police, here to arrest them all. The sound of echoing footsteps grew louder. Nash braced himself, and from around the corner appeared the FBI agent. Tom was out of breath.

"We gotta go," he said, sucking wind. "The police are coming. The guard's supervisor didn't buy our story. He checked with the police, and they said they knew nothing about a bomb threat."

"Damn! Let's move," said Sabra.

Nash took hold of the handles of Roth's wheelchair, and now the group was really moving. They rounded a corner and saw a group of confused scientists milling about outside the shrine. A different guard appeared from a small room just inside the entrance.

"Hey!" he shouted.

"Move, move!" ordered Sabra, and the four of them burst from the building and into the waning light. At the Rover, with footsteps sounding behind them, Nash grabbed the scroll from Roth and nearly threw the old man into the back of the vehicle. Nash left the wheelchair where it lay. He slipped into the passenger side while Sabra slid into the driver's seat and laid rubber, exiting the parking lot.

Nash's heart had never beat so hard in his life. In fact, he was certain he was only minutes—or seconds—from a heart attack.

"Anyone following us?" said Sabra calmly.

How could she be so calm at a time like this? Nash had no clue.

Tom looked back. "No. No one. And I don't hear any sirens, either."

"We may just get lucky," she breathed.

"But we can't go to the clean room," declared Tom. "I'll bet there's an APB on this Rover as we speak. We'll never get out of Jerusalem."

"He's right," said Roth. "Go straight to the airport, Sabra. We have to scratch the clean room and leave on my plane."

Following Roth's logic, the Mossad agent turned onto the main thoroughfare and, while Nash's heart returned to something close to normal, they hit trouble.

"Ah, hell," Sabra spat.

"What?" said Nash, wondering just how much more stress he could take.

She pointed up the road. "An IDF check point."

"That wasn't there on our way here," Nash cried.

"They like to do unannounced inspections," Sabra replied, perhaps a little too casually for Nash's liking.

"If they find the scroll—" Roth said.

"We're fucked," said Tom.

They pulled up behind the line of cars being searched at the checkpoint. A few moments later, another car pulled in behind them. "We're third in line. Anyone have any ideas?" asked the female agent.

Nash was about to speak when he saw the last thing he wanted to see in the side mirror. Flashing lights. A siren wailed.

"You have to go around the check point," Roth advised.

"Can't," said Sabra. "We're boxed in now, cars blocking all sides."

What Nash saw next froze him to his core. In the rearview mirror, the police had exited the cruiser and were now walking toward them, with guns drawn.

"Oh, shit!"

Sabra saw the police, as well. She reached across Nash's lap, flipped open the glove box, and removed a very narrow and sleek-looking handgun. Even Nash knew what it was. A Walther, the weapon of choice for Mossad agents.

Nash wasn't a religious man by any stretch of the imagination, but he found himself praying, and hard. As his mind fumbled through the Lord's Prayer, a series of events transpired that Nash would never forget.

First a man leaped out of the car next to him, shouting something in Arabic. To Nash, it sounded like "Allah Akbar!"

And now he was running through the maze of cars, weaving in and out. Transfixed by the running figure, Nash forgot about the police. In fact, he was sure the police had forgotten about them, too. Someone shouted at the running man. Guards at the checkpoint drew their weapons.

Good God, they're going to shoot him...

But they didn't have a clear shot. The man, dressed in shabby slacks and a light baggy coat, kept between the cars.

And when he was near the checkpoint he stopped suddenly. Reached inside his jacket.

And detonated himself.

Pieces of metal from vehicles in front and other parts of things that Nash didn't want to think of flew in their direction.

With the checkpoint in utter chaos, Sabra navigated her way around the destruction. Nash could hardly believe what he had seen. Cars in flaming pieces. Bloody pieces of body parts everywhere. He was literally sick to his stomach and horrified.

And as the Rover picked up speed, heading toward Roth's private plane, Nash rolled his side window down, thrust his head outside, and let the hot wind hit his retching face.

Monday
10:46 PM GMT
Rome, Italy

Zed Nash brought Douglas Peacock to a small one-room apartment off the Stazione Termini, the main train station. The area was polluted with gas fumes from the myriad of buses and cars coming and going from the station. But the apartment suited Zed's purposes perfectly well. He needed to live as inconspicuously as possible, and this afforded him the privacy he needed.

Once inside his apartment, Zed pushed aside an old stack of newspapers. He cleared a seat for Peacock, who was, admittedly, still freaked out by all the strange events that had just transpired. Zed offered Peacock something to drink.

"No, thank you," said the jittery man. "But I would like some information."

Zed ignored the question. "Then I hope you don't mind if I make myself some coffee."

Zed stepped out of the room and into a filthy kitchen. Peacock followed behind. The older man—who was easily in his early 80s and sported a full head of untamed gray hair—rummaged through a sink dirty enough to turn Peacock's hardened stomach.

"Look here," said the archaeologist. "I'd still like to know who you are and why you were there?"

"I was there to save your ass," said the man casually, not looking at Peacock. "As to who I am, well, we'll get to that."

Zed poured some thick looking coffee and powdered milk into an old brown coffee mug and slowly stirred the contents. As he did so, he looked sideways at the sweating man.

"Sit down," he said. "This might take a while."

Peacock sat on a dusty kitchen chair, swiping at it absently as he did so. Zed leaned a bony hip against the counter and watched him with some amusement.

"I've been observing you all day," said the old man, sipping his coffee. "Did you have any luck at the Vatican Information Service?"

"No. I didn't. But—"

"Thought you did."

"Wait. Why?"

"Because Vadja tried to kill you."

"Vadja?" said Peacock. "Is that the guy who's been stalking me?"

"You've seen him before?" asked Zed, raising his crazy eyebrows.

"Yes. He followed me when I was in Rome doing research on the tomb in the Church of the Holy Sepulcher."

"Ah! That explains it," said Zed. "You put your nose where it didn't belong, my friend. And now someone wants you dead."

Peacock felt the blood drain from his face. A little coffee suddenly didn't sound bad. As if reading his mind, Zed stood, washed out what Peacock could only hope was a clean mug, and poured some more coffee. He handed the steaming mug to the American.

"I'm not sure I understand," Peacock faltered.

"If you value your life, my friend, listen closely, because you very much *need* to understand."

"Go on."

"There's something in that tomb that someone doesn't want you to find."

What that something could be was far less important to Peacock than who wanted to kill him. "Someone, as in Section Eighteen?"

Zed nearly choked on his coffee. "How do you know about Section Eighteen?"

"It was mentioned in a diary that Jeremy Nash..." Peacock stopped when the realization hit him. "Are you related to Jeremy Nash?"

Zed lowered his cup to the counter with a clang. Some of the contents splashed over the rim and scalded the back of his hand. He ignored the pain. He also ignored Peacock's question. Zed's voice lowered as if speaking to himself. "Jeremy found Roth. They broke the code! Son of a bitch."

"You know Stanton Roth?"

Zed smiled. "I gave Stanton my diary to hold. Jeremy is my grandson."

"Then you know about your granddaughter?"

Zed snapped his head around and focused on the little man sitting uncomfortably in his kitchen. "What about Alyson?"

"I'm sorry to say that she was kidnapped by some religious cultists, some freaks if you ask me. If your grandson doesn't give them the diary, she's going to be killed."

Zed's eyes narrowed, bringing his bushy eyebrows together to form one long line. After a moment of silence, he asked, "Where's Jeremy now?"

"I don't know. I tried to reach my colleague who is with him, but I couldn't get through this afternoon." Peacock picked up his cell phone. "Let me try again."

"No," said Zed urgently. "No phone calls. No contact whatsoever."

Peacock put the phone down. "Then how do you plan to find your grandson?"

"If Jeremy broke the code in the diary, the knowledge of Section Eighteen will lead him here. To me."

"But if he gives the diary to the cultists in exchange for your granddaughter—"

"Jeremy is a smart boy," Zed replied. "Sometimes too smart for his own good. He'll figure something out."

Peacock stared into his coffee. "You said you knew this Vadja. Who is he?"

"He's Majestic's hired assassin. He works for the Intermarium. He makes sure no one gets anywhere near the truth of the tomb. He's quite a monster—a cold blooded killer."

Peacock's stomach turned sour and his bowels turned to something close to water. *Jesus. A hired assassin. A monster. I'm an archaeologist. This spy shit isn't supposed to be happening to me.* He swallowed hard, tried to talk, paused, then tried again.

"What's the Intermarium?" he finally asked.

"Originally it was a tool of Western Intelligence behind the Iron Curtain coordinating spying to aide the fight in the Cold War. Today, it's a pay-for-hire assassination organization."

Peacock's stomach sank again. "So just what is Section Eighteen?"

"US Air Force Intelligence," replied Zed quickly.

Peacock realized the old man's mind worked fast, and he spoke even faster. "Air Force Intelligence? I don't understand. What do they have to do with the Church of the Holy Sepulcher?"

"You won't understand," Zed answered, "until you see for yourself."

Peacock had a bad headache, and these stupid puzzle games were making it worse. Granted, the thought of a hired killer didn't help the pain behind his eyes.

"Okay, fine," he said, and decided to get back to the subject at hand. "I need to find a man named Phillip Marcus. Do you know him?"

"Yes," said Zed, bristling slightly. The name always had that effect on him. A bastard if he had ever met one. "He runs MAJIK at Section Eighteen."

"Magic?" Peacock replied. "Like rabbits in a hat?"

"No. Spelled M-A-J-I-K. An acronym for Majestic. A committee of twelve scientists, military leaders, and government officials formed in nineteen forty-seven by an executive order of U.S. President Truman. The purpose was to investigate UFO activity in the aftermath of the Roswell incident."

"UFOs?"

"Yes."

Peacock's head was spinning. "What's this got to do with anything?"

Zed smiled and thought about how much he wanted to reveal. After a moment, he shrugged and thought, *what the hell.* "I was one of the original twelve members. I was known as MJ-Twelve. MJ-Eleven, a good man named Henderson, was recently murdered. All the rest are dead except for Marcus who's MJ-One. He and I are the last of the original committee."

"And why was Henderson murdered?"

"He wanted to come clean with the truth—about everything," said Zed in his typical, rapid-fire exchange. "So Air Force Intelligence promptly committed him to a mental ward at Walter Reed Hospital—like they did to me." A devious smile crossed his face. "But I outsmarted them and escaped." Zed sipped some coffee, glancing at Peacock. "Vadja killed Henderson. I know it. And now the bastard's after me. And, from all appearance, he's after you, too. Marcus is certainly making sure no one reveals the truth."

"The truth of what? A UFO cover-up?"

"You're half right," said Zed, knocking back the rest of his coffee and looking over at Peacock with a mischievous grin. "The UFO story *was* the cover up."

Tuesday
9:00 AM GMT
London, England

As soon as Roth's plane landed in London, they headed for the clean room of Roth's mansion.

Roth laid the scroll in its protective glass case on a table brightly lit by fluorescent lights in the ceiling. He positioned a magnifying instrument similar to the ones used by jewelers to make jewelry repairs over the sheepskin parchment and turned on its soft light.

Roth proceeded to read the inscriptions on the scroll while the others waited impatiently.

After a few minutes, Sabra asked anxiously, "What does it say? Does it say anything about the Second Coming?"

Roth hushed them and continued to read the Hebrew on the tattered scroll. "Please. It's difficult enough reading this faded print."

Tom paced. Sabra waited with stoic patience. Nash found himself tapping his fingers on the leather arm of his sitting chair.

After a few minutes, Roth finally looked up. "Nothing here about Christ's return, the Apocalypse, Armageddon, or anything remotely connected to the Second Coming. Only a reference to the year 2012."

"Then this whole thing was a wild goose chase," cried Nash in frustration. "I'm going to contact Tucker and tell him we have what he wants, as worthless as it is. I'm getting my sister back."

"Hold on, Jeremy," Roth said. "Let's think this through. There still may be something here. When we were doing research on the scrolls years ago, one of the researchers discovered that some of the scrolls had been used before and that there were actually writings *under* the text."

"You mean someone had overwritten on the original sheep skin parchment?" said Sabra.

"Correct," Roth replied. "They found that by using infrared X-rays they could recover the invisible words on the parchment."

"And I suppose you have such a device?"

Roth looked over his left shoulder at a machine sitting against the wall. "That, Mr. Nash, is an infrared X-ray machine. In my business, any good clean room has one. Now, roll that over here."

Nash did as he was told, rolling the long contraption over. Roth positioned the device and slowly worked the scanner back and forth over the scroll. At each pass, line after line of hidden Hebrew text appeared on a small screen attached to the scanner.

"Now we're getting somewhere!" Roth said with glee. He studied the text, stopped at one phrase and nodded. "This is it! The script talks about the sacrifice of the Messiah, his death and resurrection," he paused and looked up at the group, "and his imminent return."

"Is there a date?" asked Nash.

Roth read some more, rapidly scanning the text that had once lay hidden. "Let's see...yes! Here it is 5707."

"Well, we've got some time, then," Tom said wryly.

"Actually," said Nash. "That would be a year in the Hebrew calendar."

"You get a gold star!" Roth was pleased. "Now let's translate that into a Gregorian year." Roth rolled himself over to a laptop on another table, typed in the Hebrew date and read the results. He turned to the group and looked very confused.

"What's wrong?" asked Sabra.

"Yes. What's the year?" echoed Nash.

"Nineteen forty-seven," Roth said sheepishly.

"Christ came back in nineteen forty-seven?" said Tom skeptically.

"That's what it says," said Roth.

"So, the Second Coming has already occurred? Damn—and I missed it."

"You didn't miss anything, Tom," said Nash. "This is clearly a joke. A fraud, and my sister's life is on the line. I've got to tell you guys, I'm pissed as hell."

Roth continued to look befuddled. "Maybe there's a mistake in the translation—"

Nash fired back. "The only mistake here is that we waited this long to get my sister back. I'm going to the chat room and let Tucker know I have what he wants."

He exited the clean room without looking back, and if the door hadn't been hermetically sealed, it would have slammed shut behind him. He *wanted* it to slam shut behind him.

God dam hermetically sealed door, he swore.

Tuesday
10:55 AM GMT
Rome, Italy

"Here we are," said Zed, as they walked from the bus station into the Piazza del Gesu in the middle of Rome.

"This?" Peacock said in disbelief. "This is where Section Eighteen is?"

Zed pointed to a pre-baroque structure in front of them. "The Church of the Gesu. The Church of the Holy Name of Jesus. The mother church of the Society of Jesus."

Peacock knew his history. "You're telling me that the Jesuits are connected to Section Eighteen? *Absolutely unbelievable!*"

"Come on," said Zed excitedly. "Let's get out of the open. There's a café across the street from the Church. We'll go there."

Peacock liked that idea. Suddenly, being in clear sight these days seemed like a very bad idea. Hell, just being *alone* seemed like a bad idea, especially with Vadja out there somewhere.

A few moments later, after sliding into a booth at the rear of the café, Zed commented, "This is where I come nearly every day."

Great, thought Peacock glumly, looking over his shoulder. *Good thing we're sticking to routine. Shouldn't be hard to find at all, especially for a trained killer.*

Zed got the attention of the waiter. "A cappuccino for me and..."

"Nothing for me," said Peacock, who wondered again if he was dealing with someone a sandwich short of a full picnic.

"What kind of research were you doing at the church's tomb?" Zed asked suddenly.

"Roth and I are trying to prove a Shroud theory."

"Ah, yes. I remember Roth talking about that. So you believe that Christ *didn't* die on the cross?"

"The markings on the shroud prove it," said Peacock, easing comfortably into a familiar subject—the first time he'd felt comfortable in many hours. "Jesus lived a long life, died, and was buried like a normal man."

"In the tomb of the Church of the Holy Sepulcher," said Zed, with a bemused expression on his wrinkled face.

"Well, yes. That's what we're attempting to prove."

"Don't look so defensive," said Zed jovially. "You and Stanton happen to be right. Jesus *is*, indeed, buried there."

Peacock's heart reacted in a strange way. It thumped once. Hard. Carefully, he pressed, "What do you know, Zed?"

The old man's face broke into a strange grin. "Jesus died, was resurrected, and came back."

"Came back? I don't understand. If he came back, why is his body in the tomb?"

"That I can't tell you. Even if I did—"

"Yeah, yeah. I wouldn't believe you. I get it. We've been over this territory before."

"I can tell you this, though," confided Zed. "I was there in nineteen forty-seven with Air Force Intelligence. I *saw* the remains in the high desert outside Roswell. I recorded it in my diary. The proof is under the Church of the Gesu, right here in Rome."

Peacock found his head shaking as if on its own accord. *Good God, the old man is mad. Isn't he?* Peacock looked at the old man again, studying the man's surprisingly calm, bemused expression. *Mad, right?*

Peacock wasn't so sure. "What do you mean, exactly?" he asked.

"In the early nineteen fifties the Air Force, in partnership with certain elements of the Catholic Church, constructed an underground bunker beneath the church and moved what was found in the high desert into it."

Yeah, the guy was nuts. Peacock was now sure of it. No, he was damn sure of it. Still, might as well humor the old bag of bones, right? He had nothing better to do, other than wait for a strangely misshapen assassin to find him. "And by *certain elements*," Peacock questioned, "you mean the Jesuits?"

"Correct. The Jesuits, or, as some call them, the high protectors of the Christian Church. When the Air Force discovered what had truly happened in the desert, they made some discreet inquiries and were put into contact with the Jesuits." Zed paused, his eyes twinkling. "And who do you think made those discreet inquiries?"

"Phillip Marcus."

"Good guess. You put two and two together."

"So, where's the entrance to this bunker?" asked Peacock.

"It's through an obscurer door that leads to the basement behind and below the adjacent rooms in which St. Ignatius—the founder of the Jesuits—penned their Constitutions and the letters that implemented them. There, down a flight of stairs, is the office of Centro Astalli, a work of the Jesuit Refugee Service." Zed paused and smiled. "Do you see the connection, my new friend?"

Outside, a car skidded to a stop. Peacock's head snapped around, and, with his heart somewhere near his throat, he turned in time to see a young man emerge from a cab.

"Well?" said Zed, nonplussed.

"Well, what?" said Peacock, forcibly calming himself down. James Bond he was not. Hell, Indiana Jones he was not, either.

"The connection. Do you see the connection?"

"Oh, right. Ah, no."

"The Intermarium was originally set up to smuggle people out of Europe. The Jesuit Refugee Service is the inheritor of that process. Do you see now?"

"Okay, fine. So why are we here?"

"We're getting in. Or breaking in. However you want to look at it."

"Breaking into what?"

"The church. The bunker."

"Oh, no!"

"Oh, yes, my friend!" said Zed, steamrolling him and leaning forward on his elbows, his cappuccino completely forgotten now. "I've been looking for a way to get into that church and down to the bunker. But, of course, that's impossible through the Jesuit Refugee Service office. But there *is* another way."

Peacock was still shaking his head, but the old man chose to completely ignore him and rambled on.

"When the bunker was being built, the builders themselves couldn't do the excavation right there in broad daylight. It would have drawn too much attention, and, of course, they would have needed to apply for all kinds of permits and such—all of which would have drawn even more attention."

"So, what did they do?" Peacock heard himself asking.

"There are little-known catacombs a hundred yards or so down from the Church itself. The builders tunneled under the Church through these catacombs and ultimately built the secret bunker. Right there beneath the church."

"Jesus," Peacock exclaimed.

"Exactly," said Zed, winking. "Now, I can't get permission to enter the catacomb. But you, as a professional archaeologist, can. And once in, we can find our way to Section Eighteen."

"We?"

"Of course we." Zed paused, picked up his cappuccino and took a long sip. "So—are you game?"

"What's in it for me?"

"You get to find Marcus."

"And what's in it for you?"

Zed's grin faded. "That, my friend, is none of your business."

Peacock knew better than to hitch his wagon to this ass, but he also had a job to do, even if it meant lurking in ancient catacombs. He sighed and nodded. Zed clapped and stood abruptly.

"Come. We have work to do."

Tuesday
11:57 AM GMT
London, England

It was almost noon, and Tucker had not yet entered the chat room. Jeremy knew he shouldn't tell Tucker about the false date of the Second Coming. He didn't want to blow the opportunity to get his sister back.

He leaned back in his chair and looked at the copy of the Shroud hanging on the wall. So, Roth said Jesus didn't die on the cross? *Next,* he thought, *Roth will be telling me that he got married and had kids.*

He was shaken from his reverie when a short piece of text appeared on the computer screen before him.

DO YOU HAVE THE SCROLL?

Nash typed back:

YES.

DID YOU GET THE DATE OF OUR LORD'S RETURN?

Nash stared at the written request on his screen for a brief while before answering. He feared—really feared—that if he told Tucker the truth, he might very well never see his sister again. So, thinking hard, he replied.

YES.

Nash could only imagine the anticipation on the other end. After a moment's delay, came the words:

THE DATE?

I'll bluff, Nash thought. *I'm holding the cards right now, right?*

YOU CAN READ THE DATE YOURSELF

159

WHEN I SEE MY SISTER.

Nash held his breath and hoped his ploy would work. A long minute later—too long—and he got a response:

GO TO THE INTERNET CAFE IN JERU-SALEM ON JAFFA ROAD ACROSS FROM THE NEW CENTRAL BUS STATION—AND ENTER THIS CHAT ROOM FOR FURTHER INSTRUCTIONS. NO ONE BUT YOU.

Nash exhaled. His ploy worked. It was time to go. He snapped shut the laptop and got up to find Roth as Tom entered the room.

"Did you make contact?" asked the federal agent.

"Yes. I have the instructions. We're going back to Jerusalem. Where's Roth?"

"In the kitchen making more tea."

Nash, feeling more optimistic than he had in many days, clapped the G-man on the shoulder. "We're getting her back. Get ready to leave."

When Nash left the room, Tom pulled out his secure cellphone, logged onto the internet, and entered the URL of a virtual private network. A few second later, his screen came up with *Server Not Found. Try Again.*

"What the hell?"

He entered the URL again. Same response. He tried once more and his screen asked for a user name and password. Once in, he started to type a message...

As Sabra slept in the seat across from him, Tom looked out the plane's window and saw the majestic sweep of the Mediterranean coastline pass below. Ahead, the Israeli coastline was coming into view. This was his queue.

He got up and walked into the pilot's cabin where Nash and Roth were flying the plane. "How much longer?" he asked Roth.

"About ten minutes," said Roth. "Please inform Sabra to get ready."

Tom grinned. "You got it, boss."

He turned and reentered the cabin just as Sabra was stirring, no doubt awakened by the grind of the engines powering down. "Are we there yet?" she asked, gently yawning and stretching languidly.

Tom caught himself staring at her lithe form.

Focus, he chastised himself. "We'll be landing in ten minutes," he said.

"Then I'm going into the back and freshen up," she said.

As she walked towards the restroom, Tom came up behind her, pulling out his pistol. She scratched her head, oblivious to his presence. He hesitated just a moment, then brought it down hard across the back of her head. He caught her before she hit the floor and dumped her unceremoniously onto a cushioned chair. A streak of blood from the back of her head smeared on the leather.

He didn't care. He had a job to do.

Working his way back to the pilot's cabin, Tom opened the

door with a bang. Both Nash and Roth whipped their heads around.

"You'd better sit down, Tom," said Roth. "We'll be landing in Jerusalem soon."

"I'm afraid that's not going to happen."

The agent lowered the gun and grinned.

Nash was having a hard time comprehending what he was seeing. Was that an actual gun in Tom's hand? Nash blinked hard, certain he was seeing things.

Roth spoke first. "I don't understand, Tom."

"We're not going to Jerusalem, Mr. Roth," said Tom. "We're going to Tel Aviv. Do you understand?"

"What do you mean..." Roth was stopped in mid-sentence when he felt the end of the cold hard gun barrel of the gun pressed against his neck.

"What the hell is going on, Tom?" barked Nash, rising.

The small weapon swung over immediately. The FBI man pointed it straight at Nash's forehead.

"Sit down, my friend," said Tom, lowering his voice. "Or I will kill you."

Nash was stunned. The tall man, a man Nash had seriously thought would be family, suddenly appeared far different. His face seemed shadowed, darker. His voice was different, too. Ominous. Threatening. He was not the same man Nash had come to know. Or *thought* he had come to know.

"I still don't understand," faltered Roth, stumbling over his words. "What's this all about?"

"It's about sticking your nose where it doesn't belong, old man," said Tom. "It's about watching and waiting for the time your grandfather would somehow contact you or your sister, Nash, and lead us to the diary."

"The FBI wants the diary?" asked Nash. None of this was making sense. And why the hell was Tom holding a gun on him?

"Close," said Tom, grinning widely. "Air Force Intelligence."

And then one thing became very clear to Nash. "So, you've been lying all along to my sister."

"Don't be so naive, Nash. In my business, lying is a given. Or, as we prefer to call it, misinformation."

"Fine," said Nash, and then he had another thought. A very troubling thought. "What did you do with Sabra?"

"Sabra's fine, although she will have quite a headache in the morning."

"So, she's not working with you?"

"You ask a lot of questions, old boy. No, she and I are not working together, and we are most certainly not working with Mossad."

Unless that's more misinformation, thought Nash. His brain was having trouble turning all this over. Thinking straight with a gun pointed at his face was damn near impossible. "Last question. Are you working with the same people who kidnapped my sister?"

"No," said Tom. "But we're after the same thing."

"The diary," said Roth.

"Yes. And now the scroll, too." Tom bent down and looked ahead through the plane's windshield. "Now turn this plane towards Tel Aviv. I have my instructions, and if you both want to live, I suggest—"

"Hang on, Jeremy!" shouted Roth.

And that's when the old man, to Nash's utter shock, yanked hard on the controls, pulling them in toward his stomach. The plane reacted instantly and, like a roller coaster ride from hell, began a steep climb up. Nash held on to his own controls and the crash he heard behind him was, on quick inspection, Tom slamming hard into the cabin's closed door.

The agent promptly dropped his weapon, which skidded into the far corner.

Roth shoved the controls back into place. The plane leveled, and now Nash was moving.

He heaved himself out of his seat, and, still a bit queasy from the aerial acrobatics, lunged for the weapon. Tom, shaking his head, did the same.

The agent beat Nash to it.

Shit.

Scrambling, Tom turned and fired blindly. The bullet ripped through the armpit of Nash's jacket—or, at least, Nash hoped it was through his jacket.

Either way, the plane suddenly nose-dived, throwing Nash forward into the controls, where he ricocheted and found himself on top of the intelligence agent.

Instinct took over, and Nash fought like a cornered hellcat. Tom was strong, so it was to Nash's supreme relief that he soon discovered he had the agent's gun hand pinned to the floor. Nash slammed the hand down repeatedly until the gun came loose. It scuttled somewhere along the floor under the controls.

"If you want to live, old boy," said Tom, breathing raggedly into Nash's ear, "then I would suggest you let me go and see to the plane."

Nash stared into the man's bloodshot eyes—briefly wondering what his sister had seen in the man—and realized with horror that the plane was still plummeting. He whipped his head around—

And saw Roth slumped over the controls, bleeding profusely from a massive head wound.

"Stanton!"

Nash scrambled his way back into his seat. He was briefly aware that the federal agent had navigated his way out of the cockpit, leaving Nash alone to regain control of the plunging jet.

Tom clawed his way over the unconscious body of Sabra, grabbed the diary and thrust it into his pocket. He gave a quick look around for the scroll but couldn't see it. He put on the parachute he had set aside without notice during the flight and cracked open the rear exit. He had no time to locate the scroll. A blast of air almost swept him off his feet as he tried to hold his balance in the plummeting jet. Without looking back and without hesitation, he dove into the sky.

Nash was sweating profusely. Next to him, hunched over the side arm of the pilot seat, was a very dead Stanton Roth.

Focus, Jeremy!

Nash did his best to ignore the sticky blood covering much of the cockpit panel and pulled hard on the controls.

Shit, he thought. *We're all over the goddamn sky. And the ground is coming up fast. Too fast!*

Nash looked at the altimeter—1000 feet, 900 feet, 800 feet.

Shit! Got to level this beast off!

500 feet—

The controls shook in his hand. The ground rose rapidly. The whole plane seemed to shudder, and Nash had a horrible image of the wings themselves being shorn off.

300 feet!

Nash could make out minute details of the approaching ground. They were coming up on a thicket of trees and brush.

And then the plane nosed up ever so slightly.

She's starting to respond. She's starting to respond!

And at 100 feet, the speeding jet finally leveled off. Nash wanted to shout for joy, but—

Gotta slow her down!

He yanked hard on the controls to approach stall speed, and he continued pulling even as the stall alarm screamed in his ears. Nash glanced at the air speed.

Jesus, we're gonna stall.

He pushed the controls forward and the lumbering jet finally leveled off.

Below and to the right was a dry wash. Nash tapped the rudder, brought the plane level and aimed it towards the flat earth.

He took a deep breath, held it, and after what felt like an eternity, the jet slammed into the powdery silt.

Tuesday
3:15 PM GMT
Tel Aviv, Israel

Tom landed safely on a wide swath of dirt and sand. He hid his parachute in a rocky chasm, procured transportation via a meandering flatbed truck filled with chickens, and made his way to Tel Aviv as instructed.

Once there, he opened his phone and logged into the secure site to report. Connection problems again—*server not found.*

What the hell is with this site the last few days? he thought.

He tried again, and this time connected. After reporting the details, his orders were confirmed, and he made his way to the agreed upon location, a street corner in downtown Tel Aviv. As of yet, there had been no news of a downed aircraft.

Nash must have pulled it off, he thought, shaking his head.

As he waited, a white non-descript van pulled up beside him and opened its side door. Tom turned to smile, but his confident demeanor turned to dread when he saw an automatic pistol pointed at his chest.

Tuesday
7:50 PM GMT
Jerusalem, Israel

Nash could hardly believe his eyes. The craft had finally stopped after slewing slightly to the side and shuddering so violently that he was certain it had rattled to pieces. To his shock, the cabin door was thrown open. He turned, expecting to find Tom there. Instead, it was the hunched figure of Sabra, holding her head and stumbling forward. Blood coated her hand.

"What the hell happened?" she gasped, stumbling. He rose quickly and caught her in his arms. He could smell the blood on her. Pulling a handkerchief from Roth's pocket he held it against Sabra's head.

As quickly as he could, he recounted the recent events. He concluded with Tom's apparent escape, since, as reported by Sabra, the side hatch was open. Sabra glanced over at Stanton Roth and grimaced.

"That son-of-a-bitch," said Sabra.

"Yes," hissed Nash. "I couldn't agree more. What do we do now?"

"Get what we need away from the plane."

They both left the cabin and scoured the craft. Nash, frustrated as hell, realized the diary was gone.

"But he left this," said Sabra, hefting the scroll, which had scuttled under some seats amid the turbulent landing.

"Thank God," breathed Nash.

"He probably couldn't find it in time," said the Mossad agent. The blood on her face had dried now, cracking noticeably where her cheeks moved.

"What should we do about Roth? Should we report him?"

"No," she replied. "We can do that later. Don't you have a rendezvous point in Jerusalem?"

Nash did, although his heart felt heavy leaving his dead friend behind, a friend his grandfather once knew.

Worry about the living, he thought. And that meant saving his sister.

Sabra held up Roth's satellite phone. "This might come in handy," she said.

Nash grabbed a bottle of water from his suitcase, and the two exited the plane into an empty, hushed land. Birds flew in formations overhead, and something scurried through the grass. A creature that was, no doubt, utterly confused by the sudden arrival of the giant metal behemoth.

Nash pointed behind them. "I thought I saw a small village just before we hit the wash. Should only be a mile or so back."

"Good," exclaimed Sabra, moving boldly forward. Nash was struck again by the woman's chutzpah, amazed and surprised by her courage. "We should be able to get transportation to Jerusalem from there," she added. She looked over her shoulder. "What are you waiting for, Jeremy? Come on."

Despite their circumstances, he grinned, and quickly caught up to her.

A hurried march to the village, a bus ride and a rental car later, Sabra and Nash found themselves sitting in the rental staring down the street at the assigned internet café.

"I want to alert my office," said Sabra, scanning the area and activating her cell, "and have a couple of agents go with you, Jeremy."

"I can't risk it," he said firmly. "Please. Just us."

She looked at him sideways, her eyes impossibly big. A little road dust glinted on her forehead.

What a hell of a day, he thought again, for the hundredth time.

He noted the lump at the back of her head where that bastard Tom had pistol whipped her. Nash found her strength remarkable. Never once had she complained of the pain, or even seemed to notice that huge goose egg on her head.

"Are you sure you don't want your head looked at?" he asked.

"No," she said immediately. "Forget my head, Jeremy. You're more worried about it than I am."

"Well, someone ought to look out for you."

She smiled at him oddly, as if his words had caught her off guard. *Maybe no one has looked out for her for a long time*, he thought. He sensed on some level that she operated alone, worked alone, and was probably often alone.

"Thanks for the sentiment, Jeremy, but we have a job to do. Speaking of which, we'll do it your way for now. But I'm going to follow you."

"From a discreet distance," said Nash. She nodded, and before he stepped out of the car, he almost—*almost*—leaned over and kissed her.

You're acting like a schoolboy with a crush, he thought. *Focus, Jeremy. You've got work to do.*

As he left the car, he was certain, judging by the way Sabra was watching him closely, that she had hoped for a kiss, too.

Focus, Jeremy!

Outside, he slung the scroll—secured in its black padded carrying case—over his shoulder and walked towards the café.

Once inside, he found an empty station by the front window and sat down at a terminal. He placed the scroll on the floor next to him, logged on, and went immediately to the chat room.

Tucker was waiting for him.

Nash expected the man to confirm he had both the diary and scroll. If Tucker did, Nash knew he had to lie.

Instead, Tucker's order was short and curt:

LEAVE THE CAFE THROUGH THE BACK
SERVICE ENTRANCE.

NOW.

Nash looked through the window of the café. He saw Sabra standing by a newsstand pretending to thumb through a magazine.

He signaled to her that he was heading towards the back of the café. She nodded.

Nash got up with the scroll, moved towards the rear of the café, and found an open screen door that led to an alley. He paused briefly, wondering if this was such a good idea. He took in some air, thought about his sister, and stepped outside into the heat. There were three men waiting for him.

One pointed a gun at him and nodded to a white van. Without a single word spoken, Nash went to the van and stepped inside. Two of the men followed him inside and slammed the door shut.

Sabra moved quickly across the street, through the café and exited the back of the building. She stepped through the service door just in time to see the white van pull away.

"Goddamn you, Nash," she said, and just as she uttered those words, a rag filled with chloroform covered her face. She struggled briefly, hitting someone hard in the face and groin, but the strong hands held firm, and soon she struggled no more.

Outside of the café, Vadja opened his cell phone and speed dialed a number. It was quickly answered.

"Yes, my son."

"They have them."

"Good. It's time for an anonymous phone call to Mossad."

Tuesday
9:47 PM GMT
Jerusalem, Israel

S abra awoke in a darkened, seemingly windowless room.

Lying on her side with her face against the cold concrete floor, she tried to focus her eyes in the dim light. Immediately, she felt a warm sensation on her face.

Warm water?

The liquid flowed down her forehead and into her right eye followed by a sudden burning sensation that jolted her up out of her stupor.

Salt?

She bolted upright and rubbed the salty liquid from her eye. And as she did so, she saw it. Above her, surrounded by strange looking artifacts, was a naked figure. A dead naked figure. Dripping blood.

The salt. My God! Blood!

Sabra found herself backing up on hands, crab-like. She wiped her mouth again, and this time she looked at the back of her hand. It was smeared with a thick swath of blood. And she was sure it wasn't her blood.

It was *his*.

She looked up again, in horror. Sabra was a trained spy and had seen firsthand many dead bodies. One couldn't be a Mossad agent and not witness and participate in the assassinations and torturing of enemy combatants.

Even with many vivid—and recent—memories of death and destruction fresh in her mind, little matched the macabre scene directly above her.

172

The room was dim, with little light. And she was certain that it was, indeed, a room. A large room. Her footfalls echoed around her as she scrambled backwards, away from the dripping corpse. The echo told her that she was, in fact, in an enclosed space. What light there was came through high windows. Sunlight. It was still daytime.

That same sunlight splashed across the figure hanging from the wall. Hanging, in fact, from a cross.

Crucified.

Oh, God.

The man's head hung on his chest. Blood flowed steadily from a crown of thorns that rested just above his brow. The skin of his forehead, she saw, was shredded down to his scalp. Dried blood was caked on his face and bare chest and down his thighs. The man wore only a soiled loincloth. His hands and feet were impaled into the wood with three rusted spikes, one each for his hands, and the third for his feet, which rested on top of each other down the center beam. Blood dripped from the spikes wounds. And, to her further horror, she saw a massive wound in the man's side.

As if he'd been stabbed with a spear, exactly like Christ.

My God!

Sabra was unaware that she had continued backing up until she bumped into what appeared to be a small wooden cot.

A hand dropped on her shoulder.

She cringed.

Her reflexes had always been fast. In fact, they were off the charts, a quality the Mossad sought. In a blink of an eye, Sabra was on her feet, spinning around in the on-guard position, ready for anything, but expecting another body. A dead body.

On the cot was a woman.

A *living* woman.

"I didn't mean to scare you. They keep me drugged. I was doing all I could to wake up. I heard them bring you in, and then I was out again. And then I heard you gasp and move around, and I was sure that you saw…him." The woman looked up to the wall.

The horror and shock of the situation had passed, and Sabra found herself studying the woman. "Who are you?"

"Alyson. Alyson Nash." She dried the tears from her eyes with her sleeve. "Who are you?"

"You're Jeremy's—"

"Yes, how did—"

"Never mind," said Sabra. "Who's he?" she asked, jutting a thumb behind her toward the wall.

Alyson shook her head, tears springing immediately into her eyes. "They did it this morning. It was horrible. They crucified him right in front of my eyes!"

Sabra sat up and took her in her arms and held her until her sobbing ceased.

"Who are you?"

"My name's Sabra. I'm helping your brother save you." The agent looked around the dingy room. The light was fading fast. "As you can see, I'm doing a bang-up job of it."

Just then a door opened, spilling light into the room. Sabra turned and watched a half dozen men march in—and one of them she was very familiar with.

Next to her, Alyson sprang to her feet. "Jeremy!" she cried.

Nash could not have been more shocked to see these two women standing before him. Only moments before, after a wild ride through the streets of Jerusalem, Nash's blindfold had been removed. As he stood in a bright hallway, blinking his eyes back into functionality, he was shocked to see a grinning Reverend Hicks standing opposite him. He had seen the same tall arrogant man interviewed on his plane flight just days earlier. Next, he was introduced to the infamous Enos Tucker. Short and squat, with closely cropped hair, Tucker projected an eerie sort of serenity. As if Nash wasn't here against his will. Behind them, the three men holding Uzis apparently needed no introduction.

Now, after being ushered into the room, Nash blinked in utter surprise and delight to see his sister and Sabra standing against the far wall. Alyson immediately rushed to his side. She threw her arms around his neck and almost tackled him to the ground. For a brief moment, he nearly forgot their circumstances and just hugged her in return. One of Tucker's henchmen separated them quickly and roughly shoved her aside.

"Are you okay, Sis?" he asked anxiously.

She nodded wildly, then pointed to the wall. "Jeremy, look!"

Nash carefully turned and followed her finger, aware that one of three very deadly weapons was aimed at his head.

He quickly forgot about the Uzi. Hell, he forgot about everything. Words formed in his mouth. Words that came and went, unspoken, until finally he was only able to utter, "*Jesus Christ.*"

"Close, Mr. Nash," said Enos Tucker calmly. "But no cigar." Tucker had introduced himself to Nash just moments before as the blindfold had been removed. Tucker spoke again, flashing Nash a chilling smile. "That would be Mr. Thomas Gray. You've met, no?"

Alyson burst into tears and collapsed to her knees.

Nash looked from his sister up to the man hanging grotesquely on the wall. His mouth went bone dry.

My God. They're animals. And then a sick realization occurred to him. *They have no intention of letting us out of this alive.*

Reverend Hicks spoke: "Months ago, we hacked into Section Eighteen's private network. It was a simple re-direct from their site to ours. When Agent Gray thought he was communicating with his superiors he was, in fact, copying us on all his updates. Thanks to his copious reports, we now know everything that you and Roth were doing." The reverend looked up at the cross. "So when he asked for a drop off point with the diary, we told him to meet us. Granted, he thought he was meeting his superiors. Instead, he met these gentlemen here." He pointed to his henchmen.

Alyson wept even harder, covering her face with her arms.

"But why did you...?" Nash heard himself stammering. His voice trailed off. Words were still difficult. The man he had come to like, then loathe, surely did not deserve the treatment he had received at the hands of these...

Animals.

"We needed a sacrifice, Mr. Nash, to bless our holy mission here in Jerusalem." Hicks walked over to the bloody body hanging disjointedly on the cross. "Mr. Gray was so kind as to complete the Shield of Christ that will protect our holy mission and ensure its success."

Nash was numb. They were all crazy. He brought himself to ignore the gruesome figure on the cross above him and said, "How did you even know about the existence of the diary?"

"Your grandfather told us, Mr. Nash," replied Hicks. He turned away from the body on the wall and now faced the group.

"What do you mean?" asked Nash. He had decided that if he wanted to stay calm—hell, stay *sane*—he had to keep his eyes and mind averted from the man hanging on the cross.

"When your grandfather decided to reveal the truth about Roswell, Section Eighteen decided he had finally become a liability. So he and some others of the Majestic Twelve were squirreled away in psychiatric facilities around the country until they could be dealt with."

"Like Henderson," Nash said.

"Yes. Like Henderson—and anyone else who came close to revealing the truth. But your grandfather was not to be denied, Mr. Nash. Even at the psych ward he spoke often of his secrets. A custodian at the ward, a member of my flock, lent an empathic ear." Hicks sneered. "Your grandfather told him everything."

Nash was not surprised to hear that. His grandfather, he knew, was a natural storyteller. And apparently the old man had been determined to let loose the greatest story of them all.

Still, Nash had questions. "What, exactly, constitutes everything?"

"What we always believed to be the truth," said Reverend Hicks. "That the incident at Roswell was *not* a UFO cover up. The UFO story was, *in fact*, the cover up."

Nash, despite the gruesome sight hanging above them and despite his dire predicament, could not restrain the inner skeptic that came rushing out. He groaned his disapproval.

"You have another opinion, Mr. Nash?" queried Hicks. The tall man clasped his hands in front of him.

"Yes," said Nash. "The real one. The U.S. Government admitted years ago that what really crashed there was a spy balloon from a secret program called Project Mogul. These balloons did exist, and may have been responsible for other UFO reports as well, including the death of Air National Guard pilot Captain Mantell. The spy balloons were meant to gather information about Soviet atomic bomb tests. During the Cold War Project Mogul had to be kept secret."

"Ah, Mr. Jeremy Nash. The great skeptic of our time. Yes, obviously you would believe a cover up."

Nash, used to dealing with those with closed minds—and, in this case, those with closed, *psychotic* minds—often knew when debating would be futile. In this case, surrounded by whacko religious extremists, he decided against voicing further opinion—even if his opinion was based upon the soundest of facts. Instead, he asked, "What, may I ask, do you believe really crashed at Roswell?"

The look on Hicks's face reminded Nash of the cat who ate the canary. "Satan's minions."

"I see," said Nash, although he had no clue.

Hicks removed an ornate cigarette case from his inside pocket, plucked a cigarette out and lit it. He drew in deeply and exhaled the smoke in Nash's direction. "Have you ever heard of Colonel Corso, Mr. Nash?"

"Of course. He wrote a popular book about the Roswell incident."

"And what did he claim?"

177

"That an alien craft had crashed, and that a handful of items from the craft had been entrusted to him while he worked for Foreign Technology in Army Research and Development at the Pentagon in the early nineteen sixties. He also wrote about how the Army had found extraterrestrial beings of some kind, two of which were reportedly still alive. And he stated that pieces of alien technology were also found."

"Correct," Hicks replied. "You seem to know about Roswell."

"I grew up there. Not to mention I've written several articles and a book debunking the entire incident."

"Then you also know that Colonel Corso never recanted his story, even upon his deathbed."

"Of course. Still, that doesn't mean—"

"And according to Colonel Corso," Hicks said, cutting Nash off, "the Army reverse-engineered the technology retrieved from the crash site. Many claim that the devices found aboard the Roswell craft ultimately became the technology of today like integrated circuit chips, fiber optics, lasers, night-vision technology, and super-tenacity fibers such as Kevlar."

Nash shook his head and fought a nearly uncontrollable desire to refute this. Now was not the time to be right.

Hicks continued, "Perhaps most chilling of all is how this alien technology has shaped the geopolitical climate over the last fifty years." Hicks leaned forward and looked straight at Nash. A hint of a devious smile crossed his lips. "Perhaps, then, we should consider the motives of the enemy in *allowing* this technology to fall into the hands of men."

"What enemy?" Sabra asked.

"The Prince of Darkness, the Father of All Lies, Beelzebub, Lucifer—the Devil."

Nash was speechless. He caught Sabra looking at him. She rolled her eyes. If the dead man hanging above her had any affect on her, she didn't show it.

Tough girl.

Hicks ranted on, "It's all here in your grandfather's diary!" He shook the small booklet in Nash's face. "We believe, and your grandfather's dairy confirms with drawings and charts, the evil tools found at Roswell were placed there by no one other than the Devil's minions, tools used to ensnare mankind and create weapons of untold destruction—tools to be used in Satan's plan to deceive the sons of God." Hicks lowered his voice. "Roswell is the key that unlocks the door to Armageddon."

Nash could no longer control himself. "Unless, of course, it really was a weather balloon."

Hicks spun on Nash. "Lies and distortion of the truth by skeptics like you are just as much a part of the deception as the actual Roswell incident. Satan's strategy includes masking the truth with confusion. If the Roswell incident was taken seriously enough, a large scale honest investigation would reveal the truth. But Satan wouldn't want that—would he?"

Nash had no clue what Satan wanted or didn't want. But since he seemed to seriously piss off the psychopath, he decided to keep quiet this time. Next to him, he sensed his sister slowly shaking her head.

Good idea. Keep quiet.

"No, he wouldn't," said Hicks, thankfully answering his own insane question. "Satan wants things to be confused. Skeptics, like you, add to the confusion."

"Thank you, Reverend Hicks," said Tucker, stepping in front of Nash. "We have everything we need except for one crucial piece of evidence. Mr. Gray hinted at it just before his untimely death." Tucker paused and studied Nash's face.

Nash, noting the wild-eyed gleam, was certain the man was dangerously unstable. Tucker continued, "What is the date of the Second Coming predicted in the scroll?"

"I'll need the scroll," said Nash. He doubted his cooperation had anything to do with his—or his sister's or Sabra's—survival at this point, although his cooperation might give them all additional time.

Hicks motioned to a henchman to hand over the carrying case. Nash promptly unzipped it and removed the infrared pictures they had taken in Roth's lab in London.

Showing the pictures to the men, he explained that the visible text on the scroll itself made no reference to the Second Coming whatsoever. However, under infrared scanning they had discovered invisible words on the parchment. He showed the two men where the hidden words spoke of the sacrifice of the Messiah, His death, resurrection, and His return.

"And this is the date." Nash pointed to a number on the film.

"Fifty-seven oh-seven?" Hicks asked, clearly surprised.

"It's a year in the Hebrew calendar," said Sabra behind them.

"And what year is it in the Christian calendar?" demanded Tucker.

Nash paused briefly, and as he spoke the dates, he savored the stunned expressions on the two men's faces. "Nineteen forty-seven."

It was Tucker who managed to speak—or shout—first. "Liar! It's a trick! Planted by you and the other non-believers!"

Nash glanced at the men holding the Uzis, who shifted uncomfortably at Tucker's agitation. Hell, Nash shifted, too. The specter of Tom Gray hanging on the wall was enough to make anyone agitated, especially in the company of two loonies.

Hicks put a hand on Tucker's shoulder. "No matter, old friend. We know in our hearts this information is false. It has to be. Therefore, as planned, we shall bring about the Second Coming ourselves."

Nash didn't like the sound of that. "What, exactly, does that mean?"

"You shall see, Mr. Nash. In fact, you will have a front row seat to the Apocalypse. But first, we will need to build the Third Temple!"

Tuesday
9:12 PM GMT
Kidron Valley, Israel

The white van, now holding Nash, Sabra, Hicks, and Tucker pulled onto a dirt road off the *Ha-Ofel Road* east of the Golden Gate of the Old City.

Nash sat with the others, catching only glimpses of bleak desert wastelands.

Good place to die, he thought grimly.

Per Hicks, his sister had been left behind as insurance. Nash wasn't sure if that was a good thing or a bad thing. In the least, they had moved her to another room, where she didn't have to stare up at the bloodied corpse of the man she had loved. Nash thought it best to save the details of Tom's double cross for a later date.

If there was a later date. At least I have my grandfather's diary.

Indeed, he had convinced Hicks earlier to return it to them. After all, why would Hicks and company need the diary if they already possessed the scroll? Hicks had agreed and returned it to him. It now sat comfortably in a zipped compartment in his light jacket. He now regretted wearing anything extra in this damnable heat.

Still, he had the diary. Why that was important, he didn't know. In the least, it belonged to Nash and his sister, and he was happy to have it back.

Several minutes later, the group was in the hills above the Old City south of the infamous Gethsemane, where Roman soldiers had captured Christ just prior to crucifying Him. The van pulled into a flat area of desert brush and came to a halt. Hicks ordered Nash and Sabra out.

"I want you to see how we're going to summon the Messiah, Mr. Nash," Hicks said. "Follow me."

Nash and Sabra, followed by Tucker and two armed men, were led to a large canvas tent. Once inside, Nash saw what looked like a portable media control console, the kind one would use at an outdoor concert. There were two parts to the console. One had a series of variable power sliding control switches, and the other, a series of buttons and LED displays.

Nash looked out the rear flap of the tent and stared at a large blue and white striped blimp suspended in the air, tethered to the ground. It looked about half the size of the Goodyear blimp.

"I see you've noticed our blimp," Hicks said.

"Hard to miss," said Nash. "What's it for? Is the Super Bowl being played in Jerusalem this year?"

Hicks chuckled. "See that clear plastic block next to it?"

It looked the size of a two-car garage.

"That innocuous looking block will be lifted by the blimp and suspended over the Dome of the Rock."

"And how will this create the Third Temple?" Sabra asked.

"Positioned outside of the walls of the Old City at its four corners are powerful water-cooled lasers. These lasers will shoot beams of light into the block, and, combined with a smaller laser shooting beams from the blimp above—"

"Creates a holographic image of the Third Temple," Nash finished.

"Yes," said Hicks. "It will fulfill the prophecy that the Temple will descend from the heavens onto the Mount as a manifestation of light and bring about the coming of the Messiah."

"And you believe that this will summon Jesus Christ and begin the Apocalypse?" questioned Sabra incredulously.

Hicks smiled. "No. Not quite."

Just then, a tall elderly gentleman with a long white beard and hair down to his shoulders barged into the tent. The man, thought Nash, looked as insane as all the others combined.

"Where's my technical staff?" the man demanded. "Where's

my pilot? And what's that thing hanging from my blimp? It doesn't look like a laser."

Hicks turned his attention to the old man. "We had to make some changes, Mr. Katz."

"Changes?" asked the crazy looking man. "What changes?" he demanded.

"We're thinking your pretty light show will not be enough to bring back Our Lord."

"I don't understand."

Tucker stepped forward. "Our men will run the program from now on, Mr. Katz. And our pilot will fly the blimp."

"But why? We had an agreement."

Hicks walked over to the end of the tent and looked at the blimp hovering above the ground. "We must remove any and all impediments to the Second Coming. And that includes the Dome of the Rock. When gone, a real, physical Third Temple can then be erected for Our Lord Christ's return.

"Remove how?" Katz asked.

"While those non-believers snicker at your feeble attempts at building a pretty hologram, we will do God's work right under their noses."

This time Sabra spoke, clearly concerned. "What does that mean, Reverend?"

Hicks pointed to the blimp again. "Mr. Katz was most correct when he pointed out that what you see beneath the blimp is not a laser. Well, not entirely. Contained within it is a state-of-the-art, thermobaric weapon." He lowered his voice and spoke in a reverent tone. "A weapon that will permanently remove the blot on Christendom forever—and usher in the Apocalypse."

"I won't stand for this," shouted Katz, his face turning an alarming shade of red. "I'm going to the police."

"You will be doing no such thing, old man." Hicks motioned to one of his men. "Take them to the van, and bring Mr. Katz with you. The rest of us have God's work to do."

Tuesday
9:30 PM GMT
Kidron Valley, Israel

Tucker removed a pistol from behind his back, and along with one of his armed men, marched Nash, Sabra, and Katz from the tent back to the waiting van. Nash was seriously not looking forward to sitting in that sweatbox—or to what might come next.

Jesus, how did I get in this mess? he wondered again. And the same answer always returned to him. His grandfather.

Thanks, Grandpa.

As they rounded a corner and approached the simmering van, the full implications of Hicks's plan finally dawned on Nash. Here, in the nearly overwhelming heat of the desert, well away from civilization, it was easy to dismiss the man—hell, everyone out here—as terminally insane. But the reality was Hicks had concocted a devious plan to wreak incalculable destruction—and in a land that was already a veritable time bomb.

Good God, he just might start Armageddon—or something damn close to it.

As they marched together, Nash leaned over and whispered to Sabra. "We have to stop them, you know. His crazy plan might just work."

"I know," she said warning him. "Stay alert."

Nash didn't know how alert he could actually stay in these hellacious conditions. The heat of the sun sapped any and all energy.

When they reached the van, Tucker motioned Nash and Sabra inside. Katz followed behind. The van felt exactly like an oven, and Nash could almost smell his own cooking flesh.

184

God, I want some water.

As if reading his mind, Tucker said, "If the three of you sit quietly, we might give you some water soon. *Might* is the operative word here."

"Now, what would Jesus do here?" Nash asked. Why he asked that, he had no idea. The words just came tumbling out of his mouth. He regretted them instantly.

Tucker, who had been about to slam home the side hatch, paused in mid-slam. And in that moment, something fairly shocking happened. Katz, for an old man, moved amazingly fast. The gray bearded man lunged for the door—

And got to it before Tucker could bring his pistol up.

Katz threw the door open, and then threw himself on top of Tucker. A shot was fired and both men tumbled to the ground outside the van. The old man jerked, then slid to the side—motionless.

Now Sabra was moving, hurling her body through the van. She hit Tucker hard, slamming him into the open-door frame.

The pistol scuttled loose, rattling across the van's interior.

Nash scrambled for it as Sabra and Tucker fought each other like two wild animals. He had a brief glimpse of the Mossad agent's face. Contorted in rage, lips bared back, she looked like a hellion. And in that instant, she clawed at Tucker's eyes in a rage, screeching like something from the depths of hell.

My God!

Nash grabbed the pistol as Tucker briefly got the upper hand and slammed Sabra hard into the floor of the van. She grunted, but then leveled an elbow squarely into the man's nose. It shattered upon contact, spewing a fountain of blood.

"Shoot her, Goddammit!" screamed Tucker.

Outside, watching and waiting for a clear shot was the young man with the Uzi. Nash did the only thing he could think of. From the interior of the van, he leveled the pistol, took aim, and fired once.

The young man jerked, and then slumped forward.

I killed him. A mixture of relief and nausea flooded Nash. He wanted to vomit.

And as Nash sat there on his knees, in shock and horror, Tucker lashed out and hit him hard across the jaw. Nash tumbled back and the gun went flying under the seats.

"Get to the blimp, Jeremy," she yelled. "You have got to stop it."

"But what about—"

"Go! Now!"

Tucker grabbed for him, but Sabra leaped on him and pushed him to the floor of the van.

Nash turned and ran, ignoring the hellacious sounds of fighting behind him.

A few beats later, Tucker had gotten the upper hand on Sabra, and he knocked her against the heavy tool chest. She lay on the floor of the van, blood running through her hair.

"Bitch," Tucker snarled, then looked towards the blimp and saw Nash running over the rise. He left Sabra on the floor of the van and took off after him.

Hicks was in the main tent, or command room as he preferred to call it. He had just given the order for his pilot to take off when he heard shots ring out.

"What the hell was that?" he asked.

"It came from the van," said the technician.

"Stay here," barked Hicks.

He was about to leave, thought better of it, and paused at the tent flap. They were close. So very close.

Nothing can stop us now—and nothing will.

"What's the status of the ground lasers and the weapon's control?" he asked the technician.

"All operating within proper limits."

"Ready the weapon for automatic countdown."

He left for the van.

As Nash ran towards the blimp he looked over his shoulder.

Ah, shit!

Tucker was following him.

Sabra! Nash stopped, almost went back.

The blimp. Damn!

He stood there briefly in the sun, gripped by indecision. He hadn't heard another shot fired.

Maybe she's still okay.

He heard her words in his head again: *Stop the blimp.*

So he continued around the rocky trail that led back to the control tent and the blimp.

The blimp was almost one hundred feet in the air.

Nash took another angle, a sharper, steeper angle down the steep hillside. He ran hard. Too hard. He stumbled once, almost pitched forward into an uncontrollable roll.

Miraculously, he kept his balance. He continued down the hillside and closed in on the blimp. His lungs were on fire. He sucked wind hard.

Good God, the blimp...it's lifting higher.

And the plastic block was rising off the ground. What the hell was he supposed to do?

Stop the blimp, commanded Sabra's words again.

And like an idiot—perhaps the world's biggest idiot—he did the only thing he could think of. He hurled himself onto the plastic block, grabbing onto the clear polyester plastic strapping that secured it.

To his utter horror, the block continued to rise, hauling Nash up with it. The hot wind picked up, tugging at Nash. His only thought was to get to the top of the block, where he wasn't hanging for his life.

And so he did just that. Or tried to.

As he climbed hand over hand towards the top of the block, something grabbed his left ankle and pulled hard.

Nash gasped and looked down.

Good God! It was Tucker.

Sabra regained consciousness, stood up, and tried to steady her feet. Katz was still. Nash was gone and so was Tucker. She stepped from the van to see the blimp cruising high in the sky.

He didn't make it to the blimp. Shit!

She looked for a weapon, found the dead guard's Uzi unnoticed under the rear of the van, retrieved it, and clambered up the steep, rocky hill.

Nash kicked hard and shook the man off. He pulled himself higher up the plastic strap of the huge clear cube. Below, beyond Tucker moving meticulously his way up the plastic mass, was the Kidron Valley passing far below. *Too far below.* Good God, he was high up!

This can't be happening. I must be dreaming.

Wind thundered over his ears. The ground passed swiftly below. Blimps certainly moved faster than they were given credit for. At least, hanging a hundred feet above the ground, it sure seemed to be moving with surprising speed.

They were on a direct course to the Dome of the Rock, which Nash could see in the far distance.

Tucker reached up again. Nash kicked hard connecting with the man's outstretched fingers. Someone was going to fall out of the sky and die. And if he was him, he sure as hell wasn't going to let this creep Tucker facilitate the process.

Nash looked to his left and saw what appeared to be one of the multifaceted grooves in the plastic block. Perfect for a handhold.

Hardly believing what he was about to attempt, Nash focused his thoughts, then willed himself to release the strap—and reached out toward the groove.

The wind hit him hard. His reaching hand missed the groove and he briefly dangled by one arm. He slammed hard against the plastic block, bounced once, then slammed hard again.

His desperately searching hand groped the plastic block, and this time he grabbed it—

Or thought he did.

"Shit!"

He lost his grip, and his left arm, holding up the brunt of his weight, gave way as well. Now Nash was sliding down the strap, past Tucker, burning his hand as he went. His right hand reached out for anything, but he continued to slide—

And just as he reached the bottom of the block—and eternity below—his flailing foot somehow wedged between the strap and another groove. With a sickening crack, he swung head over ass, and found himself hanging upside down below the block.

And in excruciating pain.

He was certain his ankle had broken. Nash tried to right himself but couldn't pull himself up without some kind of leverage. And each movement caused further pain in his ankle.

Worse, he felt himself blacking out with the blood rushing to his head. As his vision began to blur, he saw that Tucker had moved above him—and was brandishing a knife.

Hicks, sweating under the hot desert sun, cautiously approached the van.

From this angle, he could see a body sprawled across the sand, next to the van. From his position, he had no idea who it was. He fingered the Uzi in his hand and considered going back. He did glance over his shoulder and saw the blimp drifting across the sky towards its intended target.

Nothing can stop us now, he thought. *Our Lord Jesus will be returning soon. Very soon.*

This excited Hicks. So much so that he stopped and offered a little prayer. Never in his life had he felt more connected to Christ, to his God.

I am part of the plan. Part of God's plan.

Hicks always knew he was destined for greatness, even as a child. He always felt there was something bigger waiting for him.

And as he stood there upon the rocky path leading to the van, as he watched his blimp drift toward his target, and the coming apocalypse—an apocalypse that he alone had set into motion, he realized again that he had been singled out by God himself. Hicks felt privileged and honored. He often mentioned that he felt humbled, too, but that was not always accurate. Hicks, admittedly, rarely felt humbled.

He felt, if anything, incredibly powerful.

Very powerful.

There had been many who stood in his way, or tried to. He had crushed them all. And no Mossad agent or professional skeptic was going to stop him. Not now. Not when he was so close.

He fingered the Uzi and headed down the rocky trail, cautiously approaching the quiet van.

The body was one of his volunteers. A Christian warrior for God. He silently thanked the boy for giving up his life.

Hicks held the weapon out before him.

The sun shone down pulling heat into the desert. Sweat poured down the center of his back.

The van was completely silent.

A small wind blew over the desert, bringing with it a scent of something ancient.

Hicks moved carefully around the van. At the rear, he briefly collected himself, then threw open the double doors. He paused. But there was no movement or sound. He peaked around the corner and saw only the still body of the old man, Katz.

"Shit!" he blurted. Then immediately asked for forgiveness.

He dashed back to the tent.

Hicks, alert for either Nash or the Mossad agent, ducked back into his tent to find his technician sitting calmly in a chair opposite the console.

"Is everything alright in here?" He quickly scanned the room.

A female voice behind him said, "No, Reverend. Everything is most certainly *not* okay. Now drop your weapon."

He did as he was told, although he briefly consider turning and firing. The Mossad agent stepped around him. She was bleeding from a head wound—and holding one of their weapons before her. He had no doubt she knew how to use it, or that she *would* use it.

"Now Reverend," she said, keeping her eyes on him, although she seemed equally aware of the lad at the console, "you're going to shut this down and stop those lasers from firing."

He couldn't help but grin smugly. He—and God, of course—had thought of everything. "I can't do that," he replied, pointing confidently to the weapon console's LED display. "*That* means there's nothing you can do to stop our holy work. See that image there?"

The agent kept the Uzi trained on Hicks and backed over to the weapon's console. Even Hicks could see the bold red letters that read: ARMED. And below it were two LED lights—one red and one green. The green one had lettering under it that said: MANUAL. The red one had lettering that read: AUTOMATIC. The red one was lit.

"What does it mean?" she demanded.

Hicks leaned a hip casually against the console, his hands folded serenely in front of him. He was confident and relaxed. "There's a GPS device in the blimp that communicates with the lasers on the ground. It tells the lasers to activate when the blimp is exactly above the Dome of the Rock. Once the lasers fire, a countdown will commence to release God's wrath. The weapon will annihilate anything and everything upon the Rock. So you see, there's nothing you can do to stop us."

"So you say." Sabra pointed the Uzi at the technician. The tech, she suspected, was the only one who would know how to shut this thing off. "Cancel the program or die."

The tech didn't move, although sweat sprang instantly across his entire forehead. Hicks moved cautiously away from the console.

When he spoke, there was a touch of both humor and reverence in his voice. "Even if he could stop the program, he won't. He'll die for Our Lord."

"But will he suffer for Him." Sabra calmly fired a single bullet straight into the man's right boot. As he tumbled back, screaming, reaching for his foot, Sabra immediately noted the irony. His Christ had suffered a similar injury upon being nailed to the cross.

Sabra stepped forward, following the trail of fresh blood as the gasping young man dragged himself and his damaged foot away. She aimed the weapon at his other foot. "Your choice is simple. Stop the program, or I shoot the other one."

The tech, whose face had gone bone white and was already in a state of shock, opened his mouth to speak. Sabra knew there was a fair to good chance this weapon did indeed have a shut off switch. And she knew the kid would now tell her anything. Anything at all.

As the technician was about to speak, between whimpering gasps, he flicked his eyes over her right shoulder. It was then Sabra had realized her mistake. She had neglected Hicks. She had assumed she would hear the big man approach. She had assumed he would make some obvious gesture towards her.

She was wrong. Fatally wrong.

He was behind her quickly and quietly. As the kid's eyes glanced desperately over her shoulder, she spun instantly, but it was too late. Reverend Hicks was on her from behind, arms powerfully around her throat, wrenching the Uzi free. He shoved her hard away from him. She turned and saw that he had the weapon trained on her.

"I said nothing and no one is going to stop us," said Hicks, breathing hard, the short burst of energy leaving him winded.

He pointed the weapon at Sabra as he said this. She knew what was coming. One mistake was all it took for most agents to get killed. Hicks was her mistake. She closed her eyes and waited for the Uzi to fire.

It did, and it came in a long, loud burst that left her ears ringing.

She snapped her eyes open, surprised as hell to still be alive. In front of her Hicks was holding the Uzi—and looking wildly to his side. She turned to look, too.

The young tech was quite dead, riddled with bullet holes. His damaged foot was the least of his problems.

"You were right, of course," said Hicks, turning back to her, and looking about as crazy as Sabra had ever seen another human being. "If there ever was a chance of stopping the program, he was your best bet. Now, nothing will stop the coming Apocalypse."

He aimed the weapon at her face and squeezed the trigger, and for the second time in so many minutes, Sabra's luck held. He was out of bullets, having emptied the weapon into the young tech.

Furious, he heaved the weapon at her and charged. She had just ducked it when he slammed her back into some heavy crates, forcing the air out of her lungs. She had just managed to knee the bastard in his loins, although not as hard as she would have hoped when he got both hands around her neck. Powerfully strong, he lifted her by her throat up off the ground.

Squeezing the life out of her.

Tucker, lying prostrate across the top of the massive plastic block and bracing himself against one of the four plastic straps, proceeded to methodically sever the very strap holding Nash's leg in place.

Hanging upside down, a burning pain ripping through his ankle, Nash could only helplessly watch. Wind thundered over him. Nash reached up, grimacing with pain, desperate for a handhold— or to at least ease the pressure on his brutalized ankle.

And as he reached up, something happened.

The massive plastic block shifted, swaying slightly. As it did so, Tucker paused in his effort and re-adjusted his own precarious handhold.

With little thought to the potential consequences, Nash did the only thing his desperate mind could think of.

He started swinging.

At first his effort was rewarded with little or no signs of anything significant. Tucker merely held fast to his strap and proceeded to hack away at Nash's own lifeline.

The skeptic swung harder, gaining some momentum.

It's working.

Indeed, it was. Now the whole block was swinging with him—and on top of it rode Tucker. The religious fanatic halted his cutting altogether, and Nash could see the man scrambling for a better grip.

Meanwhile, he himself was swinging dangerously and recklessly out into space, held in place by only a tenuous foot hold.

Tenuous and painful.

Nash grunted—but continued swinging.

Something flashed passed him.

The knife! The bastard lost his knife!

Nash swung some more. Harder, faster. The whole thing was really rocking now.

And in that moment, Nash watched from below as Tucker tumbled over the side. Falling, the frantic man just managed to grab hold of Nash's strap.

Both men hung perilously as the blimp drifted over the landscape...

Tuesday
9:55 PM GMT
Kidron Valley, Israel

Sabra knew her mistake in letting Hicks live. *I should have shot the bastard when I had the chance.*

Now she dangled from his strong hands, her vision darkening dangerously around its edges, the pressure on her throat nearly unbearable. At the very least, he was going to crush her neck.

Beating on him had proven useless. The man seemed possessed. Instead, before the blackness set in, she looked desperately for anything she could use as a weapon.

There!

It was a hollow metal rod, perhaps an unused tent pole, and it was within reach. With the blackness rapidly encroaching, with her lungs screaming for oxygen, Sabra reached desperately for the metal rod. Her flailing fingers had just touched the cold metal when Hicks turned his head and saw what she was doing. He jerked her away and squeezed even tighter.

On the brink of unconsciousness, certain that she would never awaken again, Sabra could not have been more surprised to suddenly find herself falling. She landed awkwardly, her legs buckling. From the floor, choking and gasping, she looked up to see a sight for sore eyes.

Katz was standing over her, holding a shovel. He reached down for her and scooped her up, placing her carefully on her feet. As he steadied her, Sabra painfully took in the scene before her. The Reverend, she saw, now lay in a crumpled heap next to the dead technician. Blood pooled from around the man's badly

196

damaged head. Whether or not Hicks was actually dead, she didn't know, nor did she care.

"Are you all right?" asked Katz, tossing aside the shovel and giving her a hand.

Sabra reached for his support and found her feet, but found speaking impossible, at least for the moment. After a few sputtering, hissing attempts, she finally managed to say, "Thank you. I thought you were dead! Back there..." She noticed blood flowing from a wound in his head.

Katz shrugged. "I was lucky. Tucker just grazed me."

Rubbing her throat, Sabra staggered over to the weapon's console. "Can we stop this thing?"

Katz shook his head sadly. "I'm afraid there's nothing we can do."

She considered calling in an air strike, but there was no way the elite Israeli pilots, so good at what they do, could ever assemble in time to stop the blimp. It was, after all, only minutes away from launching its weapon.

She paused, looked out the tent opening, and saw something remarkable. The plastic block beneath the blimp was swaying dangerous.

And did she see—?

She grabbed a pair of binoculars from the console and brought them to her eyes. There were two men hanging from the block.

And one of them looked just like Nash. She watched with fascination and horror.

She lowered them. "My God," she whispered.

Tuesday
9:30 PM GMT
Kidron Valley, Israel

As he swung, Nash discovered his momentum was carrying him up. He swung again. This time harder. He reached—

And snagged the strap holding his ankle in place.

He screamed in pain.

But through it all, he held on and worked his ankle free from its prison. To his surprise and delight, he realized his ankle hadn't broken. Twisted severely, but not broken.

But he had more pressing matters.

Much like Tucker, he was holding on by only a strap—and a rapidly fraying strap at that. Because he had stopped swinging, the plastic block itself had stopped swaying. He had just gathered himself for his next step when something exploded against the side of his face.

Nash's grip faltered, but he held on in time to see Tucker's fist coming in for another blow. He ducked as the fist grazed his ear—and almost lost his grip completely.

Nash gasped and somehow managed to hang on.

Tucker, he saw, had wrapped one arm tightly around the strap, which allowed his other arm to hang free—and pummel Nash. Hanging precariously by *both* hands, Nash did the only thing he could think of.

He kicked hard with his one good leg.

It was a hell of a kick. His foot landed squarely under Tucker's jaw. The man went limp, lost his grip—

And plummeted to the empty valley below.

198

Nash, loosened his grip, swung his legs up and over the strap, and hauled himself into a sitting position on top of the massive plastic block, barely comprehending that he had somehow survived.

It's not over yet, he thought.

Indeed, just as he thought the words, something echoed loudly above him.

Gunfire?

Confused, Nash looked up. The blimp's pilot was leaning out through the cockpit's side window.

Holding a pistol.

And shooting at Nash.

"Ah, hell," spat Nash.

Nash stood unsteadily and grabbed hold of the cable that supported the plastic block.

The pilot, leaning awkwardly out the side window, took aim again and fired.

Sweet Jesus.

Where the bullet went, Nash didn't know. He had leaned backward and, still holding the cable, tried to position himself at such an angle that the pilot could not see him.

With the pilot pre-occupied with Nash, the blimp had started to descend. Indeed, Nash had a clear view of exactly where they were headed—towards the Tomb of the Virgin Mary.

We're going to hit it, thought Nash. *And the crazy bastard's not even looking.*

The large stone structure seemed to rise up from the ground to meet them. And still the bastard above him was taking pot shots.

Two of them, in fact.

Nash ducked and did all he could to keep out of range and maintain balance on the hanging block.

And then the tomb was upon them. Nash had a bird's eye view of a dark stone arch. An arch within an arch, in fact. He quickly scanned the area before them and realized they were going to hit.

He held on with a fierce grip.

The stone arch appeared just below. Nash braced himself and ignored the pain in his right ankle.

And then they hit. Hard. The block careened off wildly, with Nash holding on like some kid in a playground ride from hell.

He stood fast, gritted his teeth, held on tightly to the cable as the block plowed into the small Church where Mary lay.

Swinging wildly and holding on with all his strength, Nash had a brief glimpse of the pilot hanging out the window. Amazingly, shockingly, the man was taking aim at him again, even while the blimp continued angling down over the city.

He's out of his mind!

The next shot missed again, but it did hit on one of the straps holding the block to the cable.

A moment later, with a resounding crack, the strap broke— and the massive plastic block tumbled free. With the weight gone, the blimp rocketed up into the sky, spinning out of control.

All the while, Nash hung desperately to the main cable.

Sabra and Katz both watched the plastic block drop from the blimp and land outside the walls of the Mount.

Sabra trained her field glasses on the solitary figure hanging from the single cable.

It was Nash.

"Amazing," she murmured.

From inside the tent, the lights along the console began blinking, catching Sabra's attention.

"What's that?" she asked.

"That's the warning signal," Katz frowned. "The lasers around the Temple Mount are heating up in preparation to fire. They'll do that when the blimp is in proximity of the Mount."

"And when the blimp is over the Dome of the Rock...?" she asked, letting her voice trail off.

"The weapon will fire," finished Katz.

As he said this, the first laser fired and, ever so slowly, an ethereal blue beam of light began to appear in the evening skies above the Dome of the Rock.

"My God," gasped Sabra.

Nash looked down and saw that the blimp had crossed over the Golden Gate of the Mount.

Despite his precarious situation, he still had a job to do. How exactly this job ended up in his lap, he may never know.

None of that mattered now. He had to stop that weapon from going off.

The pilot, fortunately, had retreated into the cockpit and had somehow managed to regain control of the spiraling blimp. Nash, still hanging from the cable, did the only thing he could think of. He climbed the cable. A monstrous task made so much easier by what appeared to be handholds, all, thankfully, evenly spaced.

He pulled himself up, bit by bit.

He did this over and over as the blimp continued toward the Dome of the Rock.

And as he reached for the next handhold, a blinding light appeared directly before them. Nash squinted at the blue laser beam of light piercing the night sky.

He was now bathed in the pale blue light of the laser. He knew the weapon was set to go off.

Got to hurry!

With his right ankle nearly worthless, he continued up the cable, gasping and sucking wind as he did so.

Halfway up, with another ten feet of cable to climb, the second laser fired, adding a serene green glow to the pale blue beam.

With his skin veritably glowing and eyes nearly blinded by the light, Nash continued up.

Sabra watched Nash with a mixture of awe and alarm.

Now he was climbing, hand over hand, straight up the cable while it hung hundreds of feet above the ground. How he didn't fall, she barely imagined. Adrenalin or fear could do wonders.

Then again, Nash was proving himself to be surprisingly...

She searched for a word and was surprised when it sprang into her mind.

Heroic.

Surprisingly heroic. She liked that in a man.

Sabra adjusted the field glasses and silently cheered Nash on.

A few minutes later, nearly blinded and hands bleeding, Nash reached the gondola. He pulled himself up with his last bit of strength and flopped in through the open window.

He found himself face to face with the startled pilot, who immediately grabbed his pistol and pointed it at Nash.

Nash had just committed to throwing himself at the man when the third laser fired from the north-east corner of the Mount. The yellowish beam, which appeared behind Nash, temporarily blinded the pilot.

Nash, legs still wobbly and hands cramped, lunged forward and grabbed the pilot's gun hand. The thing went off, blasting through the floor. Nash yelped but didn't let go of the hand.

As they struggled together inside the cramped gondola, the fourth laser fired, illuminating the cabin brilliantly.

With the blimp in proximity to the Mount, the GPS status light on the blimp's control panel switched to ACTIVE as the device took control of the blimp. It positioned the blimp directly over the Dome of the Rock.

Sabra had watched as Nash miraculously scaled the remaining length of cable and clambered into the gondola.

He made it, she marveled. *Now what?*

She had her answer almost immediately. Something that sounded like an alarm clock went off. She looked over to where the sound came from and saw a red LED light blinking on and off on the weapons console. She dashed over to it. A digital countdown had begun at three minutes.

An alarm sounded loudly in the cabin.

Nash, fighting for his life, was only briefly aware that the alarm was coming from the blimp's control panel.

The pilot had pinned Nash against the console. Nash still had a grip on the man's wrist, averting the gun. But the pilot's other arm—his forearm, to be exact—was shoved up into Nash's throat.

Nash used his one free hand to level blow after blow against the side of the pilot's head, but the son-of-a-bitch wouldn't give. And now Nash was blacking out—and losing his grip on the man's wrist.

As the pilot applied still more pressure to Nash's throat, he unknowingly shifted his body weight, and thus exposed—

Nash jerked his knee up as hard as he could. How much strength he had behind the motion, he didn't know, but he did manage to catch the man squarely in the groin.

The pilot grunted and dropped the gun. Nash heard it slide briefly, and then...nothing.

It had slid through the open door.

Good.

Now, struggling to breathe through a damaged windpipe, Nash heaved his right fist into the pilot's face. He must have put more behind his punch than he thought. Or, more likely, he had caught the pilot in a very vulnerable position. Either way, the man spun around hard and flopped over the controls—

And promptly sent the blimp spiraling downwards through the beam of lasers and towards the top of the Mosque.

Nash grabbed the controls, searching for anything to right the damn thing. Before him, blinking steadily, was some sort of countdown.

1:22.

Outside was a dizzying display of lights. Nash had no idea how far away the ground was.

1:10.

And through the light show appeared the top of the Dome of the Rock.

"Shit!"

Nash grabbed the controls and yanked them up. No response. He pressed buttons and flipped switches. Nothing. The GPS was locked onto the Mosque.

0:45 seconds.

Two strong hands grabbed his shoulders and heaved him backwards. The pilot! *Shit!* He'd completely forgotten about him. Nash stumbled, lost his balance, and then his stomach leaped up into his throat—

He was falling through the open door. Worse, the pilot was *pushing* him through.

His scrabbling hand found the open door's inside handle. As he lost his balance, pitching forward into space, Nash found himself hanging by one hand—

One tortured hand that was already bruised and battered from his climb up the cable—

Wind hammered him. Surrounding him was the psychedelic light show.

The pilot turned back to the controls.

Nash, grunting through clenched teeth, tried to pull himself up. No good. The handle was already bending under his weight. It was going to snap, and it was going to snap soon.

Nash searched wildly for anything else to grab. There, grinding against his hip, was a narrow metal bar attached to something heavy.

He reached cautiously down with his left hand, found the bar, and had just looped his arm through it when the handle above snapped clean off.

He fell, miraculously not far.

Now, hanging once again for his life, Nash clearly saw what the metal bar was attached to. It was a weapon of some kind. Nothing he had ever seen before, but a weapon nonetheless.

And it was aimed at the Mosque below.

With his left arm firmly hooked between the weapon and metal bar, Nash heard, through the open cabin door above him, what appeared to be a warning sensor.

The final countdown.

He had only seconds before the damn thing fired. And he was hanging from it.

With his free hand, Nash reached for the barrel of the weapon, and was surprised and relieved to see that it swiveled easily enough.

He pulled it up, towards the blimp.

The countdown beeped loudly in the cabin above.

Hanging below and just beyond his reach, was the same cable he had used to haul himself up on.

The weapon began making a noise, a deep hum, and Nash released his hold on the bar, and fell—

He snatched the cable. His damaged hands slid down some more, then caught on one of the handholds.

Above him, the weapon seemed to briefly pulsate. He knew it was about to fire. Nash let go, and fell backwards into the night and lights, praying that they were still above the Mosque dome.

They were.

Twenty feet below, he hit it hard, slamming against the thick tile. With no handholds, he slid down the smooth surface and landed hard on the maintenance walkway at the bottom of the Dome.

Dazed and broken, Nash looked up into the night sky and

watched as the weapon's discharge hit the blimp dead center. The airship disintegrated in a ball of orange and red flames before his eyes, even more spectacular than the rippling lasers.

It seemed, in this moment, that everything had been a bizarre, albeit painful, dream.

Nash closed his eyes, and mercifully passed out.

Tuesday
10:26 PM GMT
Jerusalem, Israel

Alyson had been moved to another room.

Her mind raced. She couldn't sleep. She would never, ever forget the heartbreaking screams of the man she had loved.

Why had they killed him? And why had they forced her to witness it? Such inhuman, unbearable torture!

She turned in her cot. Her thin blanket was crumpled at her feet. She felt like she was very close to losing her mind. All of this was too much.

Just too much.

She wept again for the hundredth time.

At least Jeremy was gone. Maybe he had found a way to escape, she prayed. Maybe he would come back for her soon.

"Tom," she whispered.

She would never forget the look on her fiancé's face. She was going to need a lifetime of therapy.

There was a sound from outside her door.

Gunfire?

It came again. A rapid staccato. She was sure it was from an automatic weapon.

Alyson sat up, listening hard.

The sound of running feet. More gunfire. Someone screaming. More running feet.

Just outside her door.

Jeremy? she said to herself.

Someone tried her door handle. It was locked, even from the

outside. Alyson huddled back in her bed, subconsciously pulling her thin blanket up over her.

Another gunshot, just outside her room, and now the door burst open.

"Are you okay, ma'am?" asked a voice with a thick Hebrew accent. He was silhouetted in darkness in the doorway. She could tell, by his outline, that he was heavily armed and wearing military gear.

"Yes, what's going on?"

"Get up, we're getting you out of here."

Alyson shot out of bed, ready to go with just about anyone at this point. "Who are you?"

He quit scanning the hallway and looked at her. "My name's Ari. I'm with Israeli intelligence. I—"

And his words got cut short. He paused, tilted his head, then slumped forward.

He was, she was certain, dead.

She heard approaching footsteps approach. A second later, someone else stood in the doorway. Someone horribly scarred and repulsive looking. He stepped over the body and into the room. Fresh blood speckled and stained his fatigues. In his right hand he held what appeared to be a very old scroll.

"Where's the diary?" he calmly asked.

Wednesday
2:01 AM GMT
Jerusalem, Israel

Nash awoke in a daze. His first thought was that he was surely dead. His next thought was that surely death didn't *hurt* so much.

Indeed, his body ached all over. He felt broken and battered and wanted to go back to sleep, maybe even forever. Except he couldn't. Because of the voices. The loud voices.

He opened his eyes and saw a green canvas above him. Nash turned his head, groaned, and saw a young woman in a uniform taking his pulse.

She smiled down at him.

Nash saw that he was in a tent. Light was streaming in. How long had he been out? He had no idea. He remembered taking a beating on that damn blimp, then falling, hitting his head hard, watching the blimp explode, and that was it.

It was enough.

Too much.

I need pain meds. Bad.

The voices continued loudly. One, he was certain, was Sabra's and the other was a man's. They were in a heated argument.

"You overstepped your responsibilities, Zamir," said the man. "You got both me and Mossad in a shit-load of trouble."

"I did what I had to do, Director. We all wanted the Warriors of Christ. That was the assignment. The diary and scroll were the bait we needed."

"And you lost the scroll! The Israel Museum is raising holy hell. Even the Prime Minister is on my ass."

209

Nash found it remarkable that they were arguing in English. Almost as if they *wanted* him to follow.

Or maybe I hit my head so hard that I now speak fluent Hebrew.

"I'm sorry, Zamir, but you are now off this investigation."

"But some of my team were killed trying to rescue the girl. I want to get the people who did it. Mr. Director, I demand—"

"You demand nothing, Agent Zamir. You're off the case. We'll takeover from here."

Nash tried to sit up and managed only a loud grunt.

"Good. He's back among the living," said the Director, walking over and standing by Nash's side. He was a big man, broad-shouldered, sporting a thin mustache that didn't entirely fit his wide face. "Now tell me, Mr. Nash. What's this about a diary?"

Nash was pleased to see—or rather sense—that he was still wearing his jacket. The bulge inside was reassuring. And then he remembered Sabra's words: *Her men were killed trying to rescue the girl.*

Alyson?

"What happened to my sister? What's going on?"

Sabra came to his side, reached down and touched his head. "We tried to rescue her, Jeremy. Some of my men were killed. Your sister wasn't there. This, however, was."

She unfolded a note and held it up. "What is it?" he asked. He had a horrible sinking feeling in his stomach.

"Says that if you want your sister back you must give up the diary and that you will be contacted."

"Who took her?"

"That's what we want to know," said the Director. "Whoever kidnapped your sister killed two of my agents. We want whoever is responsible. We'll keep you under surveillance with some of our best men and watch for someone to contact you."

"I would prefer to have Sabra—"

"No. Miss Zamir is off the case," said the director firmly. "She's been dismissed. We'll put you up in a hotel in Jerusalem...and wait."

Sabra gave Nash a troubled look, and then turned and left the tent.

On her way out, she picked up Roth's satellite phone that was found in the basement with the bodies of her two teammates.

"The diary was not there, Father. I have failed you."

"But you have the scroll," said the voice on the telephone. "You did very well."

"Then let me finish the work, Father. Nash surely has the diary. I know where he is. I can retrieve it."

"No, my son. The authorities have been alerted, and he is being watched. We can't take any chances. It's best we let Nash come to us. Now return to Rome. I have more work for you."

"Yes, Father."

Nash slept through most of the day and woke up with a ravenous hunger. He called room service and ordered something to eat. That done, he took a shower and ten minutes later, while drying his hair, there was a knock on the door.

"Come in," he shouted from the bathroom.

A second or two later the door opened. "Room service," said a female voice.

"Just set it on my desk. I'll sign for it later."

Nash finished getting dressed, and as he sat down to eat, he noticed the bill. In particular, he noticed the stapled piece of paper attached to the back of the bill. He sank his teeth hungrily into an egg sandwich while pulling the attached paper into view.

He quit chewing. It was a note. Telling him to go to the Church of the Holy Sepulcher. Once there, he was to say that he wanted a priest to hear his confession. Nash had just swallowed his first bite when there was another knock on the door. He grabbed a butter knife from the tray and cautiously opened the door. It was only about halfway open when a young hotel maid pushed her way in past Nash.

"What the hell? What's going on?"

The girl turned and folded her arms under her chest. "Don't you want your bed turned down, Sir?"

It was Sabra, and she had an impish smile on her face.

Nash laughed and rushed over to her. Once there, he wasn't sure what to do next and threw an arm around her shoulders. She hugged him firmly back.

"Okay, that was awkward," she said, and punched him gently on the arm.

"Sorry," said Nash, blushing. "I'm just happy to see you."

"Always nice to be loved."

"I didn't say I loved—"

She punched him again on the shoulder. "You are so easy to tease, Nash. Are all American men as easy as you?"

He suspected she would know that more than he. He also suspected that it would be an uncommonly strong-willed man to resist her charms.

"Nope," he said. "I'm the easiest, most gullible one. At least around you."

"Ah, does that mean you like me?"

Nash blushed again and decided to change the subject. Flirting with Sabra had its place and time. He was not sure this was either. "I thought you were off the investigation?"

Her eyebrows lowered, and her mood darkened. "I am. But those bastards killed Ari and Jeron, and I'm not going to sit by nicely twiddling my thumbs. Someone is going to die."

Nash stepped back unconsciously. He had no doubt that she could—and would—follow through on her threats.

A moment later, she calmed down and smiled sweetly. "I like you, Nash. I won't hurt you. Unless you piss me off."

Nash laughed nervously. "I'll keep that in mind."

"Seriously, Nash. You were pretty gutsy out there last night, hanging from that blimp. Never seen anything like it. My God, I can't believe you didn't kill yourself."

"Lucky, I guess."

"You may have a future as a field agent."

"No thanks," he said. "I'll leave the heroics to people like you."

Sabra plopped herself in a chair. "So. Let's wait and see who contacts you."

"It already happened." Nash showed her the note.

"Then we have to get you out of here. The police have the hotel pretty well nailed down. There's undercover cops everywhere. It's a credit to my own vast undercover skills that I managed to get in here at all." She grinned at him. God, he liked this girl. "Unfortunately, you're not me," she added. "You're not getting out of here without them knowing it."

"So what do we do?"

Sabra thought for a moment. "Sometimes the best approach is a direct one. Here's what you'll do..." And she told him the plan. When finished, she told Nash to give her five minutes.

She stood suddenly, kissed him on the cheek, and left.

Nash watched the door shut behind her, glad she was gone because he was sure he was as red as a tomato.

With five minutes to kill, and hunger pains gnawing away at his insides, Nash used the time to wolf down his meal. After a veracious few minutes of eating, he looked at the time, groaned, and reluctantly left behind a portion of his goat cream cheese and bagel.

He grabbed the diary from the desk drawer, exited the room, and headed for the elevator. Once there, he glanced behind him and saw two men leave the room across from his.

He hastened his steps and arrived at the elevator just as a young woman and her child came out of it. He swept past her, apologized for his impatience, and pushed the *doors closed* button repeatedly.

He looked through the open doors to see that the two men were now sprinting.

The doors began to close. The two men picked up their pace. But they were too late. Only feet away, the doors sealed shut. Nash couldn't help but to wave and wink at the now pissed off policemen.

The elevator made its descent to the underground parking level where the doors opened to find Sabra sitting on a throbbing motocross bike, her face visible behind a slick, black helmet. Dressed now in tight jeans and a light jacket, Nash thought she looked sexy as hell.

"Here." She handed Nash a helmet. "Buckle up. Things are about to get, as you Americans say, *gnarly*."

Nash donned the helmet, buckled it on, and threw a leg over the seat behind her. "Is this standard Mossad issue?" he asked, his voice echoing loudly within the helmet.

"Nope. All mine. I do a little motocross racing on the side. Something I like to do in my spare time. You like to fly in the air. I like to fly just above the dirt. Now put your arms around my waist and hold on tight."

Nash did not feel guilty at all thinking this was her best suggestion of the day. He placed his hands around her slim supple waist and, as directed, squeezed tightly. Even through the helmet, he could not miss the seductive hint of her perfume again.

She revved the bike, popped a wheelie, and Nash was almost thrown off the bike.

Focus, Jeremy.

As she plunged forward through the parking garage, up an exit ramp and into the sunshine of late afternoon, Nash was sure Sabra was chuckling.

Wednesday
3:33 PM GMT
Jerusalem, Israel

The bike raced past the hotel.

Two unmarked cars tore out of the parking lot and followed. Sabra looked back and said loudly over the thundering wind, "Mossad. The game's afoot. They're on our tail."

Nash decided not to mention the fact that she sounded like a cross between Sherlock Holmes and Dick Tracy.

Sabra weaved her way through streets full of cars, trucks, and street vendors. Nash tried to keep his balance on the back of the bike, and each time she swerved he held on tighter. The sexiness of the situation was out the door. He was holding on for dear life.

As they rounded a corner fast, whipping past a parked police car. Nash turned and saw the officer sitting behind the wheel look up. Almost instantly, the vehicle's lights flashed.

Oh, shit.

Sabra straightened the vehicle out, gunned it, and street merchants flashed by in a blur. Nash could hear various vehicles squealing behind them.

He risked a glance back and saw the two unmarked cars followed closely by none other than two police vehicles.

We're attracting a crowd.

Nash swung his head forward again and saw that they were rapidly approaching the area off the Cardo Plaza, part of the Byzantine Road, roughly the equivalent of an eight-lane highway that ran through the heart of the city. Some of the original Roman columns were still preserved along the road.

Up ahead the road curved. Two such columns rose directly in front of them. She gave the bike some gas. Wind thundered over Nash's helmet. The off-road bike vibrated, pushed to the extreme.

Jesus, she's going too fast to make the turn.

Indeed she was. Instead, at the last possible moment, Sabra turned the bike away from the columns and down into an underground strip mall below the Cardo.

Nash screamed. He hadn't seen the entrance until the last second.

Behind them, Nash heard various vehicles skidding, and then crashing. He looked back for a heartbeat and saw that one of the unmarked cars had plowed into the side of the entrance, effectively blocking it.

Sabra never slowed, navigating expertly through a crowd of shoppers, past countless art galleries and various stores. Finally, she brought the bike to a screeching halt in front of a stunned old man, a vendor of a falafel stand.

The vendor's mouth dropped open, but then he regained his composure and promptly offered Sabra a sample. She accepted and turned off the bike's motor.

"Did we lose them?" asked Nash. His whole body was vibrating from the pulsing machine. A bug had spattered on his helmet's visor.

"Possibly," she said, lifting her helmet and munching on the falafel. She licked her fingers, thanked the old man, and shoved her helmet back down. With Nash's help, she turned the bike around and started the engine. A moment later, they were flying toward the rear exit. And then back out on the Cardo Plaza, where Sabra slipped next to a passing meat truck, effectively hiding them.

At the far end of the plaza, near the entrance, Nash saw a small pile up of cars that included two police vehicles.

They're going to throw me in an Israeli prison forever.

But luckily, they continued on without incident, and soon passed out of the Jewish quarter and into the Christian quarter. Shortly after that, Sabra stopped the bike at the end of the Via Dolorosa that led to the Church of the Holy Sepulcher.

They were right on time for his meeting.

Nash stepped off the bike on wobbly legs. He reached inside his jacket and handed the diary to Sabra. "Just in case something goes wrong, I don't want them to have it."

Sabra nodded and removed a pistol from her own jacket pocket. "Maybe you should take this."

"No. They want the diary. Not me."

She took Nash's hand. "Be careful, okay?"

Nash smiled and ran his thumb over the back of her hand as a sign of affection. "I will."

"I'll be watching you," she said.

"Lucky me," said Nash, and let go of her hand and walked up to the Church.

Nash, admittedly, felt nervous as hell. And the shaking in his legs didn't entirely seem to be the result of the motorcycle ride from hell.

As he approached the church, he recalled from his extensive reading that the structure had been built by the Crusaders. And like the Crusades, people were still killing and dying for their religion.

Nothing's changed, he thought.

He passed through the big wooden doors at the entrance of the Church and made his way passed the first of a three-panel mosaic mural on the wall. The first panel showed Jesus' family and followers taking him down from the cross. The second depicted his body being cleansed. And the third and final panel showed Jesus' burial place—the edicule—that was about twenty feet away.

Given all that had happened, Nash wondered what was hidden under that edicule.

Maybe nothing, he thought. *Then again, maybe the body of Christ.*

He moved passed the stone where Jesus' body had allegedly been washed and then headed on up a flight of stone stairs that would eventually lead to the site of the crucifixion.

At the next level, in a wide room that was surprisingly cool, Nash paused to get his bearings. He was lost. He spotted a bearded,

219

black-robed Greek Orthodox monk sweeping along the orange marble floor, heading towards him.

"Excuse me," said Nash, as the monk approached. "I'm here to do a confession."

Saying nothing, the old monk simply pointed to the brown wood stained confessional behind Nash. Nash, feeling stupid and slightly disoriented, simply thanked him. The man nodded once and swept down the stairs.

Nash walked over and entered the wooden enclosure. He noticed a padded board at his feet and knelt on it opposite a small, screened window. He waited for several minutes, fighting nerves and wondering what the hell was going to come next.

He also wondered where Sabra might be. He suspected nearby, but he didn't know for sure.

A few minutes passed, and then a few more.

Maybe he was in the wrong confessional. He was about to get up to leave when someone finally came in and sat in the priest's seat opposite the confessional wall. Nash could not make out who it was through the opaque screen. Instead, he waited for the person to speak.

"Have you forgotten the protocol, Mr. Nash?" It was a man's voice.

Nash was in no mood to do the whole 'Bless me, Father, for I have sinned' shtick. "Let's cut the crap. What do you want to tell me?"

"Do you have the diary with you?"

"Of course not. You get the diary when I get my sister. And I swear to you, if anyone—"

"Hurt just one hair on her head. Yes, Mr. Nash. I have seen those movies, too. Your sister will be fine. *If* you do as we say."

Nash's first reaction was to reach through the mesh and grab hold of this bastard's neck—and strangle the life out of him. Or at least force him to give up his sister.

"You are breathing heavy, Mr. Nash. I can hear you from here.

Let me give you some advice. We make the rules in this game. You *will* play by the rules, or we will cut your sister's heart out very slowly. And one of those rules is that you obey. Got it?"

Nash closed his eyes. "Yes, got it. What do you want me to do?"

"You are to fly to Rome. Alone. There, you will find the Church of the Holy Name of Jesus. Ask for the Office of the Jesuit Refugee Service. Knock on the door and identify yourself. They will be expecting you."

"And then what?"

"They will take it from there." The voice on the other side of the screen paused. Nash sensed the man was smiling. *The son-of-a-bitch!* "Now, go with God, my son. And do not try to follow me. Wait ten minutes and then leave. And no peeking."

The man eased out of the confessional with a slight groan, then boots rapidly retreated over the marble floor. Nash waited the longest ten minutes of his life, and then walked back down the Via Dolorosa to where Sabra was waiting.

"We have our instructions?" she asked.

"*I* have *my* instructions," Nash corrected her. "I said I didn't want anyone with me who might risk my sister's life."

"I promise I'll stay out of the way, Jeremy. Besides, you need me to get you to wherever you're going."

"How's that?" asked Nash.

"Mossad has alerted the police. By now every airport, bus station, and taxi service will be looking for you if you try to leave Israel."

Nash bit his lip and scanned the massive facade of the church. A hot wind blew dust in his eyes. Squinting, he looked over at Sabra. He really didn't mind the company. Not to mention it was looking more and more like he needed her help.

"Fine," he said. "So, what's the plan?"

"We ride out of here on my bike."

"Where do we go to fly to Rome?"

"Jordan," she said, strapping on her helmet and handing him his. "The Amman airport to be specific."

He slipped behind her on the bike and fastened his helmet. "But I still need to get new identification."

"Then we'll pay a visit to the Sheik when we get to Amman."

"You do know that I have no idea what you are talking about."

"Exactly," she said. She reached back and patted his thigh, and then kicked the bike to life.

Wednesday
3:55 PM GMT
Amman, Jordon

Nash and Sabra crossed into the West Bank through the Muslim quarter carefully staying off the main highways. They covered the fifty odd miles over rough desert roads to Amman in a few hours.

Sabra found a small hotel near the Queen Alia International Airport, and they settled in.

"You take a shower and clean up," Sabra told Nash. "I'm going to see the Sheik."

Nash was stunned by the woman's resiliency. He was exhausted, but she, minus the road dust, appeared as fresh as if she had just jumped out of bed.

"Just who is this Sheik?" Nash asked. He had already started peeling off his dusty clothes.

She grinned and kissed Nash on the cheek. "Relax. He's just a contact. I'll be back soon with your new passport."

Peacock approached the clerk's desk at the Archaeological Authority office. Once there, he explained who he was, showed his ID, and told him he was doing research for his University in London.

The young man, after bringing up the file for the catacombs, paused and scratched his patchy beard, puzzled by the annotation blinking on the file.

It said simply: *Notify Supervisor*.

He excused himself and walked over to his supervisor's desk.

Peacock watched the kid anxiously. Hell, he couldn't help but feel anxious wherever he went nowadays. The young man and someone who appeared to be his superior entered into an animated discussion.

Peacock watched, feeling more and more agitated.

A minute later, composed, the young clerk returned and said, "All is in order, Mr. Peacock." He handed him a stamped permit. "Show this to the permit office downstairs, and they will give you the keys."

Peacock, greatly relieved, thanked him and left.

When the archaeologist was gone, the supervisor picked up his desk phone and made a call.

"We're all set," informed Peacock as he returned to Zed's cluttered apartment. If the old man had been concerned about the archaeologist's safety, he showed it by lying on his bed, hands tucked comfortably behind his head. Peacock continued, "I have the permit to enter the catacombs."

"Good," Zed replied. He didn't even bother opening his eyes. "And the keys to the locks?"

"Yes, the keys, too."

"Good. We go in tomorrow. I'll go in as your assistant, as planned. There shouldn't be any trouble."

Zed closed his eyes again. "Now, get some rest, young man. Tomorrow is going to be a big day."

Thursday
7:06 AM GMT
Rome, Italy

The official at Rome's Leonardo Da Vinci airport stamped Nash's fake passport and handed it back to him without incident. Nash thanked him but didn't really breathe again until they had stepped out into the sunshine.

"Good God, that was nerve racking," he exclaimed.

"You did fine," Sabra assured rubbing his shoulder.

"Actually, the Sheik did fine," said Nash. "It's a perfect replica."

"I expected no less," commented Sabra. "He owed me one. Now let's find ourselves a cab and get to the Church."

Nash was about to ask why he owed her anything but thought better of it. They had more pressing matters. Besides, she would probably have to kill him anyway if she divulged that information.

"Fine," agreed Nash. "But remember our deal. I go in alone."

"Alright. But once I know your sister is safe, I'll call the Station Chief and have the Italian police move in."

It was a wild ride through the congested streets of Rome, with their taxi driver nearly killing them on three separate occasions, two of which involving the running of red lights.

"In Rome," said Sabra, settling a hand on Nash's tense knee. "red lights are only a suggestion."

He looked down at her hand. He was certain her gesture was meant to calm him—or, in the least, momentarily distract him from the fact that his life was in the hands of a lunatic driver. Instead, her warm touch was having the opposite effect.

Swallowing, he tried to think of something else. Now was

226

not the time to get worked up. He pointed to some traffic ahead. "Looks like we're going to be a while."

Sabra grinned knowingly, and Nash was certain she had read his mind. Or at least sensed his thoughts. "Tell me something, Jeremy. Since you're an atheist, what's the basis of your moral philosophy?"

Nash almost laughed. Her question nearly had the same effect as throwing cold water on him. "First of all, young lady, I'm not an atheist. I'm an agnostic. I don't know whether God exists or not. And I really don't care. According to Professor Huxley, an agnostic is one who believes nothing which cannot be demonstrated by the senses or intellectually comprehended."

"So, faith has no place in your philosophy."

"True. And faith is not necessary to create a moral philosophy. In fact, one can be built entirely on a scientific philosophy."

"Do tell."

"Are you familiar with the Three Laws of Thermodynamics?"

"Of course but tell me anyway. This is fun. You're cute when you go into lecture mode."

She held his eyes with her own, and it was all Nash could do to focus his thoughts. "Okay. I'll re-interpret them for you with a fresh twist."

"Oh, I love twists."

Nash sensed a sexual innuendo, but he ignored it. He wasn't sure if she was truly interested in his philosophy, bored, or a little bit of both. "Okay, well, the first law says you can't win. The second law says you can't break even. And the third law says you can't leave the game."

"That's clever."

"The laws apply to entropy and states that everything will eventually run down. The universe itself will eventually die just as you and I will die."

"Uplifting stuff, Jeremy," she laughed, winking at him. "So how does one build a positive moral philosophy around that?"

"Well, entropy is only half the story. What the Three Laws don't take into account is the concept of *syntropy*."

"Syntropy?" she questioned, and Nash was pleased when she sounded genuinely intrigued. "Okay, you got me. What's syntropy?"

"The opposite of entropy. While entropy works to tear down the universe, syntropy works to build it up. It's the creative force of the universe." He paused. The taxi crept forward. "What is the greatest example of syntropy?"

Sabra shook her head. "Got me!"

"Life! The creation of life is syntropic and anything that supports or encourages life is syntropy. Now, that's a simple example. So, to get back to your question. *How does one build a moral philosophy around that?* What, beyond the simple act of procreation, is syntropic for humans?"

"I'm all ears," Sabra replied. She also nudged a little closer to him.

"First, let's look at entropy. Human actions that harm life are entropic. These include physical harm, of course, but also emotional and mental harm and any actions that prevent the evolution of life, both physical and social. These actions either reduce the value of life or eliminate it. So, if one's moral philosophy is based on the intellectually comprehended entropy/syntropy concept, one can build a moral system that doesn't need religion or any other kind of faith."

Sabra studied him, then surprised the hell out of him by summing up his thoughts perfectly. "So, if you create and encourage the syntropic values of life, love, empathy, honesty, and all the other human values, a philosophy built on religion and the need for a God is not needed."

Nash blinked. "Yes, exactly."

"So, your philosophy is existential?"

"No. Existentialism embraces the view that the suffering individual must accept an unknowable, chaotic, and seemingly empty universe. And that's not true. The universe is filled with as much syntropy as entropy. It's our job in this life to resist the forces of entropy with the forces of syntropy—or as they say—the battle of good versus evil."

"The Gospel According to Jeremy. Has a nice ring to it," she quipped.

"Well, we've certainly arrived at the same place religion has," he said. "Embrace the good and fight the evil—but without the need for faith."

"You're forgetting one thing," Sabra pointed out. "A thing the belief in God and religion offers that your scientific moral philosophy doesn't."

"And what's that?"

"The afterlife. Heaven. The soul. The spirit. That's missing from your grand design. It doesn't account for the spiritual encounter, the experience of one with the godhead that the founders of the great religions have tried to explain to their followers."

"You're talking about spirituality."

"Correct. My father taught me the true meaning of the Torah, the Kabbalah. That's why he was so enamored with the Dead Sea Scrolls." She paused a moment. "And he was killed for what he found."

Nash placed a hand on her shoulder. "Roth spoke of the same things, this path to God that we all must find. I really don't know what to make of it. And you're right, my philosophy doesn't deal with it, but I also don't think it's a necessary subject for living in this life."

For no apparent reason, at least none that Nash could fathom, their taxi driver laid his horn down long and hard, joining a steady cacophony of blares and honks. Little good it did. They were just as stuck.

When the man was finished with his little tantrum, Sabra continued, "Are you a betting man, Jeremy?"

"I bet only on logic," he said.

"Okay, Mr. Logic. Have you ever heard of Blaise Pascal?"

"Who hasn't?" said Nash.

"Does that really mean no?"

"Of course I haven't heard of him—or her. Who is it?"

"*He* was a French mathematician and philosopher," said Sabra. "Famous for what is now known as Pascal's Wager."

"Ah, then it's a good thing his name also happened to be Pascal."

"Will you be serious, Jeremy?"

He grinned. "Fine. What's Pascal's Wager?"

She studied him a moment, squinting, perhaps gauging how serious he truly was. Nash did his best not to grin. Satisfied, she went on, "According to Pascal, there are only two satisfactory answers when the existence of God is questioned—either God exists or not. Either yes or no."

"Fine," said Nash, "So what's his wager?"

"It's not technically *his* wager, Jeremy. It's a wager we are all making. Each and every one of us. Every day. And it's not money we are wagering. We are betting our eternal souls."

Nash rolled his eyes.

"Roll your eyes all you want, Jeremy, but each of us should consider the four possibilities of God's existence."

"And what are those?"

"The first possibility is if you bet that God exists, and He does, then you go to heaven. Your winnings are infinite. The second possibility is if you bet that God exists, and He does not, your winnings are finite and thus negligible. Third, if you bet that God does not exist, and He doesn't, your winnings are finite and thus negligible. But, if you bet that God *does not* exist, and He *does*, you will go to hell and your loss is infinite."

"You missed your calling," Nash replied. "You should have been a bookie."

"It's a good way of looking at the afterlife," said Sabra thoughtfully.

"It's also a fear tactic to bring more people into churches. The reasoning behind Pascal's Wager is not sound," Nash asserted.

"In what way?"

"Pascal assumes that a God of Creation needs us disgusting, foul-smelling creatures to believe in the very being who created us. He further assumes that a God of Creation cares a rat's ass if we believe in Him or not."

Sabra looked at him for a beat or two. "Do you think I'm a disgusting, foul smelling creature?"

Nash resisted taking her lead. Instead, he said, "There's always exceptions to the rule."

Just then the driver squealed with delight, and wildly gave the taxi some gas. The traffic had cleared and they were on their way again.

They exited the cab, paid the driver, and walked into the café across the street from the Church of the Holy Name of Jesus.

"I can see well from there," Sabra said. "I'll give you no more than an hour, Jeremy. If I don't see you exit with your sister I'm calling the Mossad Station Chief. And be careful. We don't know who we're dealing with here."

"All they want is the diary, Sabra. There's no reason why they would harm us."

"I wish I had my pistol with me to give to you."

They had ditched the weapon at the airport prior to boarding their flight at the Amman Airport. Yeah, a pistol in his pocket would have felt damn nice. Nash looked down at Sabra. She reached up and patted his cheeks. He noticed, and not for the first time, that she had beautiful, almond shaped eyes. "Well, here goes," he said hopefully, and left the café, crossing the street towards the Church entrance.

Sabra took a seat in the front of the café, giving her a clear view of the Church facade. A waiter came by, and she ordered a latte

and rooted into the back of her pack to fetch some money. She found the money—and something else.

Roth's satellite phone.

She paid the waiter and turned the phone on. There were three text messages waiting for him.

Amused, she started reading them.

Peacock, who had been looking for an opportunity to phone Roth without Zed knowing, found it when they were finishing breakfast in a café across from the Church of the Holy Name of Jesus.

"I'm going to the men's room," he said.

"Hurry up," Zed grunted. "We need to get moving. The church seems quiet."

Peacock left the table and entered the rest room. He pulled out his cell and punched in Roth's number. Roth's line rang several times before a woman's voice answered.

"Who is this?" asked Peacock. "Where's Stanton Roth?"

"Who are you?"

Peacock frowned and checked the GPS monitor on his phone, a nifty device that allowed him and Roth to track each other's whereabouts.

Peacock stared hard at the face plate. Surely the damn thing wasn't working. He logged off the device, re-logged on, but got the same mystifying message.

According to the GPS monitor, Roth was here in this very cafe.

Confused, Peacock left the men's room and paused at the rear of the cafe, scanning the crowd. There were a few young kids in one corner, working together on a laptop and drinking an iced coffee. An older couple sat lazily near a window. And sitting at a small table next to the older couple was the beautiful woman he couldn't help but notice earlier.

And she was staring down at a cell phone.

What the hell is going on?

Maybe it was a glitch in the technology. Maybe the GPS device was really giving Peacock his own coordinates. Obviously, Roth was nowhere to be seen.

The pretty woman was alternately scrolling through the phone and looking out the big glass window.

To Peacock, the woman looked apprehensive, nervous.

Something is wrong.

He summoned his courage and approached the woman. She looked up at him immediately, eyes narrowing. God, she was a beauty.

Peacock, suddenly unsure how to even begin the conversation, began stammering at once: "Would you, um, would you happen to know a Stanton Roth?"

The woman shifted her weight, facing him a little more. "Never heard of him. Why?"

"I'm, uh, his friend. Doing some research for him. According to the GPS link in our phones, he's supposed to be somewhere in this café. Well, obviously, it's a mistake. My apologies."

Peacock turned and was about to swiftly escape this horribly embarrassing situation when the woman surprised the hell out of him by saying, "Have a seat."

Peacock looked back at the woman. "Excuse me?"

"Sit down," she said, gesturing to the seat opposite her. "We need to talk."

Thursday
9:25 AM GMT
Rome, Italy

J eremy Nash quickly crossed the piazza and approached Rome's largest Jesuit church where St. Ignatius Loyola, the founder of the Jesuit Order, was entombed.

Once inside, flanked by several side chapels and below a soaring vaulted ceiling, he headed down the single-aisle nave towards the high altar.

Moments later, by the entrance to one of the small chapels, he saw a sign that read: *Office de Centro Astalli.* Under it were the words: *Jesuit Refugee Service.* He knocked sharply on the heavy door. It opened promptly and a tall, muscular man stepped out.

"Mr. Nash, I presume?" he asked in heavily accented English.

"Yes."

"Follow me please."

Sabra told the nervous man of Stanton Roth's unfortunate demise. The man, after recovering from his initial shock, introduced himself and divulged that he, in fact, had been working for Roth.

"What's your association to Roth?" he asked. "And how is it that you have his cell phone?"

Early on in her training, Sabra was told to rarely, if ever, admit that she was a spy. Or, for that matter, admit she worked for the Mossad. Both revelations could be very detrimental to not only her health, but the health of her colleagues, and the outcome to many of her assignments.

So she considered her options. At this very moment, Nash was no doubt confronting his sister's kidnappers. Now was not the time to dance around the subject. Roth had obviously trusted this man—Peacock he said his name was—with some *very* personal research. Trusting her gut instinct, she decided to trust the man, too. Or, more accurately, to give him enough information to both keep him satisfied and to earn his help and trust.

And so, she told the man of Alyson's kidnapping and of Roth's unique position to offer help. She omitted key facts of the diary and scrolls, and only admitted to merely being an Israeli police investigator assigned to the case. He asked to see her ID. She showed him a fake badge, hidden in her purse for such occasions.

"Why not call the local police?" asked Peacock suspiciously. "Why is your friend going at this alone?"

"Terms of the exchange. We didn't make the rules. We have backup in place," she lied. Granted, she *was* the backup. She went on, "You mentioned you were here with someone. Who?"

"He's with me," said a voice from the door.

Sabra looked over to a sprightly old man heading their way. "And who are you?" she asked.

"My name's Zed Nash."

Something made Sabra jump at an assumption.

"Are you Jeremy's grandfather?" said Sabra.

Zed nodded.

"You're supposed to be dead!"

"I know," he smiled. "Boo."

Thursday
9:45 AM GMT
Rome, Italy

Jeremy Nash followed the tall man into a small office manned by two middle-aged males who eyed Nash suspiciously from their desks. They didn't seem particularly religious to Nash.

"This way," the tall man ordered.

He stepped through the office and led the way along a narrow hallway. They came to a flight of stairs that disappeared down into inky blackness. Nash swallowed and followed the man down, feeling carefully with his foot. They came to a landing of some sort, and Nash was utterly relieved to discover a light down what appeared to be a very narrow stone hallway.

When they reached the far end, Nash saw that the light was, in fact, from an LED display panel set into the wall. The man punched in a code, and a very modern metal door slid open.

Nash was ushered in and led down a long concrete hallway lit from above with recessed lighting set back into the ancient stone. The floor itself was dusty and cobbled together with cracked tiles. They stepped through a second metal door that opened into a bunker that clearly doubled as a laboratory. Several video screens on the wall appeared to monitor another room. One such screen even monitored nitrogen levels and other atmospheric chemicals in the room.

Nash wondered what was so special about this room and why the hell the Jesuits had such an interest in all this scientific paraphernalia. But mostly he anxiously wondered where they were keeping his sister.

God, if they killed me here, no one would ever find my body.

Nash realized he was perspiring, despite the coolness of the bunker. "What's with all the monitors?" he asked his companion standing next to him.

But the response came from behind him.

"Science, Mr. Nash."

Nash quickly turned to see an elderly gentleman, perhaps in his late seventies or early eighties, with a full head of graying hair that was cut short in a military manner. He was tall and strapping and was walking towards Nash with a confident gait.

"But let me introduce myself first. My name's Phillip Marcus, and I think you have something I want."

"First, where's my sister?"

"I'm sorry, Mr. Nash, but you don't make the rules." Marcus flicked his gaze at the tall man standing next to Nash. "Search him."

Thursday
9:45 AM GMT
The Catacombs

"Open it up," said Zed.

Peacock pulled out the set of keys he had received from the Archaeological Authority office and inserted one into a rusty lock that held together a chain secured around the iron gates of a high fence. Peacock turned the key and the lock released. The heavy chain fell free from the gate.

"We're in," said Zed excitedly.

Sabra decided that she liked the old man. And she certainly saw a little bit of Jeremy in him, although the elder Nash seemed far more heedless and reckless. She wondered again the logic of following the two men into the catacombs. The plan had been for her to wait for Jeremy outside the church. But waiting wasn't in her nature. Waiting made her crazy. She needed to do something. And helping the old man—Nash's grandfather, no less—seemed as good an idea as any.

The three passed through the gate and into a small courtyard. Sabra looked around the dilapidated opening strewn with broken tiles, crumbled rocks and weeds. "Looks like no one's been here for centuries."

"It's supposed to look like that," Zed replied. "This way."

He led the way through the courtyard, through waist high weeds, and to a broken-down section of wall. He pointed to what appeared to be a cave-like opening into the wall, with several large rocks strewn outside and inside the entrance.

"This is the way in," Zed said. "We'll have to climb over these rocks, of course."

239

"Of course," said Sabra, amused to hear the excitement in the old man's voice.

Probably hadn't had this much fun in decades, she mused.

The three scrambled over the rocks. Not only did the old man not need any help, he was, in fact, the first through the entrance. Sabra followed behind, with Peacock trailing. Immediately, she found herself in a very dark tunnel.

"Here," said Zed. He unslung his duffel bag, rummaged through it, swung a coil of rope over his head and shoulder and removed three flashlights.

Sabra clicked hers on and saw that the tunnel extended well into the darkness. The walls were roughly hewed, perhaps a combination of natural and man-made. The tunnel reminded her of a mining shaft.

"Let's go," said Zed.

"Wait." It was Peacock.

Sabra turned to the man, shining her light over him. The archaeologist was sweating profusely. Eyes wild, unfocused.

He's losing it, she thought.

"Something wrong?" asked Zed.

"Hell, yeah, something is wrong," said Peacock. He looked nervously back over his shoulder. "Very wrong. These guys play for keeps, and I don't want any part of this."

"Easy, old boy," said Zed soothingly. "There's just one more lock ahead, maybe a hundred feet up. Just open the door for us and we can take it from there."

"Sorry, old man. This is far as I go." He tossed the keys at Zed's feet. "I'm just an archaeologist. Not a damn adventurer. All this Indiana Jones bullshit is just that, bullshit."

He nodded to them, shook his head, and scrambled back over the rocks.

"Well, then," said Zed, picking the keys up with a grunt. He looked sideways at Sabra. "Are you skittish as well, my dear?"

"You kidding?" exclaimed Sabra, shouldering her knapsack and moving forward. "The fun's just beginning."

They continued in silence, winding deeper and deeper into the catacombs.

Sabra wondered how the old man was holding up. Outside of some heavy breathing, he seemed to be doing fine. *He better be fine,* she thought. She needed him, especially if she wanted to find her way back out of these damn catacombs. Already she was fighting a persistent feeling of claustrophobia.

Zed pointed his flashlight ahead. "There's the door."

When they reached it, he fumbled with the oversized keys a moment, found one that looked promising, and inserted it into the keyhole of the rusted out metal door. With a quick turn, the lock made an audible clunk as the tumblers fell into place. Zed pushed the door open. Immediately, stale air issued out, pushed forward by an inexplicable wind.

Sabra shuddered, and reminded herself that she was a fearless Mossad agent.

Sabra followed the old man through the low doorway, ducking, and pushing aside a thick strand of cobwebs that Zed had somehow avoided. Sabra hated cobwebs. As she stood straight again, pulling the damn stuff free from her hair, she suddenly gasped.

Zed spun around. "What's wrong?"

She pointed to three human skulls—all without lower jaws—embedded into the wall beside her. She suddenly felt foolish. They were, after all, just skulls and this *was* a catacomb.

Zed chuckled softly. "You okay?"

"Yes, sorry." Sabra felt herself blush. She sucked in some musty air, filling her lungs to capacity, and willed herself to calm down.

"Better now?" he asked kindly and concerned.

"Yes. It's just, you know, a little creepy down here."

"Really? I hadn't noticed."

The old man gave her a warm smile and they continued on. Shortly, after rounding a small bend in the tunnel, they entered a massive opening, a semi-natural cavern, with symbols and art painted on the walls and ceiling. Near the walls, embedded in the stone floor, were ancient tombstones covered with symbols and writing.

"Those tombs are called loculi," Zed said. "The Christians carved them out of the walls and even the floor itself." Zed continued as he shined his light around the room. "The catacombs have multiple levels, connected by light shafts. Many of these are hidden throughout the catacombs beneath thin slabs of stone—slabs that can only be described as unstable, at best. So watch your step, dear girl."

"Keeps getting better and better," offered Sabra.

Zed suddenly cocked his head, listening. Sabra heard it, too. Down one of the tunnels, perhaps behind them, had come the sound of two muffled blasts. Sabra was certain she knew what the blasts were.

Gunshots.

Zed looked at her and shrugged. Just as he did so, three more distant sounds came, each echoing through the myriad of tunnels. And now they heard something else—The sound of running feet.

Zed removed two pistols from his knapsack and handed one to Sabra.

The sound of running grew louder, each step seemingly reverberating within the cavern around them. Whoever it was, whatever it was, was just around the bend.

And in that moment, as Sabra aimed her weapon at the cavern opening behind them, a man appeared. He pulled up short, throwing his hands up to shield his eyes, blinded by their flashlights.

It was Peacock.

"What the devil is going on, man?" cried Zed, lowering his gun.

"They're behind me!" shouted Peacock.

"Who's behind you?"

But Peacock wasn't listening. The archaeologists seemed half mad with fear. "They're shooting at me! Run!"

And run he did. Wildly, blindly. Right past Zed, shoving the old man aside. Sabra followed the fleeing man as he blindly disappeared through a far opening in the cavern wall.

Sabra was about to ask if they should follow the archaeologist, when she heard two alarming things at once.

The first was the sound of more running feet coming from the direction Peacock had come.

The second was a distinct *rumbling* beneath their feet.

Sabra shined her flashlight down. Dust was shifting and vibrating at her feet...revealing the deep edges of a rectangular stone slab.

She and Zed were standing in the middle of it.

"Move slowly," warned Zed. "Very slowly."

Sabra nodded. She had never stood on thin ice before, but she sensed she was about to find out what that disconcerting experience was like. The slab beneath her, with the added weight of the old man, seemed to bow in the middle.

The unnerving shaking increased.

In the tunnel outside the cavern, the running footsteps grew louder.

Zed carefully, slowly, lifted a foot and edged outward. Sabra was about to do the same when the stone beneath her abruptly disappeared, imploding inward, bringing her down with it.

Sabra screamed, grabbing for the edge of the pit.

Unfortunately, she was too far away. Instead, her desperately flailing hand found Zed's fingers. The old man, who had just made it to safety, gripped her fingertips—but it was tenuous grip at best.

Like a pendulum, she swung toward the wall of the pit— slamming into it hard.

She gasped, the air bursting from her lungs....

And lost her grip.

The last image Sabra had before plunging into darkness was of a wide-eyed and desperately reaching Zed Nash.

Nash was suddenly unsure things would go smoothly, let alone well. Now that Marcus had the diary, the man seemed entirely unconcerned and unmotivated to produce Nash's sister.

Should have left the damn thing with Sabra.

Instead, he was only told that his sister would be here shortly. While he waited, Nash was permitted to wander the laboratory.

"I didn't know the Jesuits were so interested in science," he observed, noting the many instruments and gadgets. In one corner of the room was a sort of CT scanner. Nash wondered what the hell they used that for.

"Oh, the Jesuits have a long history of science," said Marcus idly, flipping through Nash's grandfather's diary. "We even have Jesuit priests manning the Vatican Observatory in Arizona."

"Why would the Jesuits be interested in astronomy?"

"Let's just say that if any cosmic discoveries were to be made, the Church doesn't want to be the last to know."

"What kind of discoveries?"

"Of the SETI kind."

Nash looked over at the elder man, who was leaning an elbow on a stainless steel shelf.

"SETI?" said Nash. "The church believes in aliens?"

Marcus snapped the book shut.

"Think of it this way, Mr. Nash. How would any kind of off-world contact with another civilization affect religious beliefs here on earth?"

Nash opened his mouth to respond but decided that maybe it was best to keep his thoughts to himself.

Marcus went on. "If such a discovery should happen, the Church wants a dog in that fight."

Nash nodded as if he understood. The only thing he understood, however, was that people were far too gullible.

In that moment, the metallic door banged open again, and this time Nash saw a familiar sight.

He nearly wept.

It was his sister.

She ripped loose of the dark-haired brute holding her by her upper arm and ran to Nash. She flung herself into her brother's arms and wept uncontrollably.

Nash patted her head and felt his own eyes moisten. Mostly though, he felt white-hot hate bubble up for those who had put his sister through this.

"You okay?" he asked gently, separating her enough to look into her tear-streaked face. She nodded. Tears flowed freely from her eyes, matting her long hair to her cheeks.

More hate. More anger.

Nash looked over at Marcus who was watching the reunion with a bemused expression. The diary sat, seemingly forgotten, on the metal shelf next to him.

"You have the diary; I have my sister. We're leaving now."

Nash took her hand and headed toward the lab's exit. No one moved until he reached the door. From his peripheral vision, Nash saw Marcus nod his head sharply and a guard, gripping a sleek black pistol, blocked his path.

"Tell your goon to get the hell out of our way," said Nash.

"I'm afraid I can't do that, Mr. Nash," said Marcus.

Nash spun around, his rage and anger getting the better of him. He knew now was not the time to lash out, but he couldn't keep it in anymore.

"Let me guess. We know too much. Am I right?"

"You are correct, Mr. Nash."

"And you are planning to dispose of us."

"Again, correct."

"And are you aware that at this moment Mossad agents have been tracking my every move?"

"Not your every move, Mr. Nash." Marcus grinned wolfishly. "And we both know it's just a single agent. Besides, we've taken care of her."

Thursday
11:20 AM GMT

Section 18

Sabra dropped like a rock.

Dirt, stone and debris poured down with her. Her only thought was that she was probably going to land soon—and hard. And if the landing didn't kill her, she surely was going to break every bone in her body.

Instinctively, her hands reached out for any sort of handhold.

Amazingly, her desperately searching fingers wrapped around something long and smooth. The shaft slipped through her hand, and she would have surely lost her grip if not for the knobby end that gave her a firm grip.

Sabra smashed hard against the earth wall. Air exploded from her lungs. She grunted. Debris continued to rain down on her from above, but after a few moments the downpour subsided.

Light flashed from above, perhaps twenty feet up.

The roving beam of light found her, and she saw for the first time what she was hanging from—a skeleton's limb projecting from the earth wall. The femur bone was long and thick, but the earth around it was already breaking lose.

"Shit!"

"Sabra? You there?"

"Yes, it's me. Now help me, goddammit."

"Hold on! I mean...never mind."

The light momentarily disappeared, and Sabra found herself plunged into a Stygian darkness and praying like hell to every deity and god she had ever heard of.

247

The beam of light returned, striking her in the face. "I'm going to throw you a rope," shouted Zed.

"Don't tell me about it, goddammit. Just do it!"

"Er, right, sorry."

It was at that moment that Sabra heard voices from above. Angry voices.

Things were not going according to plan.

Zed hated that. First the archaeologist had fled in fear—and then, inexplicably, returned. *And had that been gunshots he'd heard?* He didn't know, but the last thing Zed expected was for the girl to now be hanging for her life by, of all things, a leg bone.

He quickly tied one end of the rope to a massive rock slab and was about to toss the other end to the hanging Sabra when he was suddenly shoved aside. In his haste to help Sabra, and his old habit of focusing completely at the task at hand, Zed had completely missed the fact that two men had entered the cavern, one of whom was currently yelling at him not to move.

Both men had dark complexions and were well-dressed. Both were holding weapons aimed at him.

The taller of the two said something rapidly in what Zed thought might have been Italian. Immediately, the other man stepped over, pushed him back and searched him, finding Zed's pistol in his coat pocket. The man tossed it aside.

"Take him," said the first man in English. He had stepped over to the pit and was carefully peering over. Dust still swirled around the opening, churning in his flashlight's sharp beam.

A rough hand grabbed Zed's shoulder. "You come with me."

With Zed in tow, the second man stopped next to the first. Zed could see Sabra still hanging from the bone.

"What about her?" asked the second man.

"Leave her." The tall man was about to turn away, then paused. "On second thought, kill her."

The second man smiled, his blunt, broad face brightening with sadistic pleasure.

A sociopath, thought Zed.

The man reached inside his jacket, removed a pistol and aimed it down into the pit—

"No!" shouted Zed and threw himself at the man. But the taller of the two men—the obvious leader—turned and punched the elder Nash hard in the face, laying him out.

As his world threatened to go black around him, Zed thought—*They're going to kill her.*

Sabra could see the man reach into his jacket pocket and remove what appeared to be a pistol. She heard the old man scream "No!" and try to defend her, bless his heart. She heard what sounded like a punch and now the man above her, his pale face illuminated by his own flashlight, was grinning wickedly.

The Mossad agent, helpless where she hung, closed her eyes and waited for the inevitable sound of gunfire to come.

And come it did.

But from deeper within the cavern.

Sabra snapped her head up again and this time saw the short man teetering on the edge of the shaft. He paused briefly and then pitched forward, falling straight down, just missing the hanging Sabra. Rocking gently, she felt a burst of wind as he passed her. A few seconds later she heard a distant *thunk* from way down below.

Zed watched as the remaining man pulled out his gun, crouched low, and scanned the cavern.

A second shot rang out.

The crouching man screamed, dropping his flashlight and gun. As his light rolled away Zed just caught the man reaching for his neck as a fountain of blood had erupted.

Jesus Christ!

Another flashlight turned on. This time from across the cavern. And there, looking as if he had seen a ghost, was Peacock. He was holding Zed's pistol.

"I can't believe I just killed two people."

"Believe it," said Zed, after the two of them had pulled Sabra from the deadly black depths. Now the three of them were making their way deeper into the catacombs. "It was either them or us. And I prefer us."

Sabra thanked the nervous archaeologist, but Peacock only nodded absently. The pale man seemed lost in his own thoughts. Whether he wanted to or not, he was sure as hell invested in this little adventure now.

Ten minutes later, the tunnel they were following reached a dead end.

"There's nothing here," Peacock cried.

"Ye of little faith," said Zed. He stepped forward, shining his flashlight around the small, man-made chamber cluttered with rocks and boulders of various sizes. "If I remember correctly, and it's been some years, there should be...ah ha! There it is!"

Zed hurried over to a boulder about three or four feet high and climbed on top of it. He looked like a giant kid. He was even grinning like one. Sabra, once again, couldn't help but like the old man. She would like him even more, however, if he could find a way out of this cave, which felt as if it were getting smaller by the minute.

"Here," called Zed excitedly. "Behind this rock."

Sabra peered around the rock on tip toes and saw what had gotten the old man all worked up. It was an air vent embedded into the rock wall. There was also a small space behind the vent, just large enough for one person.

"This is one of the air returns for Section Eighteen," said Zed. "We go through here."

Sabra, eager to get the hell out of this shrinking room, slipped behind the rock and reached for the grate.

Just as she did so, Zed yelled, "*Stop!*"

"Why?" she asked.

"Touch it lightly. It might be electrified."

Sabra reached her hand out slowly, lightly touching the grate. Crackling energy zapped her fingertips.

"Shit! It *is* electrified." Sabra fought hard to ease her panic. She had reached a point where she truly, desperately needed to get out of this cave.

"Now what?" asked Peacock.

"No clue," said Zed, glumly.

But Sabra had an idea. She sat down, leaned her back against the boulder, and kicked hard. The grate burst inward with a rain of sparks.

"Let's go", she said, and was the first inside.

With Sabra leading the way, the trio crawled through the narrow steel duct. The Mossad agent, now further confined within the steel tube, reminded herself that she was surely only a few feet away from freedom.

At the far end of the duct, Sabra reached another grate. She gently touched it, but this one was not electrified. She peered through the opening as best as she could but, as far as she could tell, the room, whatever it was, was empty.

Adrenalin flooding her system, she pushed hard on the grate and it promptly swung open. She stuck her head into what appeared to be a dark storage room. A moment later, she pulled herself through and dropped down, relief flooding her system. The other two followed behind, with Peacock nearly falling on his head had it not been for Zed's help.

Once they were all inside, Sabra, who had taken the gun from Peacock, gently cracked the heavy metal door open. Bright yellow light flooded the small room. The agent peered though the opening and out into a hallway. A man was standing there, holding a semi-automatic weapon. She silently closed the door again.

"We have company," she reported.

"How many?" asked Zed.

"One."

"Do you have any plans?"

Sabra flashed her light around the storeroom and saw a copper pipe leaning against the wall. She hefted it. This was going to do some serious damage. She didn't give a damn at this point.

Aware that both Peacock and Zed Nash were watching her closely, she eased back to the door, cracked it open, and peered out. The guard was still there, his profile to her. Faint noises—heated talking or debate—seemed to be coming from the very room he was guarding.

Was Jeremy in there?

Sabra didn't know, but she was determined to find out. She waited quietly, unmoving. The guard hummed something softly under his breath.

And then he turned away from her, and Sabra pounced.

She was out the door in a blink, simultaneously bringing up the copper pipe. She moved quickly down the hall, and just as the guard was about to turn back, just as he possibly sensed someone was behind him, Sabra swung the pipe hard.

It connected with a devastating crash against the side of the man's head. Sabra was reminded of the sound that good China makes when it crashes. His skull, she knew, had shattered. The man was dead before he hit the ground.

She heard the other two approach behind her. Zed whistled when he looked down at the man. A pool of blood spread rapidly across the polished floor. Peacock began hyperventilating.

"Get ahold of yourself," hissed Sabra.

The voices were coming from somewhere behind the door. She cracked it open and peered inside. A flight of stairs led down. The voices were coming from somewhere at the bottom.

"This way," she whispered, and led the way down.

"Wait," said Zed.

He went back and retrieved the fallen guard's weapon. He hefted the heavy gun and looked at Sabra. "Okay, now let's go."

Nash stood with his sister on one side of the lab as Marcus and another man, newly arrived, dressed in a long, flowing priest's robe quietly discussed his and his sister's fate.

Nash scanned the room, looking for anything he could use as a weapon. Outside of a few beakers and test tubes filled with mystery liquids, he didn't see much. Besides, a man with a gun—a young kid with acne—kept a steady eye on them.

Nash patted his sister's back protectively. She nestled closer to him, burying her face in his shoulder. He was damned if he was going to let them hurt her.

As he continued scanning the room, he saw something at the far end, within the darkened shadows, that immediately drew his attention.

A door had opened a crack.

Someone was looking out through the door. Nash had no idea who it was, and wisely decided to avert his gaze, lest he drew attention to them.

He continued his slow scan of the room, aware that his own heart had suddenly increased in tempo. Was he about to be saved? Was something good, for once, about to happen?

He didn't know, but he was hopeful. Damned hopeful.

Sabra peered through the heavy door. The voices on the other side had grown quieter, and now she saw why.

Two men were huddled quietly together, while a third held a semi-automatic weapon on Jeremy and a woman, no doubt his sister.

Sabra nearly gasped when she saw Jeremy look at her. He then quickly turned his gaze away, and she saw he was savvy enough not to draw attention to them.

Good man!

Sabra felt Zed behind her, virtually breathing down her neck. The old man must have seen something that bothered him, because his breathing suddenly stopped, and she felt him tense.

She was about to have him stand back when the old man did something shockingly stupid.

He barged into the room.

Marcus looked up with a start. There was surely a ghost approaching him from the shadowed depths of the laboratory. He opened his mouth to speak, and nothing came out. Worse, the ghost was holding a semi-automatic weapon.

The guard at the far end of the room was the next to react. He was about to swing his weapon around when the ghost shouted, "Put down the weapon or I'll cut you in two!"

The guard froze, then did as he was told. He set the Uzi down and held his hands over his head.

From behind the ghost came two more figures. A woman and another man, a nervous looking fellow. Marcus ignored the other two and focused solely on the older man who was now rapidly approaching him.

"You're supposed to be dead," Marcus hissed.

"You left me for dead in that nuthouse," accused Zed Nash. And when he was close enough, the elder Nash punched Phillip Marcus as hard as he could in the face.

Nash could not believe his eyes.

In fact, he even rubbed them.

Coming from the darkness was none other than his grandfather. A man he had not seen in decades. A man who was supposed to be long dead.

Next to him, Alyson gasped, bewildered. Nash might have gasped too.

He watched in perplexed disbelief as his grandfather strode purposefully across the laboratory, holding before him nothing other than a semi-automatic weapon. His grandfather promptly ordered the solitary guard to stand down. Then the man—the same man he had been led to believe was insane, then dead, rapidly approached Marcus promptly leveling the man with a wildly thrown punch.

Alyson gasped again.

Trailing behind his grandfather was a breath of fresh air. It was Sabra and she had a pistol of her own.

Thank God!

With her was another man who seemed harmless enough. Nash ignored him and focused his attention on the bewildering scene in front of him.

"Grandfather?" he asked hesitantly.

"Good afternoon, my boy. Although you would never know it since we're buried so deep in this godforsaken place."

"But I thought you were, you know..."

"Dead? I'll explain later."

Alyson suddenly threw herself at the old man, and the two hugged tightly. She had always been closer to their grandparents. His grandfather wiped a tear off her face, then released her and turned his attention to the man still sprawled on the floor.

"Get your sorry ass up, Phillip, and tell these good people what's really going on here."

The lab was mostly silent. Something hummed somewhere, and Nash felt a brief burst of air conditioning.

Marcus stood slowly and adjusted his suit. He carefully wiped blood from his lip. The guard to his right continued standing with his arms raised. Nash used that moment to walk over and retrieve the man's discarded weapons.

"Tell them, Marcus," he commanded. "You worthless piece of shit!"

"I have no idea what you're talking about."

Nash thought for a moment, just a moment, that his grandfather was going to punch the man again. He didn't. Instead, he slowly looked more and more enraged. And crazy. Okay, that was the look Nash remembered as a kid. The crazy old man who had ultimately been sent to an institution—where he had allegedly died.

Allegedly.

"Then let me refresh your memory," said his grandfather. "In July of forty-seven, what every true Christian believes had come to pass. After two thousand years, Christ returned to earth from the skies over America."

Yes, this was definitely the grandfather Nash remembered. He felt as if no time had passed and that he was back to being a little boy listening to the old man's wild ramblings all over again.

Nash watched Marcus's reaction. The old man—once his grandfather's colleague—rolled his eyes.

His grandfather continued, his shrill voice raising an octave. "The Air Force killed my Lord and they will have to pay for it. The secret is out, and you and all the others who don't believe will pay."

"You're insane," cried Marcus. "Whoever let you out of the nuthouse made a mistake. Or, more than likely, you escaped."

Zed hit the man again, this time with the butt of the rifle. Alyson gasped. Nash moved forward, then restrained himself. Sabra watched all of this with a bemused expression on her face. She caught Nash's eye and shrugged.

Marcus had stumbled back, holding his nose. Nash was certain it had broken. As blood was pouring between the man's fingers, his grandfather looked on with satisfaction.

Zed turned to Nash. "Jeremy, I have followed your career over the years. I know you are a skeptic—and God bless you for that. You give balance to the whackos of the world."

Nash held his tongue. His grandfather continued.

"But I am speaking the truth, and it's important to me that you believe me." He turned his attention to the bleeding man who had propped himself up against a stainless steel table. "And Marcus has the proof. Show the tape of the nineteen forty-seven Roswell crash, Marcus. I know you have it here, under lock and key."

"I have no idea what you're talking about."

Zed Nash raised his weapon and touched it between Marcus's eyes. "Show them, or I will shoot you through the head with great pleasure."

Marcus swallowed then glanced over at the robed man standing in shocked silence off to one side. "Father Engle, do as the man says."

Father Engle obediently walked to one of the consoles in the lab and, after several key strokes, brought up a video. Another keystroke later and the video appeared on the oversized monitor hanging on the wall above them, with the words, *Air Force Intelligence: Aerospace Defense Command—Internal Video Surveillance: July 3, 1947.*

Despite himself, Nash found himself very curious indeed to see what was contained on this tape. He stepped under the monitor and looked up.

The film—very old and badly deteriorated—next showed what appeared to be an old version of the NORAD command room. The room was obviously on alert, and there were threat warning lights flashing around the area.

"Turn up the sound," Zed ordered.

The Jesuit priest complied, and Nash clearly heard a radio communication between the command room and fighter jets that were scrambling in response to a threat. The radio conversation confirmed that the jets were in hot pursuit of a UFO. Next, the tape became very dim and scratchy and nearly inaudible. When the video cleared, Nash could see a team of soldiers in the desert gathering up strange pieces of indescribable objects.

"The tape has been altered," noted Zed weakly. "It's missing the most important section."

"No," said Marcus. "You are simply insane. You know the report, Zed. The material found in the desert was from Project Mogul—a secret balloon project meant to spy on Russian nuclear tests. There was a miscommunication from the start that said the Air Force found a UFO."

"More lies. It's time to come clean with the truth," cried Zed.

Blood still dribbling from his nose, Marcus spun on Zed Nash. "Even if there was a cover-up of epic and, apparently, Biblical proportions, why the hell would anyone come clean now? Because a raving lunatic decided to rear his head from the grave?"

This time Zed didn't react violently. In fact, he didn't react at all. He simply turned and spoke directly to his grandson, "Jeremy, the UFO story was deliberately released by the Air Force to cover up the truth. There *wasn't* a UFO. *The UFO story was the cover up!*"

"And what was the cover up, old man?" asked Marcus. He was holding his head back to stem the flow of blood.

"You know damn well what the cover up was," spat Zed.

Nash's head hurt. He wished someone would cover up his damn ears. These two were driving him crazy.

Zed continued, "The truth of what really happened that day in nineteen forty-seven."

"That someone shot down Jesus Christ from the sky?" shouted Marcus. "Do you understand how stark raving mad you sound, old man? Tell me this. Did the Air Force also shoot down Moses—or maybe the archangel Michael? I would think that Jesus, in his perfect glory, could have deflected a heat seeking missile, especially in light of the fact that it was the Second Coming and all—"

"Enough!" screamed Zed. He turned back to Nash. "Were they going to let you out of here alive? Were they not willing to kidnap and kill Alyson to keep their secrets? Ask yourself. What are they hiding?"

Nash thought that Zed had a point. Indeed, why the threat to their lives?

"Now," said Zed, pointing to a pair of windowless doors off to the side of the room. "What's behind those closed doors?"

"Lab equipment."

"More bullshit. There's two coffins in there, and I want to see them."

He motioned to Sabra to hold the guard and priest at bay while the three men with Alyson and Peacock walked towards the clean room.

"Unlock the door and turn on the lights," he ordered.

"We have sensitive materials in there," said Marcus. "We can't just open the room up. It's a sterile atmosphere."

"I could give a shit," said Zed. He leveled his weapon at the bleeding man standing in front of him. "Open it."

Marcus took a key card from his pocket and swiped the lock. The door opened with a hiss as air escaped from the sealed room. Marcus turned on the lights and Zed pushed Marcus through the door.

Zed was right. What he called caskets were two hermetically

sealed modules sitting on low stands big enough for a man to lie in. Around the room there were pieces of silvery material in the shape of rods and small I-beams covered with strange writing that looked like hieroglyphics.

Nash had heard of strange metallic debris being removed from the Roswell crash site. Of course he had. Who hadn't? Many of the crazies, of course, believed the metal was wreckage from a downed spacecraft. Nash and other like-minded *sane* researchers believed the debris was from a top-secret weather balloon. And why wouldn't he believe the wreckage was from an air balloon? The story made sense to Nash. It was *plausible*. An alien spacecraft was *not* plausible. It was nonsensical.

And this strange material—with the equally strange writing—could have been from anywhere.

Exactly, Jeremy. Good boy. Don't get caught up in your grandfather's illusion. One always needs proof. Verifiable, unshakable proof.

"What you see before you," said Zed Nash, "is the debris from Roswell. If you need proof that this debris is from Roswell, Jeremy, I am sure there are countless records and files of this fact in this very room. Make no mistake, this material—" and Zed picked up a shiny scrap of metal, "was collected from Roswell, and it is most certainly not of this earth."

"What's this writing?" asked Nash pointing to the I-beams.

"The words of God," Zed said solemnly.

Sabra and Peacock rolled their eyes.

"No, Zed. You're wrong," Marcus replied. "The Air Force went to a toy company to make the balloon pieces. It was right after the war and the necessary materials were in short supply, so they had to use what the toy company had. The company used plastic tape with pink and yellow flowers and other geometric designs that were used in some of the toys they made. So it showed up on the tape that connected the I-beams. There's nothing alien about it."

Zed's temper rose. "*More bullshit!* He's making this stuff up as he goes along. Don't you see what he's doing, Jeremy?" Zed pleaded.

Nash looked down and just shook his head. He hated to admit it, but Marcus was correct. Nash fingered the metal. It reminded him of tinfoil, only thicker and shinier.

"It can't be cut, damaged or destroyed," Zed went on. "Or, as far as I'm aware, duplicated."

"And yet it was destroyed in a crash of some sort," said Nash. Always the devil's advocate.

"Yes," said Zed. "Clearly a mystery. But one mystery at a time, no?" He looked at Marcus. "Now open the coffins."

It was at that moment the lights to the lab went out.

Alyson screamed, and Nash could see a hunched shadow leap towards his grandfather from some hidden door to the sealed room. Even in dim light coming through the window of the clean room, Nash recognized the man's unmistakable wretched form right away.

Vadja was on Zed in an instant, seizing the old man around the throat from behind. Vadja croaked into Zed's ear. "I took care of Henderson," he growled. "Now it's your turn."

In the chaos that ensued, he saw his grandfather wrestling with the killer.

Peacock was aghast, and the little archeologist withdrew to the other end of the room. But Nash was already moving, rushing to his grandfather's aid when two shots rang out.

Thursday
12:45 PM GMT
Section 18

When he heard the shots, the guard outside the clean room saw his chance. Sabra was only momentarily distracted by the sounds, but it was enough for the guard to gain the advantage. He threw himself at Sabra who managed to get off one shot, and it was high, just above the head of the young Jesuit priest. The priest fell to the floor and scurried behind a desk.

"Get help!" the guard yelled. The Jesuit fled the room as the guard struggled with Sabra, but the combination of his strength and her surprise gave the guard the upper hand. He picked her up in his arms and threw her across the room like a rag doll. She hit hard against the wall and fell to her knees.

Dazed and confused she tried to focus her thoughts, only to be kicked in the side by the guard. She rolled over on her back ,and he immediately mounted her, pressing his body against hers. "Too bad I have to kill you. You're one good looking little bitch," he said as he ground his body into hers.

Sabra looked him straight in the eyes and spit in his face fighting to raise the gun towards him.

The guard frowned and beat her gun hand against the hard floor until she released her weapon. It went coasting across the room.

Disgusted and furious by her subservient position, she managed to get one arm free and forcibly pressed her thumb into the guard's left eye socket. He screamed in pain as she wiggled her body out from under his bulk.

"You fucking bitch!"

She crawled quickly to where her pistol was laying but before she could reach it, she felt two strong hands grip her right ankle and pull her backwards on her stomach. She turned on her back, twisting her right leg in pain but able to kick out with her left. Her kick landed squarely into the jaw of the guard who fell backwards against a metal desk. The desk slid back into a tall metal bookshelf laden with publications and scientific equipment. The whole bookshelf shuttered and tumbled down on the guard's head and shoulders.

Sabra stood up, wincing in pain, and limped over to him. He was bleeding from the mouth and the left side of his head was cracked open.

"Fuck you!" she yelled.

Someone turned on the lights. But it was the horror in front of Nash that left him momentarily dumbfounded. His grandfather, whom he had been reunited with only minutes earlier—hell, not even ten minutes earlier—lay on the sterile floor, bleeding profusely from multiple gunshot wounds.

The monster, Vadja, stood triumphantly over him, aiming the weapon he had only moments before wrested from Zed's grip. Now his grandfather lay on the floor, gasping, blood bubbling up from his mouth.

Blind fury overwhelmed Nash. Sabra, he knew, was the only other one with a weapon. Nash didn't care. He figured if he acted fast enough, moved swiftly enough, he might just get to Vadja before the big son-of-a-bitch could swing his weapon around.

Nash charged.

He quickly covered the small area separating himself and the assassin. Vadja suddenly turned—sooner than Nash had anticipated—and swung his weapon around.

Nash had no choice; he stopped dead in his tracks. His grandfather lay bleeding just feet away, and Nash had no doubt he was about to join him. Vadja grinned...and squeezed the trigger.

A shot rang out.

But not from Vadja's weapon.

The big man, to Nash's utter shock, wobbled on his feet. The Uzi dropped from his hands and clattered to the ground. A bloody dark rose appeared on his chest, blossoming quickly through his robe.

Sabra now strode purposefully across the room, holding her pistol out before her. As Vadja sank to his knees, holding his chest, he looked up.

"You whore!" he gasped.

"That was for my father," she said.

As Sabra pulled the trigger again, Nash looked away just as blood and brain matter sprayed across the sterile room. He heard Vadja hit the floor.

"And that's for me," he heard her say.

Nash saw the full cold fury capable of this woman.

She walked over to Vadja's dead body with eyes aflame and paused a beat. "Go deeper into hell, you son-of-a-bitch" and emptied what was left of her pistol into his bloody torso.

Just then, Father Engle and four guards armed with automatic weapons burst into the clean room.

They were at an impasse. Nash and Sabra faced the armed men. Peacock cowered in the corner. Three against four. Nash didn't like their odds, especially since Sabra only had an empty pistol.

On the floor next to him, Alyson knelt over their grandfather. She used her jacket to try to stifle the flow of blood. She ignored the others completely.

"Kill them," Marcus commanded. "That's an order!"

But the guards didn't move.

"I said kill them, goddammit!"

"Now is that any way to talk in the house of God?" asked a voice that entered the lab.

Nash risked a glance toward the voice as a pleasant looking man wearing the robes of a Jesuit Cardinal appeared. He looked at Vadja's body on the floor, then placed a hand on Marcus's shoulder. "There has been enough killing over this."

The four guards immediately lowered their weapons. Nash exhaled deeply, then rushed to his grandfather.

"How is he?" Nash asked his sister.

Alyson shook her head. She had their grandfather on his side, his head propped in her lap, and Nash could see the life draining from the old man's pale face. He was breathing, but barely.

"We have ambulances on the way now," said the man dressed in cardinal's robes.

Nash doubted they would get here in time.

His grandfather wheezed a breath and looked up at them. Amazingly, he smiled. He opened his lips and Nash realized the old man was trying to speak.

Alyson put her ear to his lips, listened, frowned, and then nodded once.

Zed Nash reached for his grandson. Nash took his grandfather's hand, and as he did so, he felt the life leave the old man.

Alyson used her sweater to cover her grandfather's dear old face. The man in the robe introduced himself as Cardinal Esposito. The Cardinal, an older man with serene eyes, seemed entirely too kind to be caught up in all this deadly madness.

Yet here they all were, surrounded by dead bodies and secrets.

"These people cannot be allowed to leave, Cardinal Esposito," pleaded Marcus.

The Cardinal gave Marcus a stern look. "Phillip, your assistance in this matter has produced nothing but problems for the Church. Now be silent."

"Are we free to go?" Sabra asked anxiously.

"Of course," said the Cardinal.

"They know too much, Cardinal," pleaded Marcus. "I beg you to reconsider."

The Cardinal raised his hand, and Marcus begrudgingly fell silent. "What they know is both irrelevant and improvable. I am tired of your whining and your mistakes, Phillip." The Jesuit looked at his guards. "Take him away. I will decide what to do with him later."

Two of the guards grabbed the older man, who suddenly looked small and frail. "Wait! Please. We had a deal!"

"We are done dealing with the devil," said the Cardinal. "Your contract with the Church is terminated."

"Wait—"

And with that, Phillip Marcus was dragged away.

Thursday
2:01 PM GMT
Rome, Italy

The four were now in Cardinal Esposito's immense office.

Douglas Peacock roamed around the room, examining paintings and artifacts. Nash knew some of the items, like the intricately carved rosewood cross hanging on the wall, were priceless.

The ambulance had arrived and carted off their grandfather's body. Vadja and the guard were removed as well, and now the somber group sipped tea and reflected.

"My apologies again for your grandfather," said Cardinal Esposito. "I understand he was a good and holy man."

Nash nodded again. The cardinal had said this a half dozen times already.

"Pardon me for being frank," said Nash. "But why is the Church in league with Section Eighteen and someone like Phillip Marcus?"

"There are some secrets that the church needs to keep. Sometimes we employ...others...to help us keep such secrets. But though they work for us, they are not privy to our greatest secrets. Working with Phillip Marcus, an unscrupulous man, had been a mistake from the beginning."

"What will happen to him?" asked Alyson. She was sitting very close to Nash. She had been thoroughly checked by the Church doctors and found to be in good health, although slightly malnourished. She hadn't felt like eating, but Nash made her try to eat a bagel. Even now it sat untouched in front of her.

"Marcus will disappear."

"Killed?"

"No. Of course not. But he will not be allowed back in Rome, and all his connections with the Church will be removed. He is dead to us. He is very, very lucky we do not report him to the authorities."

"But that would be more trouble than it's worth," said Sabra simply.

"Yes," said the Cardinal, and to his credit he truly sounded regretful. "I am only sorry that he caused so much destruction. It is time to move forward. Is there anything we can get you? We will provide funds and transportation anywhere in the world—"

"Cardinal Esposito?" said Nash.

"Yes, my son?"

Nash knew it was a long shot, but it was a shot he was willing to take, especially considering all that his grandfather had done to get them this far. "What's in the tomb at the Church of the Holy Sepulchre?"

The Cardinal sat back and steepled his long fingers under his chin. He smiled with genuine warmth and good humor. "My son, what's in the tomb or not in the tomb doesn't matter. Whatever rumors have been concocted—spaceships, aliens, hobgoblins, demons, cherubs, corpses, or even the Son of God Himself—is not important."

"Not important?" said Nash in disbelief. "People have killed to see what's in there. What if the bones of Christ were inside the tomb—and that he didn't ascend to heaven? That would destroy the very foundations of Christianity? I would certainly call that important."

"Mr. Nash, the Jesuit's mission is not to protect the Church's beliefs but the belief by Christians in the Church."

"What do you mean?" queried Nash.

"Jesus was not only the Son of God whose spirit became flesh to free the world from sin. He was also a teacher. One who tried to teach others that the Kingdom of God was not without but

271

within, and he tried to teach his followers *The Way* they could join him in everlasting life."

"If Jesus was only here to teach, then why all the stunts?" asked Nash. His sister slapped his leg, but Nash ignored her. He sometimes had no control over his inner skeptic. "Why the crucifixion. Why, even, the Resurrection?"

"Those *stunts*, as you call them, were a necessary part of his teaching," the Cardinal answered. "Jesus, Mohammed, and Buddha were all great spiritual leaders. While Mohammed was seen by his followers as a prophet, and Buddha as a teacher, Jesus was perceived as a savior. But Jesus' *concept* of being a savior was different than that of his followers. And to understand this difference is to understand Rome. To those living during the time of the Roman Empire, Rome was absolute and had the power of life and death over those it ruled."

"If you weren't a Roman, your life was most likely short, nasty and brutish," commented Nash.

"Exactly, which is why there were many rebellions," said the Cardinal. "All failed, of course, for the Roman legions were too strong. Still, the desire for freedom burned in the conquered peoples, and rebellions always simmered just beneath the surface. Into this environment, Jesus was born. When he claimed to be the Messiah, he was thought of by the masses as the savior that would deliver them from the slavery of Rome. But Jesus knew that no rebellion and no army could defeat Rome. Indeed, he had to show his followers that although Rome could control their *bodies*, no one could control their *spirit*."

Sabra spoke up, "You can kill a body but it's impossible to kill an idea."

"Exactly. Jesus wanted to remind his followers that they were more than what they seemed to be, that life had a meaning well beyond the physical trials of day to day living. That one could live with Rome if one gave to Caesar what was the province of Caesar—and to God what was the province of God. And to show this, he used various stunts, as you describe them, though we here in the Church prefer to call them miracles."

With an air of confidence, the Cardinal continued, "Indeed, Jesus understood that people needed to be shown a miracle before they could believe. So, he gave them one. A big one. Three days after he died on the cross, Our Lord rose from the dead."

There was a crash at the far end of the room. All heads turned to see a red-faced Peacock quickly picking up the pieces of something very old and very expensive.

The Cardinal narrowed his eyes at the mumbling man, but then turned his attention back to Nash. "Sorry if this is sounding like a sermon, but you did, after all, ask."

"You're not going to tell us what's in the tomb, are you?"

He became stern. "The tomb will remain closed to people until people return to the spirituality common to all of them.

"Returning to a personal God," Nash said.

The Cardinal smiled. "You may become an Essene, yet Mr. Nash."

The Cardinal pulled Zed's diary out of his robe. "We're going to keep your grandfather's diary. It's caused enough trouble."

Nash regretted not having it, but he understood. He nodded.

"Now, do you have the letter?"

"What letter?" asked Nash.

"Your grandfather's letter to you. The one that started you on this quest."

It was, in fact, in Nash's jacket. He was about to reach in when Alyson suddenly gripped his leg and sat forward. "I'm sorry, Cardinal Esposito, but he instructed us to destroy the letter. I'm afraid it was burned."

The Cardinal looked at her long and hard, but then finally nodded. "Pity. It could have had some value as a religious artifact. Now go in peace."

Thursday
4:23 PM GMT
Rome, Italy

They were seated again in the café across the street from the Church. It was late evening now, and the setting sun hovered just beyond the distant domes and spires.

Sabra held Nash's hand. "I'm sorry for the loss of your grandfather."

Nash nodded and squeezed her hand back. The waiter came by and dropped off their orders of lattes and crumb cakes. This time, Alyson was ravenous. She plowed through her food and even ate some of Nash's. He watched her with a bemused expression.

When she had wiped her mouth clean and picked at the crumbs around her plate, Nash asked, "What was that business about the letter back there?"

"Before Grandfather died, he whispered something into my ear."

Nash recalled the scene. He assumed it had been simple well wishes and love being exchanged.

"So, what did he say, Sis?"

"He said the secret was in the letter. His letter to us."

"Do you think it contains a hidden code?" Sabra asked. "Like the diary?"

"Could be," Nash replied. "I don't know. That Cardinal seemed pretty interested in getting hold of it. He must have suspected something."

Sabra thought for a moment. "You said you and Roth used decoding software for the diary, right?"

"Yes."

"Maybe we should run the letter through the same software and see what we get."

"Good idea. But where can we find a copy?"

"Let's find an internet café."

And they did.

The waiter pointed them to one just around the corner. Once there, Sabra did a search on Bible Code software and found a computer store nearby that, fortunately, had a copy in stock.

They hailed a cab, and twenty minutes later they were seated in front of one of the demo computers in the store. Nash scanned Zed's letter into the computer, loaded the Bible Code software demo, and ran it against the letter.

All three waited quietly, anxiously.

A few minutes later, they had their answer.

The software not only displayed a word but also a rough graphic image. The image was like an isosceles triangle minus the base with a dot within the triangle. The word beneath it was: *Talpiot.*

"What's that?" asked Alyson, pointing to the triangle. "And what is a Talpiot?"

Nash knew exactly what it was.

"The tomb of Jesus," Nash replied. "Or at least, what's claimed to be his tomb. The image you see is on a tomb that the discoverers say belongs to the family of Jesus."

"The family?" asked Sabra.

"I remember something about that," said Alyson. "It was on the History Channel or something."

"And it was a hoax," said Nash.

"Is everything a hoax to you, Jeremy?" cried Alyson.

"Until proven otherwise."

"Must be easy to be a skeptic," commented Sabra. "You simply believe in nothing."

"No," negated Nash. "I believe in verifiable truth. And when that happens, I am your greatest proponent."

"Because when the great Jeremy Nash proclaims something as true..." began Sabra.

"You can damn well believe it's true," boldly finished Nash.

"Fine," said Alyson. "But what's Grandpa getting at here?"

"This is just another one of Zed's wild goose chases, Sis. Let's drop it."

"Wouldn't hurt to pursue it," Sabra suggested. "Where is this tomb?"

"In Jerusalem," Nash said. "But there's no way I'm going back—"

Sabra took Nash's hand. "You mean you're not going to accompany me home? You mean I have to travel all by myself?"

Nash almost laughed. As a Mossad agent, Nash could only wonder how many dangerous missions she had performed *all by herself*. He already knew he would go halfway around the world for this woman—and back again. They had a connection that was deep and real, and he wanted to see it through.

"Fine," he said. "But I'll be damned if I'm going to go snooping around some dusty old tomb—"

"Grandfather died to give us this information, Jeremy."

"OK. OK," said Nash, shrugging and shaking his head.

"Great!" Alyson said. "Then let's go."

"Not you," Nash fired back. "You're going back to the States. I've worried about you enough."

"Then what better way *not* to worry about me than to have me with you?"

"I said *no*."

"But—"

"No. *Definitely,* no!"

Friday
10:23 AM GMT
Jerusalem, Israel

Nash and Sabra were once again in a cab in the crowded, hot streets of Jerusalem. With any luck, his sister's plane should just now be touching down in the States. He felt sorry for her. Alyson had put on a brave face at the airport gate, but he knew she was hurting. She had not only been kidnapped and held ransom, with her very life constantly being threatened, but she had lost a fiancé and a grandfather. And now she was going home alone. Nash promised he would look her up immediately when he returned.

Sabra held Jeremy's hand. He loved her touch. Loved holding her hand. *Damn, I have it bad for her.*

"So, where's this tomb?" she asked.

"We're not going to the tomb. We're going to the Rockefeller Museum."

"And why is that?"

"The ossuary we're looking for is in there."

"Ossuary?" questioned Sabra.

Nash looked at Sabra and raised an eyebrow. "You don't know what an ossuary is? I thought you were Jewish?"

"I know how to kill a man with my hands in four seconds."

"Point taken. An ossuary is a bone box. Early Jews would place their family bodies in a tomb—like the tomb Christ was placed in according to the New Testament—and left there to decompose. After a while when only the bones remained, they were gathered up and placed in a bone box, or an ossuary."

277

"So we're looking for the alleged ossuary of the bones of Christ?"

"Exactly," said Nash. "Of course, hundreds of ancient tombs have been uncovered in Jerusalem throughout the ages. However, in nineteen eighty, as the story goes, a construction crew unearthed a family tomb that had remained hidden since the first century. The tomb, or what is called now the Talpiot, had unusual symbols carved above the entrance. For instance, one of them was that triangular symbol we saw in the decoded letter."

"So, what was inside the tomb?" asked Sabra.

"Ten ossuaries. And what made the discovery unique was the fact that nine of the ten ossuaries had inscriptions on them."

"Why is this unique?"

"Because only twenty percent of all ossuaries recovered have inscriptions on them."

"So, these are different. Royalty maybe?"

"Perhaps. Anyway, archaeologists removed the bone boxes, cataloged them, and placed them in a warehouse. It wasn't until years later that other researchers discovered that the names on the ossuaries were, in fact, a list of the members of Jesus' family."

"And that warehouse is the Rockefeller Museum?" asked Sabra.

"Correct."

"Seems like compelling evidence," mused Sabra. "What do skeptics say?"

"Critics point out that seventy-five percent of the names occurring on Jewish ossuaries during this time period are from a general pool of but sixteen names. Individuals outside of Judea, buried *in* Judea, were named according to their place of origin. Had the names on the ossuaries been, say, *Jesus of Nazareth*, *Mary of Nazareth*, *Joseph of Nazareth*, etc, that would have made a stronger case for the tombs being the Jesus family tomb. But they were not so named."

"You're kind of smart," laughed Sabra. "I've never hung around with a nerd before."

"I'm not a nerd. I'm a man of action."

Sabra snorted.

Fifteen minutes later, they arrived at the Rockefeller Museum. Once inside, they passed by a prominent display of artifacts unearthed in the excavations conducted in Palestine during the late 19th century. They wandered through the museum, then through an inner courtyard where dozens of ossuaries were on display. The courtyard itself was graced with stone engravings by the noted British artist Eric Gill, depicting peoples who lived in the country throughout the centuries: Canaanites, Jews, Egyptians, Phoenicians, Assyrians, Persians, Babylonians, Greeks, Romans, Arabs, Crusaders, Mamluks, and Ottoman Turks.

"We need to find someone who knows their shit," said Nash.

"Is that an archaeological term?" asked a heavily accented voice behind them. "I have been told that I know my, er...shit."

Nash turned to find a tall gentleman with twinkling eyes and hair graying at the temples. Nash reddened. "We're looking for the curator."

The man nodded. "That would be me. I'm Dr. Cohen. How may I be of service to you?"

Nash introduced himself, and the curator smiled brightly. "I have read your books, Mr. Nash. We are honored to have you. Are you doing research now?"

"In a way, yes. We're looking for information on the lost tomb of Jesus."

"I see. Let's find a more comfortable place to talk. Come to my office."

The curator's second floor office was surprisingly small. Books and artifacts lined the walls. A window looked out over the bustling streets of Jerusalem. He directed them to two chairs in front of his narrow desk, which he sat behind in a squeaky chair.

"I assume you know the story up to the point where the ossuaries were discovered?"

Nash assured him that he did.

"Good. Then I will take up the story from when the museum got involved. Once the archaeologists removed the ossuaries from the tomb, they were recorded, numbered, measured, cataloged, and stored in the inner courtyard, along with tens and tens of other ossuaries."

He continued. "Now, nine of the ten ossuaries had inscriptions on them. This was rare indeed, and it immediately brought some interest to them. So the boxes were placed in a special room."

"Did you catalog the plain one?" asked Nash.

"No, not really. Without markings on it, it was of little interest. We just gave it a number."

Nash nodded. "I see."

Dr. Cohen continued, "Anyway, over the years, the elements took their toll on the nine ossuaries in the courtyard, and the record numbers disappeared. Meanwhile, more and more ossuaries were being discovered, and the inner courtyard became full. We were eventually forced to move those that bore no markings to the warehouse below, where they sit today."

"I assume there's no way to match these ossuaries to their original tomb," said Nash.

"I'm afraid not."

"Besides, the nine marked ossuaries attributed to the tomb of Christ were finally determined to be frauds. It was found that the inscribed markings on them were only a few decades old; not two thousand years old. Once that information was revealed, the museum had little interest in the ossuaries. They were collected together and put with the others in storage."

"The bones, too?" asked Sabra, who had been listing intently.

The man nodded. "They would have been taken out, boxed and stored in the basement of the museum with other artifacts. Would you like to see them?"

Nash and Sabra both vigorously nodded, and soon they were following the curator to an elevator and down into the depths of the museum. Nash knew that, on average, only ten percent of a museum's full inventory was ever displayed at any one time. Ninety percent of the goods were in storage—and often in basements beneath the museums.

The elevator stopped, opened, and the three stepped into a vast and musky smelling room. They followed the tall man past row upon row of boxes stacked high on tall shelves, and then past dozens and dozens of rows of ossuaries, all stacked from floor to ceiling.

Jesus, that's a lot of dead people, thought Nash.

The curator stopped at one particular row of clear plastic boxes. "Ah, here we are," he said pointing to a stack of boxes. Nash followed them with his eyes all the way to the ceiling. The curator continued, "The bones in the ossuary would be here, somewhere in this stack."

"You mean you don't know where?" asked Nash, perplexed.

"No," said the curator. "They were a hoax, and thus they were not given special care or attention."

Nash realized at once that finding the bones of any one individual who wasn't cross-referenced to any particular ossuary or tomb was like finding the proverbial needle in a haystack.

Or, in this case, a bone yard.

Nash sighed. "Thank you for your help, Dr. Cohen."

The curator beamed brightly and led the way back to the elevator.

Nash and Sabra were eating lunch at the museum's indoor café. School children dominated one side of the museum, loud and excited just to be out of class and on a field trip.

Sabra picked at her salad. "Well, that's that. Now we'll never know if your grandfather was right or wrong. I liked the guy. He

281

went out of his way to save my life. I'll never forget him. He didn't seem crazy to me. Eccentric, sure. But not crazy."

Nash was thinking the same thing. Indeed, he was having second thoughts of his grandfather's alleged insanity. "Maybe he wasn't crazy after all."

Sabra arched an eyebrow. "Oh? Is the great skeptic having second thoughts?"

Nash just had a wild thought, and despite his cautious nature with such thoughts, decided to voice it. "What if Jesus Christ had not died on the cross—and not risen again? And what if Section Eighteen, decades ago, had moved the body of Jesus from the Church of the Holy Sepulchre—and reburied his bones in an ossuary. Once done, they concocted the story of the Talpiot, knowing full well that the inscriptions would someday prove to be a fraud."

"And once the hoax was revealed, archaeologists would lose interest in the remains," commented Sabra.

"Exactly," said Nash. "And rebury them in unknown plastic boxes deep in the bowels of a museum. Or something like that. You know, if this were all true, the tomb at the Church of the Sepulchre would obviously be empty."

"And Christians around the world would rejoice, for an empty tomb would prove to them that Jesus Christ had risen again and ascended to heaven."

"Although it proves nothing."

"Ye of little faith," scoffed Sabra. "I just don't understand the connection to Roswell. Your grandfather believed—and rather adamantly so—that the UFO story was a cover up to the Second Coming. What do you make of that?"

"That grandfather was delusional."

"Then what was in those coffins in Section Eighteen?" Sabra asked. It was obvious the Mossad agent had a soft spot for his grandfather.

Nash played along. "Maybe little green men. Or maybe Jesus Christ and the Archangel Michael. Or maybe even Elvis and Jim

Morrison. We'll never know because I sure as hell am never going back there."

Sabra giggled. "You're beginning to sound like a conspiracy nut yourself."

"Don't say that too loud," laughed Nash. "I have a reputation to uphold."

"Hey, at least you have a lot of material for your next book, right?" she suggested.

Nash thought a moment. "It would make one helluva novel though, wouldn't it?"

"Just be sure to leave my name out of it. I'm supposed to be undercover, remember?"

"Yeah, I heard you spies were good under cover."

"You have no idea, Jeremy Nash." She leaned over and kissed him—this time, deeply on the mouth. "Now, let's get the hell out of here."

Epilogue

This is shaping up to be one hell of a shitty day, thought Jeremy Nash, gripping the arm rests of his seat.

The plane swooped and fell and did things he was sure no plane of this size were ever meant to do.

It wasn't enough that he'd spent the entire day being *interviewed* by the Israeli Defense Force about the terrorist incident in Jerusalem—a long story that Nash was writing a book about. Or that he had been awakened in Rome by a frantic phone call from his sister, Alyson—a phone call that rocked his world, a phone call that sent him scurrying off for a flight home. No, now he had to deal with this hellacious storm which was doing its best to drive the big 777 straight into the ground.

As the plane dipped again, sending Nash's stomach up into his throat area, he glanced over at some of the other Business Class passengers who were clutching airsick bags. The elder couple sitting across the aisle held each other closely, their frightened faces a matching shade of green. Nash was sure he didn't look much different. He was also sure he shouldn't have had that second helping of sushi for dinner just a few hours earlier.

Think of something else. Get your mind off your stomach. And definitely get your mind off raw fish...

Despite himself, he nearly gagged at the thought.

So, he took his mind off his stomach and onto his younger sister. In particular, her frantic phone call. What was it she had said? *Their parents murdered?* They didn't die years ago in a caving accident? Killed for something they discovered in the Hopi End Times Predictions?

Ridiculous! No. Absurd!

A Message
From the Author

I relished writing this book! If you enjoyed this first volume in the *Chronicles of Jeremy Nash*, would you consider doing two things?

First, sign up for my newsletter at www.frankfiore.com, and I'll be sure you're the first to get news on future installments in the series, in addition to info about my other titles.

Second—and this is a big request—if you liked this story, would you consider leaving a review wherever you bought this book, or on your favorite social media platform? I want as many readers as possible to discover this story, and your voice can help do that. Leave a review and tell a friend! Word-of-mouth is still the best way to introduce this story to other readers.

Lastly, *Thank you!*

Thank you, dear reader, for giving your time to read this book. It means a lot that you trusted me as the author to entertain, and hopefully excite, you with this story. Stories need an audience, and I appreciate you being my audience for just a little while. Thank you.

There are, of course, plenty of crypto-historical events, locations, and artifacts yet to be discover, examined, and explored; and lots of questions about the lives and predicaments of our main characters that need answers.

And so, dear readers, just for you, here's—

—a sneak peek at—

Seed
Chronicles of Jeremy Nash
Book 2

Grand Canyon
Twenty-one Years Ago

The dancers wore elaborately carved masks and headdresses, many with long eagle feathers extending from the crown. Jeremy had seen Hopi masks in the past, but these were markedly different. Instead of a painted face, these masks bore only a single blue star. No mouth, no eyes—no indication that they could see through the mask. The effect was surreal and a little frightening, at least to the young boy. Each dancer carried a small bell in one hand and a fistful of arrows in the other.

Jeremy found himself marveling at the strange movements of the dancers. He knew they were telling a story—an ancient story—but his young brain couldn't wrap itself around the meaning. He knew from his father that the masked dancers were believed to embody the powerful spirits of earth, sky, and water.

Maybe they are telling the story of the world, he thought.

The dancers circled each other, and as the beating of the nearby drums grew in intensity, a strange, cold wind suddenly swept low over the ground. Jeremy shivered. Others in the crowd felt it too. Jeremy saw them look furtively around.

The dancers now rang their little bells—randomly, almost chaotically. The result was an unsettling, raucous cacophony. Just as the ringing reached a fevered pitch, the ground beneath Jeremy's feet began trembling.

The dancers briefly paused. The sounds of the bells stopped.

The rumbling grew in intensity, and Jeremy's first thought was that something was going to burst out of the ground. Or a jet airplane was going to land in the middle of the Grand Canyon. And then the trembling turned into all-out shaking. Someone in the audience screamed. Jeremy's father wrapped an arm around his boy's shoulders.

One of the Kachina dancers suddenly yanked off his Blue Star mask, screaming. He fell to a knee awkwardly, got to his feet and stumbled toward Jeremy and his father. The boy stepped back in horror as the Kachina dancer collapsed at his feet, blood pouring from his nose, ears, eyes, and mouth.

About the Author

Frank F. Fiore is a five-star rated author of novels in multiple genres including Contemporary Fiction, Techno-Thrillers, Action/Adventures, Sci-Fi, Historical Fiction, and Westerns. He lives in Arizona with his fetching wife, Lynne.

Connect with Frank online at:

www.frankfiore.com

Also Available From

WordCrafts Press

Better Off Guilty
Lindsey Lamar

Muldovah
Marian Rizzo

The Transference
Jeff S. Bray

Idiot Farm
Susie Mattox

Dreamreader
Cathy Fiorello

www.wordcrafts.net